In
Search
of
Love and
Beauty

In Search of Love and Beauty

by
RUTH PRAWER JHABVALA

COUNTERPOINT
CALIFORNIA

First Counterpoint paperback edition 1999.

Library of Congress Cataloging-in-Publication Data
Jhabvala, Ruth Prawer, 1927–   .
In search of love and beauty / by Ruth Prawer Jhabvala.
p.   cm.
ISBN 1-58243-016-0
I. Title.
PR9499.3.J5   I5   1999
823–dc21   99-20011
CIP
ISBN-13: 978-1-58243-016-4

COUNTERPOINT
Los Angeles and San Francisco, CA

Visit us on the World Wide Web at www.counterpointpress.com

BOOK DESIGN BY LINEY LI

ACKNOWLEDGMENT

I would like to thank the
John Simon Guggenheim Memorial Foundation
for its generous support.

In
Search
of
Love and
Beauty

I

Everyone always knew that Leo Kellermann had something, was something, special. He himself knew it better than anyone, so he could always afford to be relaxed and confident, even when things were not going well. And for years and years they had not gone well. He had come to New York in the thirties as a penniless refugee, but he had never really had any difficulty in getting people to look after him. That was because he was so talented, and handsome, and charming—and young too, at that time; vital and young, so that everyone had wanted a share in him.

He had entered Louise's life with a phone call from her friend Regi. "An Adonis!" Regi had described Leo to her. "An Apollo! A god." Well, naturally, Louise had known to discount most of that, for she was used to Regi's temporary enthusiasms for any new acquisition—a hat, a coffeepot, or a person; just as long as it was hers. And sure enough, when later that day she met him at Regi's, she saw that he fell far short of her description. He was fair, it was true, blond as an Adonis, with round, blond curls all over his head; and his eyes were round too, and porcelain-blue; and his complexion was clear and of a pinkish hue; but he was certainly plumper and softer than a well-proportioned god had any right to be.

There was no doubt that he was very charming. Of course, it was a perfect setup for him in Regi's smart Park Avenue apartment, done up in the Bauhaus style she had brought with her as absolutely the latest thing. He was being shown off, amid coffee and rich pastries from Blauberg's, to her circle of women friends—all, like herself (and Louise), German and Austrian refugees who had managed to get their money out but felt bored and stranded. Leo thrilled them, and he knew it, and played up and shone for their benefit; and Regi looked around triumphantly—"Well, what did I tell you?"—and, without laying aside the offhand manner that was her style, egged him on to unfold talent after talent.

"And—eh—Leo—didn't you say you were with Reinhardt for a while?" "Only two years." "And that poem you published in *Querschnitt?*" "Not exactly a poem, more a play. A play in verse." "You must tell us about Freud. Can you believe it—he actually *met Freud?*" "Long ago. Before Reich. After Reich, well—" He shrugged, disposing of Freud. He often shrugged, disposing of things and people; not least of his own talents as they were brought up one by one—as an actor, an analyst, a choreographer, for a short time a political activist—he had done it all, but so far everything was only a stepping-stone, a gradual ascent toward those heights that it was his destiny to attain.

They all felt it, that afternoon at Regi's: that they were in the presence of a yet undefined genius. Fortunately, he was by no means an aloof genius. He didn't just sit there and let himself be admired. It was a two-way traffic, and while he allowed them to glimpse into his soul, he also looked into theirs. Yes, he had that wonderful gift of making each one feel—even those of them who were no longer so very young or good-looking—that he was in intimate contact with her, on the deepest and most thrilling level; and moreover, that he had absolutely no difficulty in understanding as well as condoning whatever secret, or secret longing, she might be harboring.

And while they sat there, on Regi's tubular furniture, and wondered in what way he would finally make himself known to the world, they didn't realize it was just that: in his ability to know those who, like themselves, wanted to be known, to be found out and probed to the core of their being. Needless to say, it took a lifetime of struggle and experiment and education for this special gift of his to be recognized on the scale it deserved; so that by the time he had reached his present eminence, most of the people at that original coffee party were either dead or senile or had long ago given him up as a charlatan.

But Louise stuck fast to him through all those years; or was stuck fast, for sometimes it was against her will. She could not free herself from him, nor would he let her go. In the earliest years, when he was still in New York City and didn't have anyplace else to go, he had lived with her and Bruno in their apartment; later, when he began to expand his activities to other parts of the country, he took it for granted that, if he so pleased, he could base himself with her during his visits to the city. More and more, he had better options open to him than Louise; and once he became famous, if he even phoned her, it was a big favor he did her, for old times' sake.

Here is Louise in her sixties after one such phone call. They had by this time known each other for over thirty years, and she might have been expected to take his calls more calmly. But it was not so, and she was upset for the rest of the day. He had called her from California, and the sound of his voice put her in a state, so that in self-defense she was gruff with him and said, "What do you want?"

"Want? Want? What should I want? Except to hear your beautiful voice." And he laughed his great Olympian laugh. He was extra relaxed with her—amused, mocking, affectionate—he made a show of being so: in order no doubt to point up her opposite tendency to be extra tense with him, and on her guard. So that at the end of the conversation—as at the end of everything that had ever taken place between them—he came out the victor.

"You'd think it would all end one day, you'd think it would be finished," she grumbled to herself for the rest of the day. Although she was exceptionally upright, healthy, and strong for her age, now she dragged her feet as though they wore the same ball and chain he had attached to her heart all those years ago. She shuffled around her apartment, muttering and sighing, from room to room. It was a large, lofty, old West Side apartment, which she had had for over thirty years. All the furniture—the cabinets, the velvet sofa the size of a Roman bath, the Steinway grand, which no one ever played—came from Bruno's family house in Germany. She never changed anything and didn't have the place cleaned often enough, so that the carpets, the velvet upholstery, and the convoluted carvings of screens and furniture had an accumulation of dust that seemed to add to their ponderous weight. Every now and again she declared she would change everything, including the apartment, which was of course much too big for her alone. But she never even changed the photographs, so that Bruno, her husband—long since dead—was still in his dapper forties, her daughter Marietta a girl of sixteen, her grandson Mark the cutest, prettiest little boy of two anyone had ever seen, and Natasha a baby in her pram. There was no picture of Leo; she neither wanted nor needed one.

Even after the most casual contact with him, it usually took her at least one whole day and night to get over Leo. Bruno had always pretended not to notice; and Marietta, as she grew up, had been angry with her and had shouted "You've been talking to him again! He's done things to you again!" She would clench her teeth and her fists and say "I hate him," and she did. Marietta couldn't stand Leo, she couldn't stand him near her, and whatever he did to try to win her only made her worse.

This is what had happened when Marietta first got engaged. It was long ago, of course, when people—even free souls like Marietta—still got engaged. She was at that time training to become a dancer and was living at home; but she had gone to stay with Tim's family in the country, and he had driven her back on the Sunday evening and had dropped her at the door of the apartment house. And she had come upstairs, radiant with her news. "Mother! Vati!" she had called, and then called again. There was no answer and she opened the doors and stormed from room to room, for it was inconceivable to her that there was no one home to receive the tidings she had so abundantly to give. She was on the point of opening the door of her parents' bedroom when Bruno appeared from the study. "Don't, Marianne," he said (her father was the one person unable to learn calling her Marietta, which was what she had renamed herself).

"Why, what's the matter?" Her hand was on the door knob and she saw no reason to take it away.

"Don't," he said and turned and shuffled back into the study.

She followed him. It was dark in there, for though he was ostensibly reading, he hadn't turned on the light. His book— *Hermann und Dorothea,* in German—lay facedown on the arm of his chair.

Although she wanted light—and life, always!—she didn't turn it on. She was afraid of what she would see. She came over to his chair and picked up Goethe and perched herself on the arm instead. "Vati, I'm engaged. I'm going to marry Tim."

"Child, dearest, how wonderful!"

"If it's so wonderful, why are you crying?"

"With happiness," he said and took out his big, white, monogrammed handkerchief, beautifully laundered by himself.

She remained on the arm of his chair. She burned with fury. When the bedroom door opened—and then the entrance door, Leo letting himself out—she jumped up. She appeared in the doorway of the study just as Louise was crossing from the bedroom to the kitchen, to make herself a cup of coffee. Marietta announced: "I'm going to marry Tim and I shall never forgive you."

"Ach,, tcha, child," her father protested from the dark of the study.

"Never," Marietta declared to her mother across the hall, looking daggers out of her clear green eyes, beautiful and blank with youth. In fact, she forgave her that very evening— the three of them had a little celebration, with champagne and cake; and after Bruno, who always got tired very early, went to bed, Louise and Marietta sat up talking half the night, both of them tremendously excited.

The peak of Leo's career was reached when he was seventy with the acquisition of the house in the Hudson Valley. It was a late-Victorian house—dark, Gothic, overembellished, standing on fifty acres of overgrown land with a sunken garden and a lake that had only dead fish and weeds in it. By a quirk of fate, it was Mark—Marietta's son, Louise's grandson—who had helped Leo buy the house; and just as this acquisition was the high point of Leo's career, so it was the beginning of Mark's. It was, in fact, Mark's first venture into real estate, and he had never looked back. Now, seven years later, Mark was making big deals, owned two apartment houses in the city, lived in an elegant loft, and had bought office space for his company in a sensational new architectural edifice in midtown Manhattan.

But at the time no one had wanted him to do business with Leo. Even Louise was wary of this collaboration between them. Wary on Mark's account: the boy was young, untried, whereas Leo by this time knew all there was to know about the wiles of the world and was more than willing to use them. It wasn't—she wouldn't have said—that Leo was dishonest; but he had been around too long and had struggled and lost too often to neglect to snatch at, or manipulate, whatever advantage might come his way. But how to say that to Mark, without implying more than she wished to imply against Leo? And there was the further difficulty of Mark's character: that if you said no to him, it spurred him on to yes. So Louise followed her usual policy, and inclination, with her grandson: of liking everything he did, and saying "Do whatever you like, little worm, you know best."

Marietta also followed her usual policy with her son: that is, she quarreled with him and tried to stop him from doing what he wanted. Like her mother, she knew perfectly well that this would only impel Mark further in his own direction. But she couldn't help herself. It was out of an excess of love for him; love and fear—the fear being mostly that he would turn out like Tim, his father. So whatever it was he wanted to do, her first instinct was always to try to stop him. In the present case, there were also her own feelings about Leo—"That dreadful, fearful monster—how could you, darling, even go near him?" As usual, she carried her protests too far, and Mark slammed out of her apartment and wouldn't speak to her for two days.

The third person who didn't like the Leo-Mark collaboration was Natasha, Mark's sister (by adoption). Natasha didn't say anything, but she didn't have to. He always knew what she was thinking, as she did with him. Usually she most deeply approved—admired—whatsoever he undertook, and on those rare occasions when she didn't, she tried her best to hide it. Always in vain. "Why don't you speak?" he would ask. "Why don't you open your mouth?" "But what should I say?" And she turned away her face, so he wouldn't see the expression on it; for that was always very easy to interpret. She was one of those unfortunate people who can't hide their feelings, least of all from those she loved. She tried to say it was a good idea to work with Leo, she said she liked it—so that Mark got mad at her for lying; and that threw her into despair, tears rushed into her eyes—but because she knew he couldn't stand to see her cry, she went away and locked herself in her room, and when he pounded on the door, she called from inside that it was all right, she was *not* crying.

None of them knew that Mark had been seeing Leo. It was a year after Mark had graduated. He had given himself that year off, but they all realized he was not idle in that time: Mark was not often idle, he was usually scheming something, though no one knew what until the time was ripe—that is, until he considered it ripe. If it had been left to him, they wouldn't have known about his purchase of the house for Leo until it was an accomplished fact. But of course Leo was the opposite—he wanted everyone to know what he was doing and couldn't shout it over the rooftops loud or soon enough.

He had by then more admirers, followers, some—though not he—would say disciples, than he could accommodate, so that the halls in which he gave his lectures and the places he hired for his workshops were constantly overflowing. He was not surprised when Mark began to appear in the audience and asked for permission to sit in on the workshops. Leo was used to people wanting to be near him, and although he was usually indifferent to who came and went, he was pleased about Mark. He courted her grandson's adherence to him as one more score over Louise, and—although he had long since surpassed the necessity—he could never get enough of those.

Mark also came to the Old Vienna where Leo held court at his own special table. Mark sat there and listened quietly, courteously; and Leo liked his presence so much that he encouraged him to come as often as he pleased—a privilege extended to few. But Mark, it appeared, wanted more; he wanted to meet Leo alone, without the presence of all those others. Leo made a face. "Alone? When am I ever alone? I've given up that luxury." Mark smilingly insisted, and Leo— massaging Mark's shoulder; he always like to touch people, be in touch—at last agreed, and told Mark to come early the next morning to the place where Leo was staying at the time.

This was the town house of one of his rich lady admirers. Mark was let in by the butler—whom he recognized at once as someone he had met, though he couldn't remember where. On inquiry, the young man discreetly reminded him, and they both smiled in remembrance and Mark said cordially, "Well, how *are* you?" and they reminisced a bit as they went upstairs. Mark was ushered into Leo's bedroom, which appeared to be the principal bedroom in the house. It was a very feminine room and must have belonged to the mistress of the house who had respectfully vacated it for Leo.

He lay—sprawled—in the four-poster amid floral sheets and under pastel curtains looped from the corkscrew poles. He looked like a stranded whale—Leo was huge by this time, bloated with food and the good humor engendered by his success. Mark walked around the room, admiring the paintings and the art objects; he even peeped into the bathroom, which had a *chaise perçée* and a basket piled with little soaps in the shape of fruits. Then he came and perched on the side of Leo's bed. "Well," he said, "but you're comfortable here, I'm glad to see." And he propped another fat, floral pillow behind his back, to make him more so.

But Leo looked ill-pleased; he made a face to show something was missing from his life.

"It's so tasteful," Mark urged.

"Tcha," Leo said. He added, "It smells of the five Ps." The mere reference to a dirty joke put him in a better humor. He slapped Mark's thigh and said, "You and I are the same: we don't like women."

"I thought you liked them too much," Mark said, smiling blandly the way he always did when Leo referred to Mark's own predilection.

"I need them," Leo said, "but I can't stand them. Can't bear them. They make me positively, physically sick." He thrust back the flowered sheets, and now he was like an exasperated whale flailing about among the bedclothes; but when he managed to disentangle himself from them and get out of bed, he tottered a bit, for the legs on which he supported his weight were feeble, an old man's legs. Mark solicitously helped him sit down again on the edge of the bed.

"Can't stand them, can't bear them," Leo muttered, holding his head between his hands. "I must have a place of my own."

"Exactly what I was thinking," Mark said.

It was in fact the purpose of his visit. He explained that, after attending Leo's lectures and workshops, he had come to the conclusion that Leo's work had reached a stage where he needed a communal center. In order to be brought to their full potential, his followers had to live together, work together, be together, under Leo's guidance, for twenty-four hours a day. For this, of course, they needed a house; a big house; and Mark, having studied Leo's needs, knew just the place.

Mark enjoyed arranging for the purchase of the Victorian house in the Hudson Valley; and then establishing Leo and his community in it. Leo, it turned out, was very timid when it came to taking such a large practical step; he was especially timid about risking his bit of capital—as Louise said, he had always been a miser—and Mark had to coax it out of him. Mark himself was very bold; this was his first property deal, and he managed it with ease and pleasure. In order to have his own stake in the property, he took various loans from his mother and grandmother and juggled them along with contributions from Leo's followers and with Leo's own money. He also undertook the necessary remodeling of the house. It was as solid as a fortress, with massive outer walls and crenellated parapets; the inside walls and the ceilings were covered with a carapace of oak paneling. Within this sturdy shell Mark installed a new heating system and transformed the Victorian attics and cellars into living spaces for modern disciples. Of course, all this took further loans, and Leo wrung his hands and said they would be bankrupt and ruined. Mark soothed him and carried on, supervising everything himself until he was satisfied; so that in the end Leo had his Academy of Potential Development and Mark had collateral with which to raise further loans and mortgages and launch himself on his career.

Established as the partriarch of this domain, Leo took charge of it with panache; but he still relied on Mark to look after practical details, and when anything went wrong, with the boiler, the electric wiring, the plumbing, he straightaway sent for Mark. But Mark was not easy to locate: his personal life had always been secretive and convoluted, and as the years passed and his business interests grew, his professional life also began to diverge into intricate and mutually exclusive paths. Often it took Leo days to find him, and he even had to call on Louise for help. On such occasions, this was the way their conversation might go:

LOUISE: What do you want with him?
LEO: Is he there or isn't he there?

LOUISE: That depends on what you want—no, don't
          hang up! Leo!
LEO: All right then, last chance: where is he?
LOUISE: I don't know.

This last would be in a voice sufficiently small to satisfy
Leo; and from this point on their conversation became quite
amiable and ranged over topics beyond Mark's whereabouts.
Louise was very eager and curious to be allowed to visit the
Academy of Potential Development, but Leo discouraged her.
Mark too was evasive, telling her to wait until everything was
set up; so that Leo had already been settled in there for over a
year before they would allow her to come and see the place.

Mark drove her up from the city. She commented on
everything they saw, and as the city and its suburbs were left
behind and the landscape unfolded into views of fields, river,
and distant hills, her rapture mounted; so that by the time
they arrived and Mark drove through the gates, between two
pillars topped by concrete spheres like cannonballs, Louise
was so excited that she leaped out of the car before it had
come to a standstill. There on the steps leading up to the
porch stood Leo, flanked by a few followers whom he so completely overshadowed that they might as well not have been
there.

Leo, standing in welcome on his front steps, was an impressive figure. He wore the costume he had devised for his
comfort—a long robe like a monk's, girdled by a studded cowboy belt which drooped over his low-slung stomach. Louise
rushed out of the car and up the steps to meet him. She was
in her way as impressive as he. Tall and stately, she wore a
dress of heavy plum-colored silk swathed in loops over her
breasts and hips. Her hair, disordered from the drive and the
excitement, had got loose from its pins and gave her the somewhat frantic air of a prophetess. Her voice boomed in greet-

ing and his boomed back again as they met—collided—like
two giants on the steps.

That was a wonderful day for Louise. Leo devoted himself to her entirely, and secure and proud of his possession,
took pleasure in showing her around it. He was the beneficent
deity, not only of the house and all its inmates, and of the
acres of ground that belonged to it and had been left wild and
romantic as a Victorian garden; but also beyond that of the
entire countryside rolling pale green and gold in summer sunshine, with here and there a patch of dark wood and a ribbon
of crystal water. He showed her everything and beamed as
she admired and exclaimed; and truly, it was wonderful that
all this land, wrested from Indians by Dutchmen and Scots-
men, should now belong to him, Leo Kellermann: as though
all that fighting and treachery, endurance and thrift had led
up to the high tide of history that was the Academy of Potential Development. She was as proud as he—of all this and of
him—and they wandered together through his domain without quarreling once, which was an absolute record for them;
so that it was not only a high tide of history but also of their
relationship—by this time itself a piece of history or even, so
primeval was it, of archaeology.

Natasha's first visit to the Academy was nowhere near as
enjoyable. She wasn't, of course, a guest of honor—in fact, Leo
took very little notice of her. He never did have much time
for Natasha, seemed hardly ever to see her, and maybe he
didn't—it would have been quite natural, for he was physically very large and she very small.

Poor Natasha! Her presence among them was a result of
Marietta's search for identity; or rather, Marietta's rejection
of her husband's identity. Tim's family was as American as
one could get—they had come, on his mother's side, from
Scotland, on his father's, from Ireland—and when, after less

than a year of marrige, Marietta became disillusioned with
Tim, this feeling extended itself to his family, and from them,
to their entire race and nation. Then she wanted to get back
to her own roots, though she had to disentangle them first,
since Louise, her mother, was a German Protestant, and
Bruno, her father, a German Jew. Marietta decided on this
latter part of her heritage: and when, in one of the spurts
of energy with which she followed herself through, she decided to adopt a sister for Mark, she set about finding a
one-hundred-percent-guaranteed Jewish child. This Natasha
turned out to be. But Marietta had tended to mix up Jewish
and Russian, and when she thought of a Jewish girl, it might
have been more a Russian one that she had in mind: a
Turgenev or Chekhov heroine, an embodiment of music,
moonlight, and poetic feeling. Natasha, however, was short
and thin, with thin dark hair and hair on her upper lip that
had to be taken care of; her nose was curved and so, on account of bad posture, was her spine. She had absolutely no
idea of how to dress. But her eyes were truly one-hundred-
percent-guaranteed Jewish: shortsighted, inward-looking, liq-
uid mirrors of her soul.

Growing up, Natasha had problems—as was to be expected of a young girl; what was unexpected was the nature
of her problems, for they were entirely different from those
either Louise or Marietta had known when they were her age.
At twenty-four, Natasha had never had a boyfriend, or any
other friends either; she had got into college and got out of it
again without distinction; she appeared to have no inclination or aptitude for any kind of career. She didn't need to
have; she could live with Louise or with Marietta, and she
was happy to do that: they, and Mark, were her home, her
life, everything she knew and cherished. And yet, every now
and again, she deliberately drove herself out and away from
them and made herself do things for which she had no
aptitude.

She did not look for dreadful sights, but saw them everywhere. It had started when she was a small child. One day Louise had found her lying facedown on her bed, in tears. It took some time to persuade her to come out with what had happened, and then all she could stammer was, "There's a man—"

"What? Where?"

"At the corner, sitting on the trash can."

Sobs tore Natasha apart, and she could say no more. An awful suspicion dawned on Louise: "What did he do? . . . No, you *must* answer: what did he do to you? Tell Grandma, tell Grandma!" Snatching Natasha to her bosom, she cried out in fear. "Oh God!" she implored, as was her habit, to someone she didn't at all believe in. She became somewhat hysterical herself, so that Natasha, forgetting her own feelings, had to try and calm her: "He didn't do anything, Grandma, only he's sitting there." She did her best to suppress the lump of grief that rose up in her again, but it escaped her in a cry of pain—"He's hungry!" broke from her, in overwhelmed pity for all the hungers of humanity.

It took Louise no time at all to put on her hat and gloves—she would never have gone down the street without them—and to accompany Natasha into the elevator and through the lobby of her apartment building. Natasha led her to the corner: the awful vision was still there. He sat enthroned on the trash can, like a god wafted up from its depths. He was enormous and red in the face and wore a hat without a crown on his wild hair; a pair of stiff black trousers encased one massive leg but was ripped open on the other, exposing a surprisingly soft, lily-white expanse of thigh. His trident, or escutcheon, was an empty bottle held aloft in one hand, and he was alternately shouting and singing to passersby. Louise turned away in disgust: "He's not hungry."

"He says he is"; for he was lustily thrumming his stomach to proclaim its emptiness. "And thirsty," Natasha said, tears rising to her eyes again.

"Yes, that I believe," Louise said. "I'm going to call the police . . . Upsetting you like that; what a sight for a little child to see. Tcha. Disgusting. In the middle of West End Avenue. I'll get the police right now."

"Grandma, Grandma, I'm not upset!"

Grasping Natasha's hand, Louise marched off with her to the phone booth on the opposite side of the street. Natasha continued to protest and implore; when Louise lifted the receiver, she hung on to her arm. "You can't," she said. "You mustn't." Finally, leaning against the phone booth, she brought out amid her tears: "He looks just like Leo . . . What if it was Leo?"

Louise replaced the receiver. She looked back again at the Dionysian figure on the trash can: there *was* something of Leo about him. Louise hid her face in her glove.

Natasha looked up at her in amazement: why should Louise be laughing at someone hungry and thirsty and in rags? "If it were Leo, you'd give him money," Natasha reproached. "You'd take him home and cook for him and take him to bed."

Louise's shoulders continued to shake. She opened her big purse, and Natasha was reassured. They crossed the street again. Louise thrust some coins on the man, but at the same time she showered him with homilies and reproaches which made Natasha anxiously pluck at her sleeve. But the man didn't seem to mind at all; on the contrary, he pursued them down the street with cries of gratitude and blessing, upsetting Natasha all over again because they were so undeserved.

If Natasha suffered in the streets, she suffered no less at home: and here again impotently, unable to do anything to help. She had always been used to hearing Louise fight with Leo. At one time—when Natasha was about six—Leo came to live with Louise. Terrible monster fights broke out continuously. Natasha was the only other occupant of the apartment at the time—Marietta was in India, and it was one of those periods when Mark, who pretty much took charge of his own education, had checked himself into a boarding school. Natasha was often frightened by the violence of the scenes she overheard, even though the two protagonists took care to shush each other in her vicinity. They were less careful at night when they thought she was safely asleep. Then they gave full rein to their passions, and since both of them were large and had powerful voices, the effect was loud enough to raise the dead, let alone frail little Natasha sleeping across the hall from them. One night the row was so dreadful that she made herself overcome her fear and marched bravely to the door. She found it locked, so she rattled the handle and called for her grandmother inside. It took some time for her voice to penetrate and she had to reinforce it by drumming her fists on the door. Finally, a deadly hush fell inside. Then Louise called: "Sweetheart? Darling? Is that you?" in a quavering voice she tried to make normal.

She unlocked the door and looked out. Her hair was disheveled and wild. Behind her, Leo loomed in a white nightshirt, his hair on end like a bush in flames.

"Go to bed, little worm," Louise coaxed in over-sweet tones. "Grandma is coming." And from behind her, Leo also fluted: "Shall I come and tell you a story?"

Natasha said yes, so that they would stop fighting. Leo came and sat on the edge of her bed. Actually, he didn't like children, but he could, if he wanted to, tell wonderful stories. This one was about two princesses, a tiger, and a horse, in the course of which three generations grew up and several kingdoms were won and lost. It ended happily and with the following moral: "And just because they were angry with each other and fifty years passed during which they were not on speaking terms, do you think they could stop loving each other?" Natasha was too sleepy by this time to answer. She also felt safe and snug in her bed, with Leo sitting on one side and Louise on the other. Louise held a bar of chocolate from which, during the course of Leo's story, she broke off pieces and popped them into Natasha's mouth, where they melted.

"How could it be?" Leo urged. "Even if one hundred years had passed, still they'd go on loving each other. Isn't that true?" he appealed to Natasha.

"Leave her alone, she's sleeping," Louise said from the other side of the bed.

Leo said something to her that Natasha couldn't hear properly (maybe it was in German). It made Louise laugh—she laughed a lot during those days when Leo lived with them.

But afterward, when Leo moved out—packed up his things and left after one of their fights—then it was very difficult for Natasha to do anything for Louise except climb on her lap and put her arms around her neck and beg her not to cry. And Louise tried very hard not to; she unclasped Natasha's hands, she kissed them as though she wished to eat them—she pretended to eat them like a big bad wolf, and Natasha laughed and Louise laughed, even while tears continued to pour out of her eyes.

Once Natasha had had tall dreams for herself. She had wanted to be a doctor. But she couldn't do science subjects, so that had to be put aside. Then she wanted to be a nurse. Whoever knew Natasha couldn't help smiling at that dream, for she was the clumsiest person imaginable. "Oh, my Lord, those poor patients," Mark said. He described what she would do to them, and it was true, she would. So that had to go too. Then her ambition became smaller. She wanted to do something humble but useful: useful to humanity, she thought at first, but afterward she reduced that to just wanting to be part of humanity, a tiny worker bee in its vast hive. So she took a succession of jobs—in a kindergarten, as a waitress (this was especially disastrous), in an ice-cream parlor, a bookstore, a summer camp. She never lasted long anywhere; even those employers who liked her had, in the end, to let her go. Besides being clumsy, she was dreamy and absentminded; and though she tried hard, her physical stamina was not up to her mental resolution.

The final disaster had been a job in a camp for retarded children. The campers were not really children but adults, at least in age and size. Many of them were incontinent, some were violent, others epileptic: they needed care day and night and craved affection. This latter Natasha was eager to give, but she was incapable of giving much else. She was clumsy with them. When she had to change their soiled clothes, she tugged and pulled and had such difficulty that they became exasperated and she desperate. Sometimes they hit her, and she had to hide this from the camp managers. One young woman had such love for her that she wanted to sit constantly in her lap and, though grossly fat through ill-functioning glands, insisted on being carried by her. Once, when Natasha tried to pick her up and totter a few steps with her, they both fell, the girl on top, Natasha underneath. Screaming with shock and rage, the girl seized Natasha's head and banged it violently on the floor. Someone blew a whistle; the counselors and manager of the camp came running. Natasha was rescued, and the girl had to be tied to a bed. A day later another camper threw a pan of boiling water at Natasha, and though she jumped aside more smartly than was usual with her, it became evident that she had an irritating effect on the patients, so she lost that job and Mark had to come take her away.

It was then that Mark arranged with Leo to create a job for her at the Academy. Leo didn't like it, but he rarely said no to Mark. Natasha didn't like it either. "I don't believe in his work," she said. But Mark guessed that this might act for rather than against his plan: if living at the Academy was the most unattractive prospect she had, then very likely it would be the one that, after serious thought, she would choose for herself.

She didn't know that Leo had only agreed to take her on because Mark was secretly paying her salary. Leo never paid anyone unless he absolutely had to; and mostly he didn't have to, getting all the services he needed from the people who came to train with him. It was, in fact, considered part of the training; Leo didn't believe in spiritual without physical work, and participation in lectures, classes, and workshops automatically involved participation in the household and other chores connected with the running of the Academy.

Natasha's job, thought up by Mark, was to take charge of students' files. Perhaps she was the one person in the house who could be trusted not to divulge them, so Leo agreed to let her do this. She had to keep the old files in order and type up the new ones, and she didn't mind it because she found she could do it and didn't often get into a tangle. She also didn't mind living in the attic with the other female students. Usually new members of the Academy were installed in one of the comfortably furnished bedrooms on the second floor, until the arrival of other new members, when they had to move up into the attic or down into the laundry room with the rest of the working force. But Natasha was put into the attic right from the start.

The house, large, heavy, and dark, was physically oppressive to her, and she spent as much time as she could out on the grounds. These had been left tangled and wild, and Natasha wandered along the paths winding among trees and bushes with withered berries on them; or she sat in a little broken pavilion by a body of water that had dead lilies floating on it. She liked being here best of all when the sun set and sky and water brightened and everything else darkened.

No one took much notice of her. Even Stephanie, the girl

with whom she shared one of the cubicles into which the attic was divided, was hardly aware of her. It wasn't that Stephanie was a particularly selfish girl, but she was self-absorbed: well, they all were, that's what they had come to the Academy for. Self-centered here wasn't a bad word, it was an aim, an ideal. It meant self-development, progress, even creation, and it had to be worked at. And Stephanie did work at it, terribly hard. "I've got this big block in me to overcome," she told Natasha. "A big huge block of wrong thinking and wrong living." However, it wasn't so much her own fault as her mother's who, in addition to giving her insufficient love, had instilled in her her own wrong attitudes. At one time Stephanie had hated her mother—also her father (a very successful lawyer), though less so because he was just *weak;* but now she felt sorry for them for being all screwed up. When her mother phoned, from New Mexico where she was living with a younger man, a potter, Stephanie tried to be patient with her. "Why don't you grow up, Mother," was now her only reproach. But she didn't spend much time thinking about her—not like in the past, when she had thought about her *all* the time—she couldn't, because of working so hard at thinking about herself.

Often at night, when they were alone together in their cubicle, she shared these thoughts with Natasha. Their bunk was against the wall, just under one of the round windows that lit up the attic at either end. On moonlit nights, Stephanie could be seen lying in the upper bunk, in her flimsy nightie, her hair spread over the pillow, one arm behind her head, and her eyes shining with tears of longing for self-improvement. And while Stephanie sighed and whispered her psychological secrets, there were similar sounds from all the other cubicles; and one could hear soft sounds of weeping too, for everyone was having a hard time with herself, that was why they were all there in the first place.

All, that is, except Natasha. She felt quite guilty at not

feeling guilty enough about herself: she who was worse than any of them! For they were all good at something, all were useful, and with what dexterity they cooked and cleaned and gardened and whatever other tasks Leo allotted to them. Whereas Natasha sometimes got even her files mixed up and had to call in Stephanie to help her out. And yet Natasha was the only one there who didn't sigh and confess at night but, on the contrary, lay down with a light and happy heart as if she had done a great day's work.

Marietta could never be persuaded to visit the Academy. It had been in existence now for seven years and the movement within it had grown and prospered, but Marietta hadn't been there even once. Yet she was very interested in all Mark's other ventures, knew all about his other properties, and dropped in at his office more often than he liked. But she didn't even want to hear about the Academy of Potential Development.

Leo himself issued many invitations to her—which she ignored as she did her best to ignore everything to do with him. But Leo had never given up. He loved it when people resisted him, nothing pleased him more. "It's like fishing," he said—actually, he never fished at all, it would have bored him to death, as did every sport. "It's no fun unless the fish resists; unless it struggles—flaps and fights and wriggles for its life until—yupp! you've got it: up in the air where you want it, dangling there, with all your hook, line, and sinker inside it." He tended to use this image for both his sexual and his spiritual conquests.

He and Marietta didn't meet very often, she saw to that. At most once a year—which was when, without fail, Leo came to Louise's birthday party. At one time these parties had been very elaborate, for Louise had had many friends in her youth and middle age; but as the years went by, fewer and fewer people remained, so nowadays the celebration was confined to the family: that is, Marietta, Mark, Natasha—and Leo. If she happened to be around and was on speaking terms, Louise's friend Regi also sometimes joined them. But Leo, even in these latter days of his grandeur, never failed to show up, and without being reminded. Sometimes he and Natasha were the only guests—that was during the years when Marietta was going through her Indian phase, and Mark was off somewhere on some trip of his own. Then Leo felt very bored and soon fell asleep, leaving Louise and Natasha to entertain each other.

But when Marietta was there, Leo stayed awake. It was as though her antipathy to him acted as both goad and amusement. In earlier years, he tried to get her to attend his lectures and workshops; later, to visit the Academy. She always said "I'm not your type." And he would say "Try me out," and smirk knowingly around his cigar.

But, in fact, she *was* his type. He attracted many followers who were like Marietta; that is, successful, high-strung women with problems. And perhaps, if it hadn't been for their earlier relationship, she too might have turned to Leo in her (frequent) moments of crisis. Instead, she turned in various other directions. When her marriage failed, she started a fashion business, a line in sportswear, which became very successful; for, in spite of her erratic, high-flown nature, she turned out to be a first-class businesswoman—a talent perhaps inbred in her through her father's line of German-Jewish entrepreneurs, and in turn transmitted by her to Mark. But besides outward activity, she also needed intense inner fulfillment. Leo knew it, and was ready to supply it, as he did to so many others. Marietta looked elsewhere. Above all—in reaction to her mother, for she had seen where that led—she didn't want a lover. She had her son, and that was enough for her, she said: *her* fulfillment lay in Mark. She added Natasha to him. But still something was missing, and Leo pointed it out to her year after year at Louise's birthday party. And every time he did that, she turned from him in greater revulsion,

but every time also she became more restless. So it was perhaps no accident that it was only a few days after one of these
birthday parties that she discovered Ahmed and with him
India and the particular brand of fulfillment to be discovered
there.

Ahmed was a musician and had come to the United
States with a troupe of other Indian musicians and dancers.
Marietta had attended one of their recitals to see the dancers;
although her own artistic career had not prospered, she was
still interested in all forms of dance. However, it was Ahmed
and his sarod who fired her—and to such an extent that at the
end of his recital she felt impelled to climb up on the stage
where he sat. It was a shabby little hall, which had quite
recently been a porno cinema, and the stage too was small
and shabby and so was the mat that had been spread out for
Ahmed and his accompanists to sit on. Marietta was dressed
rather smartly—she was going on to a cocktail party—but she
just hitched up the tight skirt of her dress and knelt right
there in front of everyone on her stockinged knees and bowed
her head to Ahmed and called him Maestro.

Later, she arranged for him to give her sarod lessons, and
later still, when the rest of the troupe went back to India, he
moved in with her in her Central Park West apartment. But
it wasn't him, she always insisted, it was his sarod, his music;
and not even that but the world it opened—the world beyond
world—the promise of peace and fulfillment that was like a
hand laid on her restless heart. Ahmed himself was a very
restful person; one might even say phlegmatic. While he
plucked the most melting, alluring, ethereal sounds from his
sarod, he himself sat there completely impassive, with a dead-
pan expression on his face. If he felt that he was ravishing his
audience beyond their endurance, he might permit himself a
flicker of a smile and one naked toe to twitch under him, and
that was all. His manner off the platform was equally imperturbable. Perhaps that was what drew Marietta—herself so

infinitely perturbable. Otherwise it was difficult to know what she saw in him. He was far from a romantic figure: small, thin, grizzled, he was in his late forties and already a grandfather several times over.

He was glad to move in with Marietta. He liked life in the West. He drank Scotch, smoked incessantly, and watched late-night movies on TV. When Marietta had a crisis of some sort, he wasn't in the least upset. He didn't expect her to be anything but irrational. He stroked her as he might a cat, and she curled up beside him as though she were one.

He was also a good intermediary between her and Mark. Mark was ten years old at the time, and as once it had been his greatest bliss on earth to lie in his mother's embrace all night, and to help her dress, and to be her inseparable companion—"She'll make that boy into a homosexual," Leo had warned Louise—so now his favorite occupation was to tease her, contradict her, make her mad. They fought incessantly. Ahmed took it all in his stride—he knew about mothers and sons, how alternately they adored and exasperated each other, and he also took it for granted that the relation with her son was the strongest in a woman's life. He helped her by entertaining Mark—whom he liked as he liked all children, naturally and without fuss—and he took him and Natasha out to see cartoon films at which he laughed more than they did.

But one day he decided it was time to return to India. It was impossible to tell whether this decision was the result of slow gestation or came to him on a sudden impulse; nor was it clear whether it was due to homesickness, or because he was tired of New York, or of Marietta. He didn't give her much time to get used to the idea. One day she came home from her showroom to find him packing. He was leaving the next day.

Five months later she followed him to India. Ahmed wasn't distressed by her surprise arrival. On the contrary, he seemed to like it. He at once began to spend a lot of time in

her hotel room, enjoying once again the Western luxuries he
had missed since his departure from New York. He took her
everywhere and was proud to be seen with her. Fair and shining, she was like a trophy he had brought home from his
foreign tour, or a luxury article he had smuggled past cus-
toms. Her enthusiasm over everything amused him. How she
exclaimed! And at what he considered such common, every-
day things, one was almost ashamed of them. She adored,
simply adored, the bazaars and the merchants sitting inside
their booths amid their goods: copper pans, or silver orna-
ments, textiles fluttering in the wind, gaudy sweetmeats—such
colors, she had never seen, never dreamed such colors! She
liked the smells, too, of incense and clarified butter, and even
the denser ones of rotting vegetables and more sinister rotting
things—even those didn't bother her, for she regarded them as
part of everything: as the beggars were part of it all, and the
corpses on the pyres, and the diseased people healing themselves in the sacred river, and the very fat priests.

Ahmed's friends invited her to be with them at their all-
night music sessions and to drink opium dissolved in almond
juice and milk. They appreciated her cries of "Fantastic! Fab-
ulous! Oh, Ahmed, it's too much!" They took her boating on
the crowded river, drinking and playing music like a royal
party. The women in Ahmed's family also enjoyed her company. Crammed together in inner rooms, they were avid for
outside entertainment. Marietta was a show for them: they
admired and enjoyed everything about her—her lithe figure,
her blond hair worn loose and long, her scanty summer
frocks. And she let them touch her to their heart's content
and slipped off her costume jewelry for them to try on. She
watched them cook and ate in abundance and pretended she
was interested in the recipes. She wondered and wondered at
everything and exclaimed and shone with joy so that there
was absolutely no language barrier—feeling streamed out of
her. And she detected a deep understanding in them, for in

spite of their secluded lives, they were intelligent women and sharp and worldly. They probably guessed Marietta's relationship with Ahmed and took it for granted: everyone knew what men did once they were out of the house, and who could blame them for what they did as far away as abroad? No questions were asked. Marietta loved their acceptance of everything—of their condition, their womanliness; she felt they were deeply intuitive and above all wiser than anyone she had ever known. She longed, for a while, to be like them.

But although, after the first visit, she returned to India every year for a period of six years, she never again spent much time with Ahmed's family. Instead she traveled around, mostly on her own, mostly in planes and hired cars. She wanted to see everything but as herself, making no attempt to merge with people and landscape. She enthused about Indian materials, but when she had clothes made out of them, they were to her own design and Western taste. She never took to a sari or any other form of Indian dress, and her sandals remained Italian and high-heeled.

She met other Western women traveling around India. Some of these had attached themselves to a guru, or were going around in search of one. Marietta was interested in their quest, as she was interested in everything else she met with, and occasionally she followed them to their ashram. But she could never stay there long. It was too vapid and inaesthetic for her and not what she had come to India for. The ashrams always seemed to be situated in dust bowls, and the followers of the gurus had the same drained, infertile air as the landscape. As for the gurus themselves, although they varied in personality, there was something about all of them that reminded her of Leo: not so much in themselves, as in the effect they had. Moreover, while Marietta kept excellent health all through the rest of her travels, every time she visited an ashram she got some infection; so she stopped going.

Whenever she arrived in a big city, she at once checked

into a luxury hotel. There she had long, cool showers and trays sent up to her air-conditioned room. Young men whom she had met came to visit her. They were eager Indian youths who were excited by being in an expensive hotel, and also by her. They examined the clothes she had unpacked and sprayed themselves with her scents. They slept with her and were ashamed if their lovemaking was too frenzied to be sustained. But she didn't mind—it wasn't for sex that she liked being with them, it was for themselves. They were charming and pure.

When Mark grew up, and before launching himself into the property business, he traveled a great deal and to all sorts of places. Sometimes his family would hear from him in California, and then from Mexico, or from Paris, from Rome, from Istanbul; they never knew from where it would be next. Not that they ever heard much—a phone call, a postcard, and that was all. They didn't know what he was doing, or whom he was with, and he discouraged questions. All he allowed them to do was send him money, and sometimes he applied to his grandmother for it, and sometimes to his mother; each thought it a privilege to supply him. Then one day he would turn up again, as unexpectedly as he had departed.

His absences were prolonged and hard to bear for all three women. The worst of it was that, even when he did come home, they never knew when he might decide to be off again. Once, when he had been back less than two weeks from a three-month absence, Marietta came home from her showroom to find him packing up again. He said he was leaving for London in the evening.

She stood in the doorway of his room and said, "You've got to be joking." Her voice shook.

His reaction to her presence was to perform his task a trifle more slowly, deliberately, thoroughly. Mark was always thorough and deft. He had small, neat hands, and it was a pleasure to watch him do anything; he himself took pleasure in his own dexterity. He smoothed his shirts, he fitted his socks into carefully prepared interstices; his suitcase was laid out as exactly as a diagram.

Marietta tried to calm herself by showering and changing. She made herself fragrant with soap and talc and toilet water; she brushed her hair—still blond, though no longer naturally—she wore a long loose robe of pastel silk. All the time she was alert to sounds from Mark's room. She heard him move about and once he talked on the phone, laughing his light, pleasant laugh. She had to restrain herself from rushing in there and snatching the receiver from his hand; she had tried that before, in their life together, and it had not done her any good. Her heart beat loud and sharp. She lay down on her sofa and tried to at least look relaxed. She shut her eyes, she waited for him.

When he strolled in from his packing, he seemed pleased to see her so apparently calm. He touched her robe: "Nice. Is it new?" he rewarded her. She opened her eyes and looked into his. "I bought it months ago. I've worn it hundreds of times." He turned away.

Marietta's apartment was as light as Louise's was dark. She had low, deep furniture upholstered in raw silk, a shining gold Buddha, and on the walls some exquisite gold-framed Indian miniatures. Her Oriental rugs bloomed with delicate floral motifs. One wall was entirely taken up by windows, framing her view of Central Park. Mark stood against this and looked over the wide green vista and the blue reservoir. He could feel his mother behind him, her gaze into his back, so that he resisted turning around for a long time.

"Why London, could you tell me?" she said at last.

"I have to go." He spoke in a firm, kind voice and turned back into the room. He was anxious above all to avoid a fight, not for his own sake—all he need finally do was pick up his suitcase and go—but for her: so as not to leave her in the painful way he had to once or twice before.

"You don't have to go at all. Not at all." She sat up on the sofa: "You're getting more and more irresponsible. You're going to be like your father. You're never going to do anything."

Mark shrugged; he could take that lightly, for he knew it wasn't true. He wasn't in the least like his father. She knew it too; she knew him to be like herself; part of herself.

"Come here," she said. "Sit here. No, I'm not going to make a fuss. I only want to talk to you. Come on."

He approached warily. When he was close enough to grab hold of, she resisted the temptation and waited with bated breath for him to sit beside her. Her heart beat terribly hard with this effort at self-control, it was like a stone flinging itself against her ribs.

"When you're not here," she said when he was perched, somewhat cautiously, beside her, "I wait for your calls—rare enough, God knows. Any news of you. Yes, yes, I know, darling, I shouldn't, but there it is all the same. I do it. . . . Don't sit like that, poised for flight, it's too—" She laughed to swallow up that last word, and the laugh ended on a sob and she raised her hands as though to clutch the front of his shirt but let them fall again and lie, veined and fine with beautiful rings, in her lap.

"My goodness," Mark said. "What a fuss. As if you'll never see me again; as if I'm going forever. As if I'm shipping out to Australia instead of a quick trip to London."

"How quick?" she quickly pounced, so that he closed up again, guarded himself. She put her hands before her face and her shoulders shook; she wept like a little girl.

He was moved by both pity and exasperation; the latter was stronger, but nevertheless he gathered her into his arms. He said, "Why do we have to go through this every time?

Every *time?*" With her face buried against him, he stroked her back. He rather liked doing that—he had always liked it—feeling her slender back through the fine silk, it gave him a luxurious sensation; but at the same time he turned his wrist to look at his watch. She held herself stiffly, wanting this to go on forever but knowing that it would stop very soon.

Natasha came home and found them like that. Mark looked at her over their mother's back; he usually managed to make her understand without having to say anything. She understood now. She went into his room, she saw his packed bags. She sat down for a moment on his bed; but she didn't bother him with her feelings—which was just as well, for he had his hands, literally, full with his mother.

"I feel so strange nowadays, darling," Marietta was whispering into his shirt where her face was hidden. "Sort of trembly all the time—can't you feel it? . . . What do you think it could be? Could it be my menopause?"

"What, already?" he said, for she was in her early forties at the time.

"I haven't been very regular these last months . . . You know how I'm like clockwork, usually." He did know, he knew everything about her, there was no intimate detail she spared him.

"Maybe you're pregnant."

"Oh, sure." She gave a sarcastic laugh. It wouldn't have been impossible—except that she was certain it was; as if any of those people could impregnate her, those short-term boyfriends who had succeeded Ahmed. She allowed them to stay with her sometimes, only to turn them out as soon as Mark needed her for anything, even if it was nothing more than to accompany him to a show. "I should see a doctor," she said. "I mean, in case it's something really awful."

"You should." Again he turned his wrist to glance at his watch.

"You don't think it could be?"

"Menopause?"

"Something really awful."

He had a plane to catch, a friend to meet at the airport; it was not the time to discuss his mother's internal problems.

"Do it some more, darling," she said, for he had stopped caressing her back. "It really makes me feel better, calmer. You're the one person in the world who can make me feel calm," she pleaded.

Natasha came out of his bedroom. She was carrying his suitcase; it was bigger than she was and pulled her sideways and her face into a grimace of strain. But she struggled on manfully.

Mark let go of Marietta and jumped up in relief. "Put it down!" he cried to Natasha. Of course she wouldn't—Natasha could be stubborn where it was a question of self-immolation—and he had to compromise with her by allowing her to carry his portmanteau. All this got him naturally into the swing of departure and farewell to Marietta. Natasha accompanied him down into the street and waited for a cab with him and helped him into it; and received his cool kiss and stood there to wave; while he drove off, relieved, looking only forward now to his journey and his friend, while Natasha went back up to do what she could for Marietta.

Louise had grown up in a suburb of the town of D— in Germany. Her parents had a villa with a garden in which grew apple and plum trees. Every day Louise got in the tram to go to her school in D—. From the time she was thirteen— like most big girls she developed early—there was always some boy waiting near the tram stop to catch a glimpse of her. Sometimes he got on the tram, to have the pleasure of riding with her and furtively watching her. Another unknown boy might be hovering at the other end, waiting for her to get off. Louise didn't mind, and learned to expect it. But it made her carry herself in a certain way—with her head held high and her bust thrust out, looking neither right nor left and apparently unaware of anything going on around her. She often tossed back her head so that her thick pigtail swung around; when she put up her hair—she never cut it, even when everyone else went for the Eton crop—she still did that, only now her coils of hair swayed like a crown on her proud head. By this time it was not boys but dashing young men who waited for her. Some of them were quite bold, though always respectful, and they approached her and dared to ask for a rendezvous. At sixteen she had her first affair of the heart, with a young medical student as romantic as herself. It was very beautiful but had to end when he was recalled on the death of his father to manage his family's estate in Silesia. Fate tore them apart, her heart was broken, but only for a while.

The town of D—— had an excellent theater as well as opera house, and Louise was a devotee of both. She and her friends gathered up in the "gods" to cheer and bravo their favorites and clamor for encores and curtain calls. Afterward they appeared at the stage door to ask for autographs, and Louise only had to be seen to be asked out to after-theater suppers with the actors. By this time she had an inseparable companion—they called themselves The Inseparables—in her friend Regi, also very handsome though a completely different type. Regi was tall, thin, nervous, with short skirt, short hair, and a cigarette in a holder. She was sharper and more daring—altogether more modern—than Louise, but they made a good ensemble and a welcome addition to the town's more advanced circles. But although they sat in smart cafés and visited expressionistic painters in their studios, they did not in any way behave cheaply. Both had to be home at a certain hour—their fathers sat up for them—and they attended serious classes in art history, cordon bleu cooking, and eurythmics. They accepted this routine for, while allowing them to be bohemian in their leisure time, it kept them basically bourgeois and unspoiled for the advantageous marriages to which their looks entitled them.

So it happened that, when Bruno Sonnenblick first saw Louise at the Opera, she was exactly what he took her for: a pure young girl. He wouldn't have settled for less; he hadn't waited this long for less. Bruno was thirty-six years old—eighteen years older than she, today he would have been over a hundred! He was a director of his family firm of thread manufacturers and lived with his widowed mother in the family mansion in the Kaiserallee. Every day he was driven home from the factory in a Mercedes-Benz to lunch with his mother, and then she saw to it that his nap was not disturbed. Only she herself came tiptoeing in, to replace his freshly laundered shirts or arrange gloves and spats on their appointed shelves. It could not have been easy for her when Louise entered the picture. But there was no help for it: Bruno was hotly in love.

Every day flowers, chocolates, and the Mercedes-Benz came for Louise. She moved into a box at the theater, and supper afterward was alone with Bruno in an alcove at Schwamm's. He ran the entire gamut of breathless courtship, but best of all were the letters he wrote when he had to leave on a business trip abroad. Yes, it was these letters that won her. They were written on pale stationery with the family watermark; they were entirely legible, for his handwriting remained as neat as his English suit, his spats, and Homburg hat, even when he was swept away by passion:

Most Deeply Beloved,
As I sit here in my hotel room overlooking the Hyde Park, your goddess face and form rise before my eyes and so overwhelm me that at this very moment I feel tempted to fling myself on the carpet and kiss it in ardent gratitude! Such gratitude at your blessedness and that the light of it has come

*to shine in my life. It is too much to grasp. Until the day I
beheld you, I did not know that the human beings could live
in bliss on earth. I did not believe in heaven—I have confessed to you, dearest, my views on religion—but now I believe in heaven on earth. Thanks to you, my goddess,
immortal thanks . . .*

Shortly after Leo first met Louise, he moved in with her
and Bruno into their West Side apartment. Those were
strange times for all of them, when they were refugees who
had lost their first hold on life and were trying to establish a
new one. This was exciting as well as devastating for those of
them still young enough to start again but for those who were
not, like Bruno, it was only devastating. He shuffled around
the apartment like an old man. It was the one place that felt
familiar to him, for not only was it filled with his family
furniture but it also had the same high ceilings, vestibule and
corridor, and sliding doors between the living and dining
rooms as the house in the Kaiserallee. He tried sometimes to
go for a walk by himself but came back very soon and waited
till Louise was free to take him. She loved this new city and
felt herself to be growing and learning in it as much as Marianne (later Marietta) who had been a baby when they
brought her.

Louise considered it a privilege when Leo decided to
move in with them. The apartment was dark, but with him in
it the effect was as of shutters flung open, light streaming in.
He did have a tendency to leave every door wide open—even
bathroom doors sometimes!—enabling him to move from
room to room in an unimpeded sweep. He needed free space
and had in fact a theory about the stultifying effect of closed-
in architecture. But he had theories about everything. He
brought a lot of people in, very interesting types, and there
were tremendous discussions and working out of plans and
differences of opinion in which Leo's usually prevailed. Every-

one was finally ready to give way to him not only because he shouted louder—though that too—but because he really knew better, felt more intensely, was willing and able to carry through. At that time his principal aim was to develop an awareness of three-dimensional living in a civilization which was hopelessly crippled in all its responses. Through the theater, though reaching far beyond it, he intended to train initiates and form them into a movement which was to be socially, psychologically, and—why not?—biologically revolutionary.

They all sat far into the night around the dining table from the house in the Kaiserallee, fortified by a continuous supply of Viennese coffee, lemon tea, petits fours, and sweet liqueurs. Louise never got tired of sitting there listening, sometimes clasping her hands in wonder at what she heard. Bruno was next to her, and when she got particularly excited, she squeezed his knee. For him it was a double pleasure to be present, for his own sake, and then to see her so alive, so caught up. Of course he got tired much earlier than everyone else, but she would plead with him "Just five more minutes, Brunolein, you *must* hear this"; so that he made an effort to keep awake, though not always successfully.

By the time Bruno's last illness was diagnosed and an operation performed, he was too weak to survive it. He lay in the high hospital bed, white and emaciated but somehow looking young, boyish almost, in his cerulean-blue pajamas and his eyes luminous as they followed Louise around the room. The nurses adored him. He never asked for anything, and when his lips moved to form a request, it was always and only Louise he wanted. She bent down to hear him and he tried to bring out words of endearment, smiling ruefully at himself because he was too weak to complete them. And tears like molten lead surged into her eyes and she could hardly wait to get out into the corridor. There she leaned against the wall, but its cool gray stone gave no relief. She stood there in grief, despair, and repentance till a nurse came out and said "Louise, he wants you," smiling at such childlike attachment from the dying old man.

After her father died, Marietta temporarily locked up her apartment and moved herself, Mark, and Natasha in with her mother. Unfortunately just at this time her husband, from whom she had been separated for several years, made one of his periodic attempts to persuade her to return to him. He did this regularly—she never knew why, because he wasn't any happier with her than she with him.

Tim was a weak person, but when he wanted something he could be very persistent. He pursued Marietta with endless telephone calls; he followed her down the street, jumped into cabs with her, barged into her showroom, turned up at her business lunches. He came up to Louise's apartment at two o'clock one morning. As soon as the bell rang, Marietta knew it was he, and she called to her mother not to open. But he rang and rang till Louise got up and let him in. He walked past her into what she still called her salon (pronounced in the German way as "zalong"). He sat down on the sofa with his legs crossed, as relaxed as a casual afternoon caller. He was completely drunk, but the only sign was that he moved very slowly and carefully as though afraid of breaking something.

At the time of Bruno's funeral and in accordance with some custom she vaguely remembered from his family, Louise had shrouded all the mirrors in the apartment. Afterward she had not uncovered them; perhaps she forgot, perhaps she just did not want to see herself. Marietta too was glad not to see herself in mirrors. Both women looked tragic and neglected, shut up together in the dark, high-ceilinged apartment. It was dim, dusty, and disheveled even during the day, and how much more so at two in the morning. But Tim didn't seem to notice; he sat there, elegant and completely at ease—the only bright spot in the room in his pale-gray suit and striped shirt and Countess Mara necktie—and said, "Couldn't I have a drink?"

"Why don't you go home? Why don't you go away? You know she doesn't want you," Louise said in the toneless voice she had during those days.

"Whatever you've got," he pleaded. He really couldn't stand it anymore but got up to open the sideboard. All he found was an opened bottle of sweet red wine and, clicking his tongue in pity, he poured it into a glass. He made a face as he drank it, but it was better than nothing, so he refilled it again.

By this time he had forgotten what he had come for. He moved around the room, so slowly that it seemed to take him an age to get from the sideboard to the grand piano. He swayed somewhat, but that was the way he always moved—maybe because he was so tall and willowy, like a reed that any breeze could ripple. He sat down at the piano; he opened it; before Louise could stop him, he began to play. He had a really nice touch on the piano. He played by ear and always the jazzy, catchy tunes he heard in the piano bars he frequented; he only had to hear them once and he could play them.

And he really liked playing, and listening to himself. He entertained himself so well that he completely failed to hear Louise's protests; or the wail that Natasha now set up from Louise's bedroom where she lay in her cradle. There was something terrible about Natasha's crying as a baby. They all dreaded it. It sounded like the weeping of an old woman rather than a child, full of hopeless grief; and once it started it went on for hours. Only Mark ever managed to sleep through it; and now his father to play through it.

Marietta got up and went into Louise's bedroom. She picked up Natasha and walked up and down with her, to no avail. Louise joined her, she too rocked and shushed and

clucked, but Natasha cried louder, and that made Tim play
louder in order not to be drowned out. Marietta couldn't
stand it anymore—she went into the salon to try to stop him.
He did look strange, enjoying himself so much in that desolate room with the shrouded mirrors and the chandelier dim
against the windows growing smoky with dawn.

"Listen to this, Mari," he said. "Don't you like it?" And
he began to sing the words as far as he remembered them:
"Parrot," he sang, "why only Pretty Polly dear, what's wrong
with sweetheart love and sugar bun—" and forgetting the rest,
he supplemented it with la-la-la and swaying and smiling,
encouraging Marietta to join in with him. When she shut the
piano, wedging his hands under the lid, he left them there
and looked bewildered. "What did you do that for?" he said.
"Open it, or I can't go on playing." He was so drunk he no
longer knew what was going on, or why he had come, or
anything. He waited for her to reopen the piano lid, and
when she wouldn't, he did it by himself. He went on playing;
at least it drowned out the baby's crying. But he stopped
before Natasha did and slumped over the keys, bringing out a
fearful sound that almost matched hers. He was asleep and
muttered when Marietta tried to wake him. So she left him
and returned to the bedroom she shared with Mark. She lay
next to him—how peacefully he slept—and pressed herself
against him and hid her face in his sweet warm hair.

The Old Vienna first opened its doors in the thirties at
the time when they all arrived in New York as refugees. In the
beginning they laughed at it for the crudity of its effects—the
deep-blue buttoned banquettes, the velvet curtains with gold-
fringed valances over panels of white lace, the chandeliers
hanging down as thick and fast as paper lanterns. But the
place turned out to be so comfortable, the service so good,
the management was so affable, not to speak of the Viennese specialties—the coffee with whipped cream, the strudel,

nockerln, and all the rest of it—that everyone just kept coming, and it was crowded from the time it opened at noon till it
shut at two in the morning. Louise and Regi often went there,
either for a tête-à-tête or to meet other friends in their circle;
and it was they who first brought Leo at a time when he
couldn't have afforded to come on his own. Afterward of
course he became almost the reigning deity of the place.

Louise and Regi had their first quarrel about Leo in the
Old Vienna. It was their habit to meet there at least once a
week for afternoon coffee and "to talk things over." What
they talked over on that occasion was Leo's classes which were
about to begin. They were his first experiments in a lifelong
series of training programs and workshops—his trials and
errors, as he called them, toward the evolution of a life-philos-
ophy (though he hated that word) which in the end cul-
minated in The Point.

The point at issue between Louise and Regi on that afternoon was where these classes were to be held. At first he
had agreed to hold them at Regi's and she was annoyed that
the venue had been changed to Louise and Bruno's apartment where he was then living.

"But Regi, darling," Louise tried to soothe her, "it
wouldn't be convenient for you. . . . You know you like to
sleep late. And what when you have to sort your laundry?"
she said, smiling on this last, for it was one of their private jokes, Regi sorting her laundry meaning Regi having a
lover in.

But Regi continued to pout. Pouting rather suited her,
she had that sort of mouth; also, ever since the age of thirty
she had been a redhead, and redheads were expected to be
sulky. "He isn't going to hold classes all day, is he? We could
arrange about the times."

"Can you honestly see Leo arranging with anyone about
his times? You know what he's like, what sort of a *tornado,*"
Louise said, and laughed out loud.

"Well, of course, with you spoiling him. He doesn't have it so easy with me, I can tell you." Regi tossed her head and looked more sulky. She and Louise were always somewhat on display at the Old Vienna. They were perched on little chairs at one of the round marble-topped tables for two set up in a row along the center of the restaurant. Their legs were too long to fit under the table, so they kept them crossed outside, long and smooth in silk. Both were elegantly dressed—Louise in one of her sober, well-cut suits of very expensive material with a fox-fur piece around her neck; and Regi much more flamboyantly in a long-skirted, clinging crepe de Chine dress with masses of jewelry hung like booty all over her.

A waiter approached their table with a note. It happened regularly, and the only question was for which one of them the note was intended. This time it was for Louise; she read it and tossed it in the ashtray. "I told you, Heinz," she spoke severely to the waiter, "not to bring me these things."

"What can I do," the waiter said. He leaned over the table, not only to brush it with his napkin but also to whisper to Louise: "He says you are the most beautiful woman he has ever seen."

"Ridiculous," Regi said, stubbing out her cigarette on the note in the ashtray. "Which one is it? One of those decrepit pieces of furniture against the wall, I expect."

"The gentleman on the right over there," Heinz whispered.

Only Regi turned around to look. She saw a smart, bold Viennese gallant—there were still plenty of them around in those days, sitting in their favorite cafés all day on the lookout for women with whom to have a liaison or just a rendezvous. Regi turned back contemptuously.

"I don't know why you have this fatal attraction for all the dear old gentlemen," she told Louise. "You should *see* this one: why don't you have a peep? He's smiling all his gold teeth at you."

"I'm not interested."

"No. I think nowadays you are only interested in Leo."

This upset both of them: Regi because she thought it was true, Louise because Regi was going too far.

Assembling her dignity around her like a shawl, Louise said: "Of course I'm interested in Leo. Aren't you? I thought we were both interested in his work."

"Well! Good heavens! Who introduced you to him in the first place? Who discovered him: you or me? I must say! Ridiculous!"

"Keep your hair on please, Regi."

"Sometimes you're so irritating, I'd really like to scream. I would scream too, if we weren't in public."

"Go on. Do. I think you ought to."

"Do you think so?" Regi asked. "Are we supposed to act out in public too?"

They huddled closer around their little marble table and fell into a deep discussion. To the Viennese gentlemen watching them from all around the restaurant it was clear that they were talking about affairs of the heart. But actually they were discussing Leo's theories which were changing their lives. They were both in their thirties and several years older than he was; they were married women—in Regi's case already twice, and twice divorced: they had a lot more money than he and were at that time among those who had the privilege of supporting him. But none of this detracted from his authority over them, and they had absolutely no hesitation in putting themselves—their personalities, or inner beings, or souls (except that he disliked that word)—into his hands.

A compromise was reached about his classes. Since Regi's apartment was starkly modernistic with a lot of empty space, it was more suitable for the physical expression classes; while the theoretical lectures remained at Louise's. Both represented important, indeed, inseparable aspects of his work.

At that time his teaching was still loosely attached to the theater—though the theater only in so far as it was a symbol of Life; and in his theoretical classes at Louise's he taught that the actor—*mutatis mutandis,* the human being—could only express those passions which he had absorbed into himself through his own experiences. Leo would call on someone, anyone, at random—and how their hearts beat, for who would it be today?—to relate some personal experience in illustration of the Passion which was the topic of the day. One day it might be Jealousy, or Wrath, or merely Irritability, another Love. It was discussed, expounded on, at Louise's, and then at Regi's it was acted out. With all her tubular furniture pushed out of the way, and only her white wolf rugs scattered over the parquet floor, the students gave strenuous physical expression to the chosen Passion; not only in their own characters but assuming those of others as different from themselves as might be—shoe clerk, masseuse, streetcar conductor; and further, not only as human beings but as animals too, so that, for instance, on the Day of Wrath there would be such roaring as of lions, such bellowings of bulls, chatterings of monkeys, shrieks of hyenas that nervous old ladies in the rest of the building would call through the intercom to complain to the doorman who came up to ring Regi's bell.

Leo's classes became popular, so that soon Louise's apartment was too small for his lectures, and Regi's for his physical workshops. He took a large open rehearsal space in a building converted into an experimental theater. Around this time, he began to prepare his students for public demonstrations. These were not to be regarded as a contribution to theater—he was moving farther and farther away from that— but as a demonstration of his work in the field of existential experiment. He discouraged students with an interest in or talent for acting in favor of those whom he called "blank

pages": that is, those who were willing to give themselves over
to his exercises for their own sake—to lend themselves, body
and soul, to his experiments.

This Louise and Regi were fervently willing to do. On
the other hand, they were by no means blank pages but had
very highly developed temperaments of their own. The same
could be said of all Leo's students—both at that time and,
indeed, at all times. Maybe that was why they were attracted
to him in the first place, because they had proliferated into
such complicated personalities that they could no longer
manage themselves and felt the need to hand themselves over
to someone else, someone stronger. It was part of the challenge of his work; but it was also part of its difficulties, and
from this time on he began to have what he called his "escape
hatch" to which he could retreat from the demands of his
emotionally charged students.

His first escape hatch was a small room at the top of the
experimental theater building. He allowed his students to fur-
nish it with the sort of things he liked and needed—a leather
couch, framed etchings of Gothic edifices, a comfortable armchair, many reading lamps, and a phonograph on which to
play his favorite Wagner and Beethoven records. It was a
cozy, masculine den, and his students took an eager pride in
getting it ready: but when it was, they found themselves
excluded with a big LEAVE ME ALONE sign which he had
scrawled on a piece of brown paper and tacked to the door.
They could do nothing but stare at it.

Although Leo moved some of his personal possessions to
the escape hatch, he still kept most of them in his room in
Louise and Bruno's apartment. This suited him—especially as
they did not charge him any rent—and it also suited Louise,
for that way she could still think of him as living with her.
She lay awake at night, waiting for him to come in. For the
rest of her life she remembered those nights of waiting, with
Bruno asleep next to her. Often she couldn't stand it anymore

but got up and moved from room to room and looked out the windows into the deserted lamplit street below. She always ended up in Leo's room, moving around it, touching his things, experiencing its emptiness suffused for her with the feel of him. Overcome sometimes with emotion, she stood leaning her face against the cold window glass. The building opposite was the same heavy, scrolled, turn-of-the-century apartment house as her own; here and there in its dark granite mass a window was lighted up like a watchful eye. The silence in her own apartment was as deep as its darkness, and Bruno slept and slept—or she thought he did. Once, though, when exhausted with watching and waiting, she came and sank next to him again, she saw that his eyes were open and as wakeful as the windows opposite. It was a shock: "Bruno?" she said, but at once his lids extinguished his gaze, and she saw that he was breathing regularly in peaceful sleep, so she must have been mistaken.

Louise and Leo had become lovers within a week of his moving in with her and Bruno. For her it was a secret that she carried within her like the gardens of paradise—green, blooming, watered by eternal springs; birds sang perpetually. One day she couldn't stand it anymore—she had to unburden herself: of course to Regi, and in the Old Vienna.

But Regi, as soon as Louise had made her tremendous, her tremulous, confession, just laughed: "You don't by any chance think no one *knows?*" When she saw the expression on Louise's face, she laughed more. She made a production of it, throwing back her head and opening her mouth wide with all her healthy teeth and palate flourishing within. Of course the men all around looked at her, hungry as wolves.

"You're wonderful," Regi said.

"You mean you guessed?"

"Guessed!" Again Regi laughed, but only for a moment. Then she turned serious and cynical: "Well, what do you expect—what would anyone expect—when someone like Leo moves in with someone like you?"

Pained and bewildered, Louise protested: "But he's my teacher. Mine and yours."

"Yes, some teacher. Listen," Regi went on, "I know Leo. And I know you."

"No, Regi, that's not fair."

And it wasn't: Louise was by no means promiscuous. In giving her hand in marriage to Bruno, she had given herself totally: first as chaste bride, then—after the birth of their daughter (it took eleven years till Marietta was conceived)—as housewife and mother, the Ceres of his household. She adored Bruno, no other man but her husband had ever counted for her.

"Oh, I'm not blaming you," Regi said, blowing cigarette smoke into the air, worldly-wise and tolerant. "It was inevitable. I was just waiting for it—ever since you told me what you told me."

For in one of their tête-à-tête sessions at the Old Vienna, Louise had confessed to Regi that now she and Bruno were as father and daughter, or brother and sister, or was it mother and child?—anyway, all possible combinations except husband and wife with each other. Louise had not complained: it made no difference at all to her feelings for Bruno whom she loved as before.

"If it hadn't been Leo," Regi said, "it would have been someone else. Well, naturally, what are you, a nun or something?" She was quite indignant on Louise's behalf.

But now Louise got really angry: "You don't think, you're not thinking, that it's nothing more than—with Leo and me—" She couldn't even bring out what she had to say and ended up with "How horrible of you."

Regi shrugged her slender, crepe de Chine shoulders; she lighted another cigarette; she recrossed her long legs by the side of the little marble-topped table. "Sometimes you talk like a child."

But just now Louise could hardly talk at all; she continued to stammer, partly in anger, partly in frustration at being unable to express the height and depth of her feelings. At that moment the waiter came up with a note. It was for Louise—tears of rage rose in her eyes, she tore the note across and across and threw the pieces on the deep-pile rose carpet. How handsome she looked as she did this, how brilliant her eyes were, and her bosom heaved like an opera singer's: her gold-toothed, bald-headed inamorato across the restaurant thrilled at the sight of his own rejection.

She jerked her head in his direction: "I hope you're not mixing Leo up with one of those. And I hope you don't think there's anything vulgar going on."

"I told you: I'm not blaming you. I never thought it was vulgar when you made your pass at Leo—well, yes, of course you did, my goodness, what else was it?" Now it was Regi who was angry, whose eyes blazed; but unlike Louise's eyes, full of fire, Regi's were of ice, glinting green: "From the very first time you saw him at my place, from that first afternoon, I could see it: what was going to happen; what you were after."

"Lies, lies," said Louise, shutting her eyes.

"But I'm saying: it's not your fault. How could you help it? You were ready for it. And I was happy for you; I was glad. I'm still glad," she said, crushing her cigarette in the ashtray in a rather vicious way.

Louise gathered up her handbag. She buttoned the coat of her two-piece. She rose with a resolute air.

"But what's the matter?" Regi inquired, looking up at her. "Can't we even talk frankly with each other—I thought that's what friends are for? Oh, all right, go then, if you want to, but don't forget it's your turn for the check this week."

Louise opened her purse; she placed money on the table

regally. And regally—tall, full-figured, crowned with a wide-
brimmed hat—she walked out of the restaurant. She did not
hear Regi call after her, "You can take the change from me
later!" Nor was she in the least aware of the tide of interest
and admiration that followed in her wake. As soon as she
disappeared through the revolving door, this tide turned and
swept back toward the marble table where Regi now sat
alone. Regi had picked up and counted the money and put it
away in her alligator bag; she called for more coffee with
cream; she recrossed her legs. Men straigthened their neckties.
With a click of her gold lighter, Regi lighted another cigarette
and rounded her mouth to blow the first smoke ring into
the air.

    Forty years later, Louise and Regi still met at the Old
Vienna, though not very regularly. Regi lived mostly in Florida now, and when she visited New York, she didn't always
bother to call Louise. But when she did, they usually arranged to meet at the Old Vienna, and as before they oc-
cupied one of the little tables for two ranged down the center.
And as before, they drew many glances—only now not because they were handsome but because, perched among the
crowded tables, tall and old and odd, they were impossible to
overlook. And Regi, though still retaining the bored manner
she had developed for social occasions, was at the same time
avidly alert to everything going on around her.
    "Why do you still come here?" she asked Louise, though
she herself had never suggested another meeting place. Her
eyes roved around, rested on Leo's old table in the alcove:
"Because of him, I suppose."
    "He's hardly here now. He's at the Academy."
    "Academy," Regi said. "Ridiculous. Who's ever heard of
such pretentiousness. . . . And I hear the girls are getting
younger and younger."
    "You're looking well, Regi," Louise said.

"Because I look after myself well." Her eyes rested on Louise; she smoked disdainfully. Louise still wore one of those same dark suits Regi remembered from years ago, and the same big hat to go with it; only now her hair, too thin to keep pins in, straggled from underneath. Regi herself had given up on her hair and wore a tall red wig; her brand-new dress was silk and of electric blue, and her jewelry was bigger and more fantastic than ever.

"And now you've sent your granddaughter to him too. Even if she isn't your granddaughter." Regi had never given her approval to Natasha's adoption.

"She's working in the office," Louise said. "There's a lot of secretarial work."

"In the first place," Regi said, counting off on a skeletal forefinger, "she can't do secretarial work."

"Natasha is very hardworking." But Louise sounded neither convinced nor happy. She didn't know why Natasha had gone to stay at the Academy; she wished she hadn't. It was true, Natasha couldn't do secretarial work; Leo would get angry and yell at her whenever she bungled something, which would be often.

"In the second place—" Regi said; she was ready with another finger to count off, but then she couldn't remember what there was in second place. Her eyes began to rove around the restaurant again; when she caught a curious glance at herself, she put on the contemptuous expression with which she had always warded off a pass. "Such awful types come here now," she said. "I wouldn't be seen out dead with any of them. And the waiters are just useless, no good." She clawed at a passing one, pointed at her empty cup: "*If* you're not too busy, thank you, and can spare a little time for me. I'm going to the theater tonight," she told Louise. "A musical, you know how I love them. Jerry is taking me—you remember Jerry?"

"Yes," Louise lied. Regi always had some young man

around whom she paid as little as she could get away with, so
they changed frequently.

"You do? How can you? I only met him last week . . .
Oh, I suppose you're mixing him up with Chuck. Well, Mr.
Chuck had his good-bye and good riddance, we've seen quite
enough of that one, thank you very much. . . . Oh, by the
way, he said he knew your Mark."

"Why not? Mark knows a lot of people."

"I wouldn't like him to know someone like Chuck; not if
he were *my* grandson. . . . I have such a pain here, Louise, it
shoots right up my thigh."

"Pain," Louise said. "Who doesn't have pain."

"I have my checkup regularly," Regi said with a proud
sway of her wig. But next moment she looked at Louise with
eyes which were quite appealing and humble: "It couldn't be
anything bad because Dr. Hirschfeld gave me an absolutely
clean bill. He said I was remarkable . . . But it keeps coming
back." She put out her hand to a waiter again, but he escaped
her nimbly, swaying sideways with his tray. "You don't know
how lucky you are, Louise. All you have is toothache."

"And heartache," Louise said—as a joke, trying to cheer
her up.

But Regi took her seriously: "Well, now listen, the time
for that sort of thing is really finished. There's a lot of it going
on in Florida, but I keep myself absolutely away from it. And
if you hear people talk about me with Jerry or anyone, you
can take it from me, there's nothing of that sort. He's just a
nice boy who helps me out sometimes. I might get him to take
me to Dr. Hirschfeld again tomorrow, if this doesn't get better. . . . Oh, God, you're looking over there again. I can't
stand it."

Louise took her eyes away from Leo's table and murmured, "There's such a nice couple sitting there, do you think
they're husband and wife?"

"Husband and wife. Whoever is husband and wife nowadays . . . I'll tell you something, Louise: I'm tired. I'm tired of it all."

"So am I," said Louise, but in such a different tone that Regi had to put her right at once: "I mean of all that sort of nonsense. The you and Leo sort of nonsense. And while we're on the subject let me tell you something else: from now on, I don't want to hear another word about the old monster. I just don't want you to mention him in my hearing ever again. I don't even want you to *think* about him when you're with me. Is that absolutely clear? Ridiculous," she finished off.

But once upon a time, Regi had felt differently about Leo. Louise didn't remind her—and Regi didn't want to be reminded—of the night she had found them out. It was a night when, Leo having failed to come home for almost a week, Louise did what was forbidden to her: she tried to track him down. In an uproar at her own daring, she telephoned the escape hatch. But there was no answer. She let it ring and ring; then she tried several times more. The result was always the same. There was a rushing in her ears, or was it a storm in her brain. She lay down next to Bruno asleep. The storm did not abate. She got up, tried again; at the other end the phone rang and rang in an empty room.

Then she became reckless. She telephoned Regi. It was three in the morning but Regi answered quite soon, and wide awake. ". . . Know where Leo is?" she echoed Louise's question. She put surprise into her voice but did not take much trouble to make it sound genuine. "How should I know a thing like that?" she drawled and seemed to be smiling—possibly at someone else there in the room with her.

Years and years later—two generations later—Regi told Mark about that night, and its aftermath, and how jealous his grandmother had been. Regi laughed at the recollection: "She always took everything so *seriously*. For me it was only an episode, short and not all that sweet, but for her . . . Well," said Regi, patting down her wig, "each one to his taste, or whatever it is they say."

Mark listened to her with pleasure. He always liked listening to Regi and getting her view of the past. When she was in New York, he often visited her in her apartment—the same apartment where Leo had held his first classes. Although she only used it for a few weeks in the year, she kept it because by present-day prices it was what she called dirt cheap. She never allowed anyone else to stay there. When she left, she simply lowered the blinds, and when she returned, she opened them again. She still had the ultramodern furniture of the thirties, all glass and tubular metal legs; the same white wolf rugs yawned on the parquet floors. Over the marble mantel hung an expressionist portrait of Regi in the nude. "Do you really like it?" she asked Mark who always spent a long time looking at it. She felt it didn't do her justice, although she knew by now that it was worth a great deal of money. It had been painted by a German artist who later became very famous. He had been madly in love with Regi—crazy about her, she told Mark—but she hadn't had much time for him. "I don't know why you think it's good," she pouted at the picture which showed her geometrically elongated, with green eyes spilling all over the place, and breasts like little icebergs.

"This is what I really looked like," she said. She drew his attention to a studio portrait which showed her contemplating in profile. When he admired it, she got into a good mood and brought out her albums. There was Regi in a swimsuit, and Regi in her leopard-skin coat; and motoring in an open sports car, and off to a masquerade as a chimney sweep in tight black silk. Louise was with her in many of these early photographs, and other girls in very short skirts. There was a New Year's Eve party where everyone held a champagne glass and blinked at the light of the flash. Another time they were on the beach wearing colored swimming tubes. All the young men were dapper, with a tennis racket in one hand and the other around a girl's waist. In some of the pictures they kissed the girls but no one was serious for their eyes were swiveled roguishly toward the camera and some of the young men winked.

"Yes, we were so romantic," Regi said, "so romantic it isn't true." She looked at Mark sitting next to her, turning the pages with such pleasure. "And what about you?" she said, digging her forefinger into his ribs. "Don't say you're not romantic."

"No, I'm not saying that," Mark smiled.

"I should hope not. You can't fool little Regi. I can always tell."

"Tell what?"

"What, he asks. What do you think?" She massaged his thigh which he obligingly kept still beneath her old, old, speckled hand. "Yes, it sticks out a mile when a person is romantic; when that person lives for love." She smiled into the distance but next moment she took her hand from his thigh after giving it a hard, rather spiteful little pinch; she sighed. "You should have known me at that time, what's the use now," she said and shut her album with a snap and was in a bad humor for the rest of his visit, as though somewhere she had been cheated, shortchanged.

But she was right: Mark was of a very romantic disposition. Regi often teased him and tried to get him to confide in her about his affairs. "You can tell Regi," she coaxed him, and afterward she boasted to Louise that he did tell her. But he didn't; he was secret as the grave.

In his younger days he had been promiscuous. He had started when he was in school, had really got into his stride in college, and then through his restless years of travel. But although in those days he had frequented bars and beaches, this was not his chosen way of life. Mark was serious in his approach: it was love he wanted, he craved, and he was ar-

dent and tireless in his pursuit of it. He met with many disap-
pointments, drained cups of bitterness to their dregs, but his
ideal was never dimmed. This was always embodied for him
in youth and beauty—it was only there that love for him was
to be found. Yes, he believed in the beauty of the soul, but it
was necessary for him actually to see it embodied in physical
form. In earlier days, his chosen partners had been of his own
age, but once he got into his early thirties, he preferred boys
who were considerably younger. He looked very young himself: he was fair, compact, quick-moving, rather short in stat-
ure—his height was his grandfather Bruno's rather than his
tall willowy father's. But although he looked so boyish, the
role he liked to assume was a paternal one. Perhaps because
he had always had his women—Louise, Marietta, Natasha—to
look after and play the father to, so that he was used to being
depended on, educating, guiding.

His latest lover was a youth called Kent who suited him
better, he thought, than anyone he had yet met. It must be
admitted that he had thought this more than once before, but
had been disappointed. Kent fulfilled the first requisite to
perfection—he was beautiful. Immensely tall, with broad
chest and shoulders, he appeared very manly; but although
his head was as perfectly modeled as his figure and sat on his
shoulders like a Roman emperor's, his lovely eyes and mouth
were full of a soft, feminine expression. And as if all this were
not enough, he was also intelligent and talented. It was his
ambition to be a photographer, and Mark was eager to help
and encourage him. Kent had already been helped and encouraged by a previous patron, a much older man who was a
documentary film maker. Mark had met both of them at the
opening of a new gallery, and at once the skirmish had begun.
The older man was desperately in love with Kent, but Mark
was desperate too. When the older man became too hysterically importunate, Kent began to hate him and begged Mark
to rescue him. This Mark was glad to do; and he was also

glad to replace the cameras the previous lover had bought
with more advanced and expensive equipment. Although
there were some ugly scenes when Kent moved out of the
other man's loft and into Mark's—at one point it almost came
to the police being called in—in the end the older lover had
resigned himself, as perhaps he had already learned to do
from previous occasions, and Mark and Kent began their life
together.

Mark's loft was in a late-nineteenth-century building
which had once been a warehouse. Each floor had been
bought separately and converted into an apartment, and
since two of the owners were interior decorators and one was
an architect, they vied with each other as to the beauty and
ingenuity of their conversions. Mark had the topmost story—
an enormous space into which his architect had been able to
fit as many rooms as into a complete town house, though at
the same time leaving it open to a surge of cityscape. The
warehouse windows, tall as a cathedral's, gave out onto a
different scene on every side. There were round water towers
and a round Greek Orthodox church, a Romanesque tower,
an unconverted warehouse and another converted one, a
neon-lighted airline, a building with a silver spire, another
like a black glass pencil with an adjacent Gothic old hotel
mirrored in its side—all crowding and jostling together as they
rolled away toward the horizon where the river flowed into
the sea.

Mark left early in the mornings, leaving Kent to spend
the day as he pleased. When Mark came home again—quite
late, for his business drew him into many activities—he often
found Kent in the darkroom he had fitted up for him. They
were both excited by the work Kent was doing, but sometimes, as they looked at the photographs together, Mark's
eyes strayed from the work of art to the artist, inspiring him
with a different ardor. And often Mark wished he were an
artist himself—for instance when he left in the mornings and

gave a last look at Kent still sleeping in the bed they shared. Although this bed was high and gilt and luxurious, Kent, lying naked on the designer sheets, looked as innocent and pastoral as a boy lost in a wood and sleeping on moss.

Over the years, Mark had worked out a compromise with his mother. She had had to accept the fact that he had his own place; that he was not to be pursued there; that he would be with her when he could—certainly whenever she truly needed him; but that in return not too many demands should be made on him nor questions asked. It had not been easy for Marietta to accept these terms—yet in the end she did, and was perhaps even glad to, for fear of having to accept others that she didn't even want to let herself know about.

Natasha moved more freely in and out of the different areas of Mark's life; probably because he felt safer with her. In earlier days too, when he had gone off on his various trips, although he never told Natasha where he was going or with whom—she didn't ask—he always took care that she had a number where he could be reached if absolutely necessary. Natasha never told Marietta that she had this number, for she knew that if she did, Marietta would very soon have found it absolutely necessary to use it.

Now, in these later years, Natasha did not tell Marietta about her visits to Mark's loft, nor about his friends whom she met there. Some of these friends she did not like, though she never told Mark so—not even later when he broke with them. And she was wary of those whom she did like because she knew from experience that sooner or later something would happen and Mark would suffer. It was strange, his suffering— she had seen it since he was a boy at school and had quarreled with his friends there. Even then it had struck her as so at variance with the rest of him, or with that aspect of him that they knew at home: where, always, from childhood on, he was strong and resolute and manly. But when his friends were cruel to him, he wept—yes, Mark wept like a girl! And at such times there was nothing she could do for him, though she would have undergone any torment suggested to her to save him from those unbecoming tears.

She met Kent shortly after he had moved in with Mark. Afterward Mark asked her, trying to sound casual the way he always did when he introduced her to a new friend: "How do you like him?"

"Yes, he's nice."

" 'Nice.' What a word."

He turned from her as though she were not worthy to be talked to any further. But she couldn't bring herself to say more, for fear of what might happen later and what she then might have to retract. Besides, she knew he would return to the subject—and of course he did, just five minutes later.

"Do you think he's handsome?"

"Very."

"Yes." And Mark smiled into the distance as though he saw Kent there in all his glory. After a while he said, "But it's not only looks, you know. He's very talented too. It wouldn't surprise me at all if he turned into a really good photographer. I mean, really great. Famous." Natasha tried to make the right noises but obviously did not succeed. Mark began to sound testy: "Well, you saw his pictures. What did you think? You must have *some* opinion," he said when she thought nothing.

"You know I don't understand these things," she excused herself; and it was true, she didn't, she had no appreciation of visual art at all.

"No, and you won't learn. You won't make an effort."

She knew he was cross with her because he wanted her to say more, to be more enthusiastic, to sing Kent's praises; nothing less at this stage would have served. But she couldn't, she wouldn't, though she minded him less than some other friends whom Mark had taken to live with him in the past.

* * *

Mark didn't remember much about Tim, his father, who had died when Mark was seven. It was a characteristic of Tim's family that in the last few generations the male members of it had died young and either violently or under mysterious circumstances. Tim's father had driven his car over a cliff; his grandfather had died by drowning in the ocean at Southampton; and Tim himself had combined both these violent deaths by falling with his car, one perfectly still summer night, into Lake Kennebago after a party in a cabin there.

Another characteristic of that family was that none of them had ever really gone in for a career, either in business or in the professions or any occupation whatsoever. This may have been in reaction against their ancestors who had very strenuously made money in farming, property, and whatever trade had been currently profitable. They had built themselves handsome classical houses, but since their descendants applied themselves to spending rather than making money, these were gone now—either torn down, or fallen into decay, or taken over as institutions. And besides the houses and the fortunes, the family itself had disappeared. The only relatives Mark ever knew were his father's mother and two sisters, Mary and Evie. These three led spare but active lives in a converted farmhouse standing on the few acres of land which were all that was left of the original family holdings.

As a boy, Mark sometimes went to stay with them, but he always got restless and left earlier than intended. He missed the city and his two homes there—Louise's and Marietta's—and his life with both these women and with Natasha. It was only when he was grown up that he began to think more about the other side of his family. Then it was too late. The mother had died of a carefully concealed cancer when Mark was twelve; Mary had gone to live on Martha's Vineyard where she set up in the antiques business with a friend; and Evie had to be checked into a mental home for a while, from which she emerged only to take an overdose of her tranquilizers in an apartment hotel on West Twenty-sixth Street. Their house was sold and its contents scattered among family members who turned out to be more numerous and to have stronger claims than anyone had suspected. Mary even had to fight a lawsuit with one very clamorous cousin over a Federal chest of drawers. By the time everyone was through, only a few pieces were left for Mark; but these he cherished, and when he grew up, carried them to the various lofts in which he established himself.

He also developed an attachment to his father's part of the country that became in due course proprietary. It was here that he found the house for Leo's Academy; and when he came to visit there, he drove around the countryside and got out of his car to look not only at houses with a view to acquiring them but also at the landscape, as though he wanted to buy that as well. It pleased him to think that a part of him belonged here; and often on a summer day he parked his car on some overlook and got out and filled his gaze with the view of grassland shimmering green and yellow in the sun and cows grazing as peacefully as the clouds that floated in the sky above them. When he got back into his car he drove slowly and lingered especially through villages where the white clapboard houses—some of them converted into antiques shops—clustered around an only slightly larger church, also white and clapboard with a modest spire attached to it vertically and a modest green graveyard horizontally.

As he drove, Mark liked to daydream that he had spent more of his boyhood here than he actually had. He had never stayed long enough with his paternal grandmother to make any friends—these he made in the smart prep schools he attended—but imagined what it would have been like if he had, and what sort of boys they would have been who knew how to do all sorts of country things. And more and more it was this sort of boys, or as he imagined them, whom he chose for his closest friends: fair, wholesome, Anglo-Saxon, from simple families from somewhere within the heart of the country; so that, in being with them, he also felt he was acquiring a greater share of something—a landscape, a country, a way of being—that he longed for but only half possessed.

"Are you sure you want that?" Mark asked Kent as he watched him open a bottle of Sauterne.

Kent didn't answer; he didn't have to, the way he poured himself a very full glass was in itself enough.

"You ought to have a glass of milk or something," Mark half scolded, half coaxed.

Kent lay on a sofa, drinking his wine and sinking into one of his silences. Mark had learned to live with these silences, though he still wasn't sure what they portended. Sometimes it seemed as though Kent were thinking nothing at all; but then again it might be that he was descending into deep, dense territories within himself that he couldn't share with anyone. The only thing one could be sure about was that he didn't like to be disturbed—Mark knew that perfectly well, but he was always doing it.

"You ought to be reading something," he said. "There are all those copies of *Art Forum* you haven't even opened. What's the matter with you? I thought you were supposed to be interested. I thought that's why we got all those subscriptions. I thought you wanted to learn." Mark could hear himself, and he sounded like someone else—like his own mother, like Marietta when she was trying to get some reaction out of him, Mark.

And predictably, just like he himself did with her on such occasions, Kent got up and announced: "I'm going out."

"Where? Where are you going?"

"Out." Kent spoke in an accent as flat as the midwestern plains his forefathers might have come from. Actually, he wasn't sure where they came from, for he had never met his father and in fact didn't know who he was.

"Don't be silly," Mark said. "You know perfectly well all these people are coming. Lincoln and Christopher and all . . . What, you don't want to be here? I think you should. You certainly should. It's time you mixed with a finer type of person." Mark hated this phrase and himself for using it. But he couldn't help himself—it was too exciting to have Kent towering over him in this way, scowling. He kept his eyes fixed on the glass of wine in Kent's hand; he wanted to bring him to the point of smashing it to the floor and stamping on it, perhaps even first flinging its contents in Mark's face.

Sensing that this was what he was being tempted to do, Kent carefully put the glass down. He went into the bathroom and stood in front of the mirror, regarding his chin. But he left the door open for Mark to follow him.

"You don't have to shave," Mark said. It was surprising how rarely Kent did have to shave—for such a rugged type, his beard growth was scanty.

Kent's answer was to plug in his razor. Mark, contradicted, put in his place, sat on the rim of the tub and watched him go through this manly activity.

"I want to talk about the weekend," Mark said after a while. He sounded carefully casual, though it was always an important subject between them. Ever since they had been together, Mark had tried to make it an axiom that their weekends belonged to each other. But Kent, stubbornly resisting the assumption, never divulged his plans till the last possible moment; mostly he had none, but he didn't admit that, any more than he admitted Mark's right to include him in his.

"I thought we might go to the Academy," Mark said. "Just for an hour or two to see Natasha, and then there's something else I want to do. I'll tell you when we get there . . . It's a new project," he dangled. "We could leave on Friday evening."

"I'm busy Friday."

Kent went into their bedroom, Mark trotting close behind. Kent really seemed to be getting himself ready to go out; he drew a comb through his hair, flung a fatigue-style Italian jacket over one shoulder.

"Lincoln and Christopher are expecting to see you. They especially said. They like you. Even if you don't like them."

"I don't."

"No, and I know why. Because they make you feel inferior, uneducated, which you needn't feel at all, Kent. You have such tremendous potential. Everyone says so. I wouldn't be at all surprised if finally you beat everyone at their own game."

Kent, not interested in any of that, went back into the living area where he recovered his glass of wine.

"Don't have any more of that," Mark said, following him still. "It's not nice for you to be drinking in the middle of the afternoon. I mean it," he said—so sincerely that Kent defended himself: "What if I'm thirsty?"

"Then drink milk, I told you. Or a Tab or something. But milk is best, a growing boy like you," he said with husky tenderness; and on the wave of that went on in a rush: "I really do have this new project I want you to know about. We could check in at the Blue Boar Inn—you liked it there, didn't you? It's comfortable anyway, and not too pretentious for a place like that. You'll come, Kent, won't you?"

"I might," Kent said. "I might not."

"What sort of a damn-fool answer is that?"

"Damn-fool answer to a damn-fool question," Kent said, and then he barked out a laugh at his own (unwonted) display of humor.

"Sometimes I think you're just a big lout. A big stupid lout, you know that? And put that down," he said, looking at the glass in Kent's hand. "Just put that right down."

In reply Kent was about to lift the glass to his lips—but Mark, always much quicker, put out his hand and held on to the other's wrist. And they both looked down at Mark's small square trim hand holding on to Kent's wrist which was bony as a boy's and stuck out of his sleeve. His arms were so long, he never could get shirts to fit him.

"Let go of me," Kent said.

Mark wouldn't; he began to breathe somewhat heavily, waiting to see what was going to happen. They stood holding on to each other as if in combat. Then Kent wrenched his wrist free with a jerk that made the wine in the glass spill out. It spilled over Mark, but it was unclear whether this had been deliberate on Kent's part or not. Mark looked down at himself and then up at Kent. And this look sparked Kent off further and he did what seemed expected of him next—he smashed the glass on the floor and crushed it with his heel. Now it was Kent who was breathing heavily.

"Great," Mark said. "From my Tiffany set."

Kent crushed his heel on it again. Watching him, Mark wanted to beat his fists against his friend's chest—but also to get down on his knees to him and say my darling, my love, my best beloved boy.

When he got to the Academy, Mark found Natasha sitting on a mossy bank by a brook. She was alone and completely idle, but when she saw him she started up and scrambled quickly to her feet, stumbling a bit in her eager clumsiness.

"I was just going back to the office," she excused her idleness. Her eyes shone and shone at Mark's unexpected appearance. She looked at him the way no one else in the whole world ever did: not like Marietta wanting to possess him but with pure selfless joy in his presence.

How wonderful it would have been for both of them if he could have taken the same pleasure in her: could have, for instance, sat beside her on this bank, and with the background of the water trickling over stones, told her all about his new project. If only it could have been she with whom he

wanted to share it more than with anyone; instead of thinking all the time of Kent, who had at the last moment refused
to accompany him.

"Do you want to get in the car with me?" he said to
Natasha, in the rather dampening way he used whenever he
proposed something he knew would give her immeasurable
pleasure.

In the car she sat beside him as stiff and silent as a child
who dares not disturb a preoccupied elder for fear of having
an outing curtailed. And Mark *was* preoccupied, biting his lip
as he drove, on the one hand trying to suppress thoughts of
Kent, on the other to suppress his irritation with her for not
being Kent. And after a while he did become more serene: the
effect of driving through this beloved countryside, and also of
Natasha's happiness as she rode beside him, staring in front of
her except for an occasional glance she stole at him.

Every few miles they came to a little town or village
facing the highway with an open store selling farm-grown
fruit and vegetables, an oil company, a real-estate agent, a
diner, or a lumber yard. They turned off one such stretch of
road and drove into a deserted byway full of little openings
disclosing lush green dells. Then they came to a wider opening which must have once had handsome gates and still had a
little stone gatekeeper's cottage to one side. They turned in
here and bumped along an overgrown driveway winding upward till it reached a tall, narrow white house with a classical
portico. "Oh," said Natasha, "the burned house."

It wasn't all that burned. There had been a fire here a
year ago—deliberately started, it was rumored, by its owners
for the sake of the insurance. The fire had caused more excitement than damage, and the local fire engine had turned out
smartly, bringing the town and all its children in tow, and the
whole thing had got photographed and written up in the
local paper. Only the rear portion, which was a later addition
to the house, had been damaged, and if the purpose of the fire

had been to collect insurance, then its perpetrators would have been disappointed. At any rate, the house was now once again up for sale—as it had been for the last 150 years, changing hands over and over again, sometimes with only a few years' interval. No one seemed to know what to do with it.

Mark wanted to buy it. This was his new project, which he unfolded to Natasha. He wanted to buy it not as an investment but for himself and his friends on weekends and summer vacations. He planned to repair and restore it to what it had been in its heyday. Natasha listened to him with the same respect and enthusiasm with which she had listened to him from their childhood. She didn't always understand his plans, but she always admired them. Now too she was nodding in rapturous agreement with what he said, even though she couldn't really enter into his reasons. This may have been because she herself had no desire to acquire anything, and she certainly had no feeling for this strange, half-ruined mansion and the land on which it stood. After a while, he fell silent and preferred just to sit there on the steps of the portico. From here he could overlook what he intended to make his domain, for the house was perched on an eminence from which it sloped on one side into a little wood, on the other to a lake. Mark half shut his eyes—against the bright sun, partly, but partly also to shut Natasha out. She was so entirely the wrong person to be there with him. Her *appearance* was all wrong: her back as bowed as a seamstress's, her pale ghetto complexion, her dark inward-looking eyes—no wonder that she had no feeling for this land or any conception of what it might be like to own it.

It was not for her but for Kent that he wanted it; and it was of him that he thought as he sat beside her. He wanted to put Kent back into his boyhood surroundings—or rather, what he liked to think of as his boyhood surroundings: though really he knew that Kent had grown up among the disused factories, vacant lots, and coin laundries of a decayed nineteenth-century mill town, and didn't belong here any more than Natasha did.

Leo's room at the Academy was not called his escape hatch, but it still had something of that character. Certainly it remained the place in which he shut himself away from his followers. To them, it was more in the nature of his den, or lair, where he crouched; and woe to anyone who intruded on him there unbidden. But sometimes some of them were bidden, and when they emerged—some starry-eyed, some in bewilderment—it was usually difficult for them to talk about what had happened in there. One night Natasha's friend Stephanie was summoned, and when she returned she flung herself facedown on her bunk above Natasha's. Natasha got up to look at her and, seeing her shoulders shaking, put out her hand to touch her in sympathy; but when Stephanie raised her face, it could be seen that she was not crying but laughing.

It was only several days later that she revealed the events of that night. She and Natasha were in the garden—most of the younger students spent whatever time they could out there rather than inside the heavy old house. The grounds covered fifty acres, and now in the summer they were green and dense, with little paths opening out into clearings in which stood a sundial, or a drinking fountain, a cluster of apple trees, or a statue of a girl with a bird. And everywhere there were Leo's students, and even when they couldn't be seen, hidden in the smothered turns and twists of the garden, they could be heard laughing and calling to one another as they performed their allotted tasks. Those working in the house also sometimes appeared at the windows, ostensibly to shake out dustcloths but taking the opportunity to linger there and lean out between the shutters.

Stephanie and Natasha were in their favorite spot by the side of an incline; a stream trickled down one rocky side and into a brook curling within a narrow cleft below. They might have been sitting by a waterfall plunging from a rock into a ravine, except that it was all on a miniature scale. There was also a tiny pavilion, but on this warm summer night they preferred to sit on the ground with their backs against a tree. Another friend was with them, Jeff, who worked as a handyman around the place.

Suddenly Stephanie flung herself facedown on the moss. Her shoulders shook the way they had done the night she had been with Leo, so Natasha guessed she was thinking of that. At last Stephanie said, "He's so *fat*"; and this thought rendered her speechless for some time longer.

It seemed she had been called that night to sleep with Leo. His bed was, as usual, made up for him on his leather couch (the same couch he had had in the escape hatch but now cracked and wrinkled like old skin and even ripped here and there). Stephanie was told to get in with him and lie against the wall. The couch was not very broad and Leo took up practically all of it, so that Stephanie had to lie sideways and pressed flat; and Leo, pushing himself against her, pressed her even flatter. She thought she would surely suffocate. It was not only that she lay there overwhelmed by Leo, but the entire room—his den—appeared to be closing in on her. The air was dense, for prone to colds, he did not often open the windows and he was constantly brewing strong coffee and smoking or half smoking his cigars.

Nothing happened for a while. Leo did not speak at all, though he breathed very heavily and sometimes grunted. Then slowly his breathing mounted until, with one giant grunt, he heaved himself from his back onto his stomach, slipping Stephanie beneath him. He lay on top of her and all his organs pumped like bellows. His body was mighty, overflowing, of an insufferable weight: so that it was the stranger to feel his male member against her thigh, tiny and soft as a baby's and as sweetly impotent. It was then that

Stephanie began to laugh. She tried to convert these sounds
into ones of pleasure, but Leo had heard too many of those in
his life to be fooled. He rolled off her—she thought she would
die of relief—and told her to go away. He wasn't angry but
displeased with her; he called her light-minded, a fool.

The next day he had called her again—but only to explain that the whole thing had been a test: not for her but for
himself, to ascertain whether he could withstand the temptation of a young girl beside him. As she had witnessed, he had
passed with flying colors, so he would like to know what the
hell there was to laugh about. Well, there wasn't really,
Stephanie admitted, in telling this story to her two companions; but her lips were still twitching, and she concluded over-
solemnly, "I guess it's a pretty stiff test. You have to hand it
to him."

Jeff made a guttural sound and, frowning with concentration, began throwing pebbles into the brook below. Jeff
had a lot of thoughts—he was bursting with them usually—
but he didn't believe in sharing them. All discussions were
carried on within himself, in fierce and silent concentration,
and he didn't let anyone in on them until he had reached his
own conclusions.

"I've heard of that test," Stephanie tried to draw him
out. "They all do it. It's part of the whole thing, like the forty
days in the desert." Jeff only frowned more and threw more
pebbles, so she went on: "Just because you don't believe in
him anymore, that doesn't mean he's all phony. You're just
being subjective, Jeff."

It was true that Jeff no longer believed in Leo or in the
Academy and was only waiting for the next thing, whatever it
might be, to turn up so he could leave. Meanwhile, he was a
much better handyman than any of the other, serious students, so Leo didn't mind having him around, eating and
sleeping for free.

Jeff did not defend himself against the charge of subjectivity, but carrying on the argument inside himself, he got more and more excited and threw pebbles in fast succession; so that Natasha, afraid he might run out of them, began to hunt around to build up a new supply for him.

She liked being here with these two. She admired them both. She had never before become friendly with two such people; it might even be said that she had never before been so close to anyone outside her own family. And sitting like this in the open at night, with stars tangled among the leaves and branches of the trees, was also new to her.

"It's easy," Jeff said at last. "Anyone can do it."

"*You* can't," Stephanie said. Half turned away from him, she lifted her arms to do something to her hair, thereby pointing the profile of one little breast in his direction.

He took care not to look at her but at Natasha, and he said to Natasha: "Come here, I'll show you. Come on, don't be shy. I won't hurt you."

Actually, Natasha was not shy with him. Trustingly, she did what he said: lay down next to him, facing him, their two bodies glued together. He put his mouth on hers. She was not uncomfortable. His lips had a fresh taste to them, and there was also a nice smell about him, as of apples and hay. He put one arm around her, to hold her closer. She felt protected by him and safe and was almost sorry when, in conclusion of the demonstration, he let her go.

He appeared to regard his point as proved and went back to tossing pebbles. But Stephanie plucked a blade of grass and applied it to the back of his neck; he continued to concentrate on his task with the intensity of a fisherman. "My turn," she said.

"Split, will you. Beat it. Go on, you heard me."

Stephanie smiled to herself; so did Natasha, at the two of them. They all three knew that there was every danger of the test not working between Jeff and Stephanie. Quite often, when they sat here either in the evenings or when they had

time during the day, they made love to each other. It was a
very natural need that arose between them. The first time she
had been there with them, Natasha tried tactfully to absent
herself. "It's okay," they had said, courteously inviting her to
stay. And it *was* okay—it was just one more activity that went
on in the summer grass at the edge of the brook, among the
birds and insects. And it was okay too when sometimes he
came up at night and they did it in the bunk above Natasha,
under the window filled with moon; and indeed the noise
they made was preferable to that of the other people sleeping in the attic, so that Natasha was glad when their tossing
and heaving drowned out the sleepers suffering from guilty
nightmares.

Leo called Stephanie several more times in the night,
and the same thing happened each time: she laughed and he
kicked her out. But he was never really angry with her, and
she continued to be one of his favorite students. It was
strange, how indulgent he was with these young students who
came to him. He even waived their fees when they couldn't
pay him, and that was something really unheard of with him.
In earlier days, if anyone pleaded inability to pay, he
shrugged and said "Bad luck." He wouldn't even allow a
postponement of payment—"The thin end of the wedge," he
called it; it was an expression he often used and in connection
with other matters.

A word might here be said about Leo's fees: actually, he
didn't charge fees—he accepted donations. These varied according to what he estimated a person ought to give, and in
fact the amount was part of the therapy. It usually took him
some time to assess this amount, just as it took him some time
to assess each applicant's need; and both were a secret process
that went on while the newcomer was being made comfortable in one of the second-floor bedrooms of the Academy.

Some people went away, deciding that Leo was not the answer for them, whereupon he would shake hands with them heartily, almost as if congratulating them on their escape: but if there was a committal and the person decided to stay, then Leo would say all right and he would narrow his eyes and get very businesslike: revealing his diagnosis and its suggested cure—that is, the psychospiritual exercises on the one hand, the size of the donation on the other.

But Leo had mellowed: Louise and Regi and their contemporaries would have been amazed to see the indulgence he showed to his young students. He moved among them with an air of benign blessing, in his brown habit with the silver ornament around his neck and the buckled cowboy belt hanging low over his stomach. He loved to watch them at their occupations and encouraged them by tweaking a firm young cheek here or buttock there. His presence among them, his approval, made them so happy that they redoubled their efforts, whether this was cleaning the house, cooking, gardening, or—a new project of his—bottling fruit for sale. Sometimes he called them all to sit around him in the sunken garden, and then he would say "Sing, children," or "Tell me stories"; and these would always be their own stories, their lives up to the moment of regeneration—that is, up to the moment when they had joined the Academy.

It had been very different in Louise and Regi's time. Of course he was different then—he was young, younger than most of his students, and stormy. Those terrible rehearsals they had, before one of their public performances! He had worked out a series of group dances, based on his psychological exercises but also of intrinsic aesthetic interest. He had choreographed them, worked with a composer on the music, designed the costumes and the scenery—he was not a Renaissance man for nothing—and he spent weeks rehearsing his students. That was as terrible a time for him as for them. He was literally in their hands—or rather, in their whole bodies which he was working to shape into living symbols to illustrate his ideas.

Their rehearsal space was a studio in the old converted theater building he had rented. At one end of the long room the composer sat at an upright piano while Leo was perched on a high ladder-chair from which he could overlook the students at the other end. Hopping up and down on the top of this chair, he uttered foul German curses translated into English. Sometimes he fell into such a rage at their ineptitude that he threw whatever was at hand; while they, holding on to the long white robes he had designed for them, had learned to skip smartly out of the way.

The day of performance approached. The theater, in the same building as the rehearsal space, was booked; the students went all around town to paste up the posters Leo had designed, and to hawk the books of tickets he had allotted to them. It was a small hall, but on the great day was never quite full. This was the fault of the students—they tried hard to sell tickets to genuine spectators but the price was steep for those days (five dollars) and interest not widespread, so that they usually ended up buying quite a few themselves. On the day itself, Leo was cool and very efficient—which was just as well, for no one else was. Practically single-handed, he put up the scenery; he tested and fixed the lights; he hovered over the piano tuner; he spotted and dealt with incipient cases of hysteria; he could even be seen kneeling with pins in his mouth to fix someone's hem. So that at last it was always and only due to his efforts that the curtain parted almost on time, revealing the symbolic scenery. Sometimes this was just one pillar with a broken wall attached, sometimes a series of orbs stretching away into a similitude of infinity. Winding in and out of these props, and to the accompaniment of the pianist perspiring at his upright, Leo's students performed the motions into which they had been trained. Leo himself stood to one side, dressed in the same robes as the performers except that his were black where theirs were pure, purest white. After each dance, and with the piano beginning to spell out the rhythm of the next, he explained the meaning of each item— the way each represented a separate passion of the microcosm worked up to a pitch where it was ready to take on universal significance and merge into the macrocosm: culminating in the final dance—an ensemble called The Spheres of Eternity— in which the separate groups of dancers formed themselves into one full circle, symbolizing the harmonious absorption of the individual into the universe.

The applause at the end was hearty. The audience was mostly comprised of friends and relatives of the performers, so that their enthusiastic clapping may have been partly in re-lief—not only that the performance itself was over but also the weeks of ordeal which had preceded it. At any rate, the spec-tators, descending with their kisses, congratulations, and flow-ers into the basement where the dressing rooms were fitted in around the boiler system, went home satisfied; but for the performers there was a celebration arranged by Leo at the Old Vienna—a celebration which usually turned into a last ordeal for at least one of them.

At first everything went very festively. Several tables had been joined on to Leo's, so that they extended in a long row from his alcove into the center of the restaurant. The place was packed with other after-theater parties; the waiters ran around, shouting to each other in various European lan-guages; the chandeliers blazed once from the ceiling and twice in the mirrors; huge trays were carried from the kitchen to reload the trolleys of pastries and hors d'oeuvres; everyone was shouting at the top of their voices, both in excitement and in order to be heard.

Leo's party was the most festive and the most excited. They gulped cold wine too fast so that their sensations were heightened and some of them were quite drunk. Leo himself

drank enormous quantities of alcohol, and his face, with a
cigar stuck in it, flamed. He was still a young man at that
time and a great dandy in his tuxedo with a gardenia in his
buttonhole. The students allowed to sit with him at his round
table were handpicked. They were watched enviously by
other, less favored ones who had to make do with seats at the
joined-on tables: enviously but also apprehensively, for everyone knew that one of the chosen had been placed there in
order to be made the scapegoat of whatever failure had
marked that evening's performance. The routine was always
the same: when everyone's good mood was at its height, Leo
addressed a remark to one particular person at his table. At
once everyone fell silent.

One year it was Louise's turn to be the scapegoat. This
was the year that Regi had become Leo's favorite. After the
first shock, and scenes, and despair, Louise had settled down
into resignation. She was still part of the group, she still saw
him almost daily, he still kept some of his clothes in her apartment. It had to be enough. Love made her humble, and she
persuaded herself that it was. She thought he was pleased
with her for her acceptance, and he appeared to be; and she
was sure of it when she was chosen to sit with him at the
round table for the after-theater supper.

Leo made jokes. He was in capital humor and teased a
girl who had almost tripped during one of the dances when
the laces of her ballet shoes had come undone. "How do you
expect me to raise you to a higher level of being," he deplored, "when you haven't even learned to tie your shoe-
laces?" "Oh, Leo," protested this girl, blushing, shy and
happy; she was a very young girl and a great favorite with the
others. They joined in teasing her, enjoying her confusion, her
blushes, her bliss (of course she was in love with Leo). And
Louise too enjoyed it, knowing so well how the girl felt. She
put out her hand to ruffle her hair: "Leave her alone," she

said, "she's just a baby. Why don't you pick on someone your own size?" she joked to Leo.

But he did not joke back. Instead his good-humored smile faded, he took the cigar from between his lips, and fixed Louise with a steady stare: "All right, I will," he said.

It was strange the way the rest of the people in the restaurant carried on as though nothing were happening. The waiters still shouted and the conversations and laughter and greetings continued; but it was only a tide lapping at the edge of their row of tables. Here they sat frozen in an island of silence: some still held the stems of their glasses where they had been twirling them; half-drunk bottles were placed in a row along the middle of the tables but no one dared refill an empty glass; they were all turned in their chairs toward the round table where Leo had begun his inquisition. They held their breaths. Leo did not raise his voice by as much as a decibel, but he could be heard distinctly down to the very end of their tables, completely drowning out the surrounding noise.

"You're no baby," he said to Louise—and she wasn't: she was a blooming matron in a plum-colored evening gown. "What happened to you? During the Interior Storm?" He pointed out some faulty footwork she had committed in the course of that number—maybe she had, maybe she hadn't, she couldn't remember; she could only gaze back into Leo's cold, compelling eyes, and feel the silence of the others surrounding her.

"You ruined it," Leo said in a voice as flat as his stare. "You ruined everyone's work, including mine." He shrugged his shoulders, plump as a woman's, broad as a man's; he wasn't angry, not at all; he was resigned; he had expected nothing better.

"I don't blame you," he said. "I blame myself. Will I never learn?" he ruefully asked. "People are what they are, I can't change the leopard's spots—no, not even I," he joked at himself, but no one laughed.

"Let's look at your spots, Louise," he said, with a sigh that this should be necessary. But it *was;* it was his responsibility to spot psychological failings, both for the sake of the individual and for that of the group. His hands were folded on the table; he spoke in a conversational tone, into the air, without emphasis. He brought out all Louise's faults—her jealousy, her possessiveness; he dwelt on her limitations, such as her bourgeois housewife mentality. Louise sat at the table— the way she had been taught as a girl, with a good straight German back—and made no attempt to defend herself. How could she? She knew it was all true, and that she was all ego.

Louise now entered what was known in Leo's group as the D phase—Depression, Discouragement, and Disgust (with self). Also Disappearance from Sight: she was expected neither to see Leo nor to join in group activities until she had sufficiently worked on her imperfections (or, as a later generation would put it, straightened herself out). During this time, she drew closer to Bruno than they had ever been before; even closer than during the first years of their marriage, for at that time she hadn't needed to lean on him as she did now. She threw the weight of her misery on him—and how glad and willing he was to receive it. He didn't know what had happened, only that she had come home to him and they were a family of three again—he, she, and Marietta (or Marianne, as she still was at that time)—and not just a part of Leo's movement.

Marietta used to like coming home from school at this time because she knew Louise would always be there. She adored her mother. Louise was a tall woman, but for Marietta she had absolutely mythological proportions: in fact, when she learned about Juno, Minerva, Ceres, all those goddesses, it was always Louise she saw in her mind. Louise had a firm tread and a ringing voice, so when she was home, she filled that apartment, big as it was. And she always had plans, she always knew what to do, and Bruno and Marietta followed. When she felt like hugging them, they stood still and smiled while she squeezed them with all her might. They tiptoed around her when she wept; and when she raised her head and wiped her eyes and said "Let's go and see the tapestries at the Metropolitan," they fetched her hat and coat and put them on her and then got ready themselves as fast as they could. Even at her most miserable—and this she was during these weeks—she might at any moment sit down at the grand piano which she couldn't play and bang out enormous chords and sing arias, out of tune but as if she were the greatest diva in the world.

During this period of compulsory Disappearance from Sight, Louise realized that it wasn't her work with the group that she missed but only Leo himself; and that it was her attachment to him which was the cause of the imperfections she had to struggle against. Helped by Bruno and Marietta, she did struggle, and felt herself becoming calmer and happier. When members of the group began to phone her to ask whether she felt ready to rejoin them, she was short with them; and when they tried to argue, she slammed down the phone.

However, when one afternoon Leo rang the bell of her apartment in his unmistakable way—in a series of short buzzes like electric shocks—she realized she had been waiting for him. Also, that she had long ago decided what to do. She went to the door and called to him: "Go away—I'm through." He went on buzzing.

Afraid that he would disturb Bruno's afternoon nap, she opened the door a few inches; only to have Leo push from the other side till he got in. He walked straight into the salon while she followed him, protesting. He said, "These are for you"—presenting her, for the first and last time in their life together, with a bouquet of flowers.

"Leo, it's no use talking: I'm not coming back to your group."

"I don't want you for the group. I want you for myself. You'd better put those in water, I paid good money for them."

She was glad of something to do and when she returned with the vase, she kept her back to him while she arranged the flowers. She was in a storm of emotion—but at the same time she felt like laughing because his bouquet, which was very thin and straggly, looked so incongruous in the tall cloisonné vase in which she was arranging it. He came up behind her and pressed her closer against the table where she stood. He murmured down the back of her neck: "I've missed you."

"No, Leo, leave me alone. Let it end now."

"You're warm like a bed with a woman in it. What a relief after Regi."

"Go away, Leo. Please."

Stepping back to release her, he said, "On one condition."

"What?" She turned around to look at him.

"Here," he said, indicating his lips for her to kiss; so she turned back again to the flowers. After a moment's silence, she said, "Wherever did you get them? They're half dead."

"Oh, really? Cheated again. Turn around."

"No."

So he came close again and began to tickle her. She screamed, as he knew she would; she was terribly ticklish. She gasped, "Bruno's asleep—no, Leo, stop. You—must—stop."

He retreated, but when she turned to look, there he stood with his finger pointing to his lips again.

"No," she said.

He crooked the fingers of both hands and wiggled them at her in a tickling motion so that she screamed before he even touched her.

"You'll wake Bruno," he warned; and again pointed to his mouth.

She felt she had no choice—she had to go to him and press her lips where he indicated; and as soon as she did so, he grasped her tight, and she groaned; though before going under, she murmured, as if to save herself by deprecation, "It's only physical, that's all it is." "Oh, yes, *only*," he murmured back.

So it was that, when Marietta returned from school a few hours later, she found Leo there again. He was on the sofa with one arm laid along the back of it and his legs stretched out before him. His thighs bulged in English pinstripe; he wore silk socks with clocks on them, and white and tan shoes. He was holding forth about something or other, and Bruno was nodding in his polite way and also throwing in little affirmative comments to show he was listening attentively; and Louise was standing near the sofa with her hands clasped before her and her eyes fixed on Leo sprawled there. She didn't even see Marietta come in—not till Leo turned his head; and Leo looked at Marietta in the way he had that always made her wish her skirt were longer or her legs less long and bare. And he greeted her—again in his usual way, as though they were the same age. Marietta didn't answer, she went straight across the carpet and stood by her father's armchair. Bruno put his arm around her and told her to curtsy— he always told her to curtsy when there were visitors, automatically using the exact same German phrase and intonation he had heard his mother use with his sisters. He kept his arm around her and continued to make polite listening sounds to Leo, apparently unaware of how stiffly Marietta held herself within his embrace, or how she glared across at Leo. Louise didn't seem to notice either—only Leo did, and he

smiled at it. He went on talking to Bruno and Louise, but the
smile on his full red moist lips was for Marietta.

There was something enchanting about Marietta as she
grew up. She was light and very stylish, and her movements
were graceful in an entirely unselfconscious way. Everything
about her was unselfconscious: because she really didn't think
about herself but about higher, abstract things; about ideas,
in the platonic sense. When she wanted to be a dancer—that
was her first ideal—it was not for personal ambition, not even
for personal expression: it was to forge herself into an instru-
ment, or to contribute herself as a medium, through which
everything that was beautiful could pass.

She believed of course in love, but had not much time for
men. That aspect of love was for her embodied in Leo and
was detestable. When she married, her husband Tim was predictably as different from Leo as anyone could be. Less
predictably—for she loved her parents—his ancestry and background were far removed from her own. But perhaps this was
a need of her nature, the same need that afterward drove her
to India to immerse herself in different forms of life and en-
thuse over different expressions of it; to glory in variety.

When she was first married, Marietta loved to accompany Tim on visits to his family in the country. She read
everything she could about the land and its history, reaching
back to the time when the Indians had owned it, and its first
Dutch and British settlers, and all the families, including
Tim's, whose names recurred over and over on the grave-
stones in the two cemeteries. At that time, what was later the
house Mark wanted to buy (the burned house) belonged to
someone very rich connected with films who used to give big
weekend parties. Tim's family did not attend these parties
and always referred to the place as the Van Kuypen house, as
though Van Kuypens were still living there. In fact, they had
lived there for hardly two generations. The first Van Kuypen,

a hosiery manufacturer as well as landowner and influential politician, had built it for himself during the early years of the nineteenth century. When he died, the property as well as the hosiery business were both flourishing, but within a decade his sons, who lacked his ability to make money but surpassed him in spending it, had run both into the ground. By the time the grandsons came of age, the house had passed into the possession of another local manufacturer and potentate—the owner of a sawmill—but his family repeated the history of the Van Kuypens, and the taste for pleasure exceeding that for business, had to sell off within another generation. All this time Tim's family were industrious tenant farmers leasing their land from whoever owned the Van Kuypen estate. While the landlords went down, the tenants went up. They became judges, bankers, one senator, one of the wives an ardent abolitionist. Toward the last quarter of the century they themselves acquired the Van Kuypen house and land: but that was their high-water mark from which they receded after another generation, for the same reasons as the previous landlords—that is, the sons proving more sophisticated and less industrious than the fathers. They had retained their former farmhouse, and it was here that they remained when the mansion swam all too soon out of their possession; and it was here in this commodious, converted farmhouse—where no evidence was left of the family's farming activities but only of their sophisticated city living—that Tim's mother lived with her two daughters at the time of Marietta's marriage.

After the first few months Marietta ceased to enjoy her visits there. Each member of the household except her appeared to be totally engrossed and enclosed in a separate pursuit. There was Tim in his chair in the front parlor, with a glass and decanter beside him, his legs crossed and swinging one foot as he listened to his favorite records on his phonograph. His mother spent the day in endless domestic activity, polishing the silver, bottling fruit from the garden, sorting out

her linen closet. The older sister, Mary, tramped around the
yard in rubber boots, deciding which trees needed pruning
and which spraying; or she would roar off in the ancient family pickup and return with some old door or mantel to lug off
and store in the barn. The younger sister, Evie, went for long
walks by herself, sometimes stooping to pick up a fallen leaf to
take home and press in her book of poems or memoirs. If the
three of them happened to encounter one another around the
house, they never failed to exchange a friendly comment,
even though for the most part each was too preoccupied to
hear the other.

They met at dinner, a formal meal in the dining room
for which the three women changed from their old skirts and
cardigans into dowdy frocks. They were tall women with big
limbs and sagging bosoms; they looked alike and also had the
same ringing voices speaking in accents that were more English than American except for certain characteristic flat and
elongated vowel sounds. And indeed they all, including Tim,
seemed very English—but English of a bygone age, even of the
eighteenth century, when women were mannish and eccen-
tric, and men, pretty as girls, dissipated themselves into an
early grave. Marietta could find no place for herself in this
family group. Nothing was more boring to her than the conversation around that dining table—except perhaps the food.
She was accustomed to Louise's lavish meals, and it was extraordinary to her how sparsely they ate and how satisfied
they seemed to be with this economical fare. "Hm, *good,*
Mother," Mary would comment, chewing on the tough meat
and vegetables boiled long in water; whereupon the mother
expatiated on how much she had paid for what they were
eating, and from there generally on the high prices everyone
charged, and from there on every prosaic triviality that came
into her head. No one else talked much, but she talked cease-
lessly.

Later it occurred to Marietta that she was doing it to

keep up the appearance of a solid family at dinner around that solid table laid with the family china and silver, and the portraits of ancestors—the senator, the abolitionist—looking down at them from the walls. Tim was already quite drunk by the time they sat down to dinner; and as the meal progressed, and he filled and refilled his glass with the wine which was much better than the food, he became cross-eyed and disheveled to the point of disintegration. But he continued to sit bolt upright and to smile without cease like a well-bred dinner guest. If he mumbled something, his mother immediately answered him as though it made perfect sense. In the same way, if Evie acted strangely, or even if—as sometimes happened, quite suddenly and unexpectedly—she threw a tantrum, the mother would handle that too as though it were something entirely ordinary that went on every day of the week at every dinner table around the land.

One night Marietta ran away from the house. She had had to help Tim undress and go to bed, and afterward she couldn't bear to lie next to him. She felt trapped with him in their bedroom—narrow and sloping like all the upstairs rooms and too small for the furniture in it: the high mahogany four-poster, the carved chest-on-chest, a walnut armoire that had a strange smell in it as of dead people's clothes. She sat by the window and looked out over the landscape: the fine tall trees, the handsome houses separated from one another by respectful acres, in the distance the Episcopal church with Tim's ancestors in its graveyard. It was all as alien to her as this room with Tim slumped on the bed; so that suddenly she jumped up and, not even bothering to pack her clothes, she went downstairs and let herself out the front door. She got in her car and drove straight to New York, not stopping till she came to her parents' apartment where she went up in the elevator and rang the bell, once, twice, and when she heard Louise come out of the bedroom, she called softly, "It's me"— shutting her eyes with relief and impatience as she waited for her mother to unlock and unbolt the door. She didn't know it yet, but she was already pregnant with Mark.

Marietta had a tendency, which got worse as she got older, to brood. She lay awake at night doing it, and it continued all day and washed like turgid water through all her activities. She was good at what she did—dealing with buyers and manufacturers, attending fashion shows and business lunches—but she wasn't engrossed by it. It was all just a skill she had, a sleight of hand, like her social manner which was charming and serviceable but had really nothing to do with her. By nature she was solitary, and most of her evenings were, in fact, spent alone. She didn't feel like talking to anyone, except that there was usually something very urgent she had to say to her son. Often Mark wasn't home, but she didn't leave any message on his recording machine, she only hung up in disappointment. Occasionally, another man answered and then she would hurriedly say "Tell him his mother called," mumbling somewhat in embarrassment. Once or twice she said nothing but hung up like a secret caller.

She brooded about Natasha's absence. She didn't know why Mark had chosen to place her with Leo, nor why Natasha chose to stay there when Marietta wanted her at home. And now Mark kept going out there too and was even thinking about buying a house in the area. Marietta was very much opposed to this idea. She didn't know what he needed a house for, and when she fought with him about it, she said "And why *there,* of all places?" She had made this same objection when he was buying the house for the Academy. She thought they had finished with that part of the country— Tim's family's—and couldn't understand why Mark should want to start the whole thing again.

Thinking about all this, Marietta couldn't sleep and she paced up and down, smoking many cigarettes. Little pulses beat inside her, all through her body and also inside her head, and she didn't know why: she had always felt intensely but not like this, with these physical symptoms which made her twitch as with electric currents running through her.

As usual when she couldn't bear to be on her own, she took a cab across town to be with her mother. It was past midnight, but she found Louise as awake as she was. Day and night were really the same in Louise's apartment. With the chandeliers blazing, Louise was walking around making tall pots of coffee for herself, as absorbed in her own thoughts as Marietta was in hers. In her youth Louise had resembled a Wagnerian singer, but now in her late seventies she was more like a French tragic actress: tall, stately, draped in dark silk, her white hair disheveled, she appeared always to have heard some terrible tidings. Yet at the same time there was also something cozy about the way she sat there drinking coffee as though it were the middle of the afternoon.

"Of course, no use arguing with him," Marietta was complaining about Mark. "No use asking him anything. Impossible even to talk to him. I tried to call him; no answer, just that idiotic machine; one of these days I'll go over there and kick it to bits."

"Child, child, darling," Louise murmured.

"And who are all these people he hangs around with? I mean, if they were decent, nice people he'd *want* us to meet them . . ."

Louise stood over her and stroked her hair. Marietta laid her head against her mother and shut her eyes. "I don't know what's the matter with me," she said. "Do you think it's the menopause? Blood pressure? I feel like I might split apart, blow up. What is it? I don't know."

Louise laid her hand on the twitching pulse in Marietta's cheek. "It's nothing. It's nerves. You're so highly strung, darling, it's your temperament." Louise was a strong, healthy woman herself, and she was confident that Marietta was the same. All that milk Louise had drunk while she was carrying her! All those fried potatoes she had eaten! It was almost fifty years ago but the effect of it, she was sure, was built into her daughter's bones.

The Van Kuypen house had been on the market when Leo and Mark were looking for a place for the Academy. But Leo had rejected it: "I get bad vibes," he had said (he liked using the slang of whatever generation was current). The late-Victorian house they eventually bought suited him much better. When Mark said that that gave *him* bad vibes—because it was so ugly—Leo said no, it was a healthy place. It had been built as a summer home by a wealthy New York wholesale grocer, and there were still photographs in the house of the whole family arriving for their annual vacation in carriages overloaded with children in sailor suits, nursemaids, pets, steamer trunks, and leather hatboxes. The pleasant aura of these summers had remained intact in the house because, according to Leo, nothing worse had happened to the family than that they had gone out of business and died of natural causes.

When Mark proposed to buy the Van Kuypen house for himself, Leo was another person who tried to discourage him. He shook his big head and pushed out his underlip: "Leave it alone, Mark," he said. "Let it rest." He didn't approve of people trying to buy back their own or someone else's ancestors. "That's not the way it's done," he said. There were, however, a growing number of people in the area who were trying to do it. Rich and restless women from New York bought up dingy cabins and spent a fortune refurbishing them and restoring the fittings to the exact period detail, down to the locks and hinges, and hiding their stereos inside seamen's chests. But when their labor of love and ingenuity was finished, they still found themselves with plenty of money and energy left over; and it was then that, eager to work on themselves instead of their houses, they turned up at the Academy to put themselves in Leo's hands. But he wasn't, as he put it, having any. "First get rid of all that shit," he said—and they did, cheerfully sold the refurbished cabins to other rich New Yorkers and moved themselves up into Leo's attic.

But Mark was not to be dissuaded. He was raising part of the payment on the Van Kuypen house by taking out a mortgage on the Academy, and for this he needed Leo's signature. He didn't want to burden Leo with the details, for he knew how much Leo hated and feared all business matters. There was a scene every time Mark came to see him, with Leo complaining—about the house, the expense, the repairs to be made. Leo said he was an old man, he couldn't cope with any of it, it wasn't fair to saddle him with these problems. Mark calmed him. He asked to see the contractors' estimates and bank papers and bills and everything else that was disturbing Leo. As a matter of fact, Leo had laid it all out ready for him to see. Leo was very methodical about papers, especially those relating to money matters. He was also cautious but not shrewd—at least not shrewd enough. He had never quite understood the terms under which he had acquired this house, nor how much of it belonged to Mark's firm and how much to Leo's movement. He watched Mark run his expert eye over all the papers, and after a while he asked, "You're not cheating me, are you?"

Mark looked up. Their eyes met. Leo's were sunk in flesh, wise and ancient as an elephant's, whereas Mark's were green and beautiful, a lover's eyes. Mark looked away first; he smiled. "What if I were?" he said and turned over another paper.

Leo sighed with a great shudder. "I know," he said. "It shouldn't make any difference to me. But it's the way I grew up. Everyone forgets that I grew up too—yes, pardon me, I'm human too, I have my conditioning. Why shouldn't I be my father's son, just like everyone else? My papa was a clerk in the mayor's office and naturally he thought a great deal about his pension and his savings. He had to have them, like lung and liver, and so do I. I'm a petit bourgeois, Mark, I worry about these things. And something else that's worrying me is that I may have to live forever—don't laugh! Sometimes it looks like I may have to go on and on, and how can I, without pension and savings." He appeared entirely serious; but next moment he became playfully rueful: "*And* I'm in love again. Isn't it terrible? Really shocking, not to say ludicrous. No wonder she laughs at me." He smiled, thinking of Stephanie's laughter. "Yes, yes, ludicrous," he went on, "but also, Mark, a little bit beautiful I think. Isn't it beautiful to see a very old tree with a big fat gray trunk and out of it sprouting the greenest, the tenderest little shoots; shy little harbingers of spring," he said, and lay there on his leather couch, smiling like a German uncle.

Mark took out the mortgage papers. At once Leo collapsed and became a mass of weary old flesh: "Must you, now? Must you spoil my mood? . . . What is it, anyway?"

Mark tried to explain, and for a while Leo tried to follow, but Mark went into more and more detail and quoted higher and higher figures, with complicated calculations which Mark loved to do, which were easy and joyful to him, but which addled Leo completely, so that he gave up and cried out for Mark to stop. "Well, just sign here, then," Mark said.

"I don't have a pen, Mark."

"I have." He thoughtfully pressed it into Leo's hand which was, however, shaking so much that Mark had to guide it.

II

Usually when Mark arrived at the Academy, it was after a fight with Kent. His heart was breaking, but he was used to that; ever since he could remember, he had suffered in this way from the boys he loved, and he had developed a stoical front with which to cover up. His lips were set, his eyes rather cold as he drove himself the two hundred miles from the city to the Academy.

His manner when he got there showed no trace of inner turmoil. He was, as always, jaunty, courteous, and alert. But there was no fooling Leo. It was dark inside his den and he lay inert and sagging like some superannuated circus animal on his leather couch. But with only one look at Mark—"Ah," Leo said, "love trouble again."

It might be said about Leo that he cared far too much about himself to bother about anyone else; and it was true. But it was also true that he could look deeply into others and see what was going on there. It was an instinct he had, a skill, a gift, something almost extraneous to his own personality which he himself acknowledged to be that of a monster egotist.

Another paradox about Leo: one could say—many did say—that he was vain, greedy, and worldly, but all the same he seemed positively to run away from his own success. Popularity, adulation bored him. He had always been very attractive to a certain type of high-strung, high-bred girls; with these he relished behaving in a very crude way, and then enjoying the pale, pained smile with which they pretended not to mind. When they were at their most soulful, he was at his most down-to-earth; he became a peasant and a simpleton; he was loud and vulgar and embarrassed them in public places; and when none of this worked—and it never did, on the contrary—he finally sent them packing by telling them they were the wrong type for him and were harmful to his work.

It was not only people of whom Leo grew tired—or, he himself would have said, outgrew—but also his own ideas. In the past, just when his theater movement was beginning to attract wider attention, he was ready to abandon it. This was what really broke up his affair with Regi. For a while they had got on very well together. It was a relief for him to be with her, for unlike his other followers, she did not press him too closely, either physically or in any other way. On the contrary, she didn't like him to come too close to her, and when he what she called "bothered" her, it was always either too hot, or time for her to have her nails done or her legs depilated. This amused him, he called her iceberg and shivered—"Brrr"—when he came near her. She was frank about it, she said she never cared much for that stuff; it was intellectually, she explained, that he attracted her. This amused him even more; he really enjoyed Regi for a time. And she adored the success his movement was beginning to generate. She constituted herself his general business manager and put up the students' fees and cut down the theater owner's. When both these affected parties complained to Leo, he shrugged them off—it was the time when he was losing interest anyway and was content to leave everything to Regi. What she enjoyed most was the publicity angle and really worked hard at it and was in seventh heaven when she managed to arrange an interview and photographs with the *Herald Tribune.* But although on the appointed day the students were all keyed up and stood tense and ready in toga and sandals to demonstrate their exercises, Leo refused to appear. When Regi knocked on the door of the escape hatch and fluted sweetly through it, "Leo, we're ready!" all she got in reply were some loud, caricatured snoring noises.

Well, she wasn't the type to put up with this sort of behavior and it wasn't long before she was declaring herself completely disgusted with him and all his ideas—and, moreover, with the intellectual life in general. She said it was all a lot of nonsense and rubbish and maybe all right for women who didn't have any social life, but Regi herself had plenty of that, thank God, and other things too; and indeed, shortly afterward she married a rich fur dealer—it was her third marriage—and went on an African safari for her honeymoon. As for Leo, he disappeared for many months, and when he re-emerged it was with a new form of expression for his philosophy.

During the many years of its formation, Leo's philosophy passed through a variety of stages before reaching its culmination in The Point. One of these stages came out of his contact with Marietta's Indian lover. Leo was in his fifties when he met Ahmed. No longer the large blond florid youth who had been introduced to Louise as an Adonis, he was already potbellied and short-breathed. He had not yet evolved his final costume—the monk's robe—but he had by this time laid aside his sharp, pinstriped English suits in favor of bib overalls over a striped sweater. This somewhat childish mode of dress, combined with his huge head from which tufts of gray hair stuck out like a prophet's halo, gave him a very odd appearance. And the followers by whom he was surrounded—or patients, depending on whether one regarded him as a guru or psychiatrist—were also very odd: they were the usual people he attracted, a motley crew with motley problems of sex, drugs, nerves, religion.

All this was astonishing to Ahmed, but he reacted to it as he did to the many other astonishing features of American life (including Marietta): simply by laughing and shaking his head. And when he got to know him, he really liked Leo whom he found to be a jolly companion. Sometimes Leo sent all his retinue packing, and then he and Ahmed would just be two men together, drinking and talking about women. They both enjoyed that in their different ways. But most of all Leo loved Ahmed's music. Ahmed practiced for many hours during the day, alone in Marietta's apartment while she was in her showroom; and Leo would come and join him there to listen to him. They sat in her penthouse apartment—so lightly furnished that it seemed to have more flowers in it than objects—facing each other sitting on a rug on the floor. Leo listened with great attention; he had learned to sway his head like an Indian and also to exclaim at certain moments of high art. He loved the expression on Ahmed's face while he played: Ahmed seemed to be listening to something beyond himself and trying to reproduce the celestial notes he heard there. He was a shriveled, aging, insignificant little man but when he played like that he was as tender and exquisite as a youth in love. And what to say of those moments when the music reached some point beyond human capacity or comprehension? Then Ahmed's smile was a mixture of joy and pain as if it were a form of suffering to endure so much bliss.

Leo tried afterward to recall, to analyze, to isolate and fix those moments. He asked questions which Ahmed couldn't understand, let alone answer. They reminded Ahmed of Marietta in bed with him, asking "Do you like it? What do you feel? You must tell me, Ahmed, you have to." He never did—he couldn't—but it didn't matter since she was so busy telling him what *she* felt (actually, she was rather frigid). He tried to say that it was wrong to talk so much, but she didn't know what he meant, and he had no ability to explain anything in words. With Leo, he didn't need to, Leo understood him through his silence. "You're right," Leo would say when Ahmed failed to answer him. "A hundred percent right. One shouldn't think but be. Not talk but feel, feel, feel." Ahmed thought that Leo himself was much better at feeling than other Westerners: in the way he enjoyed the music, or the way he ate—loudly, and grabbing right and left—and the hoard of dirty stories from several continents he knew and relished.

When Leo asked Ahmed about his music: "Is it of the senses or of the spirit?" then Ahmed understood him less than ever. He had no conception of any division between the two, and if he had thought about it, he would have said, surely the one is there to express the other? That was what his music was for—he knew this so deeply that he had absolutely no thought or words for it. But Leo was fascinated by this question, and probing into it, he evolved a new theory which he tried out in practice, the way he did with all his theories, on his students. For his students were his test tubes. What he needed to carry out his experiments was the person; the personality. And by this he meant the whole of a person, all of him (or, more frequently, her). He tolerated no half measures.

Ahmed's music opened up Leo's Tantric period. He taught in his lectures that there were ascending levels of being, and that each level had to be thoroughly explored and exploited before one was ready to rise to the next. In practice, what it came down to—later he modified this considerably—was that while one was on the level of the senses, one had to fulfill them to the brim: so that at this time, his students were encouraged to try out some very physical experiments on themselves. Although he had left the art of the theater behind him, Leo had retained the rehearsal space in the theater building: only now, instead of their dramatic exercises, his students could be seen to go through some more direct experiences with each other. Not all of them could rise to the rigors of these experiments; although willing to transcend themselves, for some of them—like those pale, high-strung girls of good family—their limitations, or inhibitions, were too rigid to be overcome without severe psychological strain. These weaker students fell by the wayside, but Leo had expected that: it was one of the risks involved in his game of higher evolution.

He himself took no part in these experiments. He didn't have to, since he had never had any difficulty in living up to the full potential of his senses. As it happened, this was a relatively calm period in his personal life. Perhaps he was settling down. He still had his escape hatch in the theater building, but he also lived in several other places—rather grand places belonging to rich women students for whom it was a privilege to entertain him: there was a town house on Fifth and Eighty-first, another house in Vermont, a third in New Hampshire. He kept clean clothes and possessions in all of them, and went from one to the other as the spirit moved him. He turned up at Louise's at intervals too, though by no means regular intervals.

Except on her birthday—he was always to be counted on for that. She had her sixtieth birthday around the time of his Tantric period. By now she was no longer one of his disciples—although he had returned to her after the scene at the Old Vienna, he had never invited her back to his workshops. She was his private, domestic life to be kept apart from his professional activities; and it was as a family member—an uncle to Marietta, a great-uncle to Mark and Natasha—that he turned up for the sixtieth birthday party. He was the only male left in this family group of women and children. Bruno and Tim were dead; Ahmed had recently gone back to India. Regi was one of the celebrants that year; she and Louise were on speaking terms.

By this time, on account of Mark and Natasha, it had turned into a children's party. Louise had extended the dining table to its full length to hold the array of gateaux and pastries she had ordered from Blauberg's. Mark and Natasha sat there with napkins tucked under their chins, stuffing themselves on everything within reach in between bouncing balloons up to the chandelier. It was the same long dining table, the same dark, over-furnished dining room where those exciting evening talks had taken place at the beginning of Leo's career. Now the only grown-up sitting at the table was Leo himself, for he was the only one who loved cakes as much as the children did.

The sliding doors between the dining room and the salon were open. Regi, who was unfortunately suffering from a migraine, lay on the high crimson velvet sofa in the salon, piled around with cushions made in fine needlepoint by various generations of Bruno's female relatives. Louise tried to massage her temples with eau de cologne, but Regi said she didn't do it right and pushed her hand away. Actually, Regi's migraine was psychological as much as it was physical. She felt the weight of too many birthday parties, and altogether too much that had been and gone. Two years earlier, her third husband—the fur dealer—had died, leaving her rich but restless. For the first time she was finding it difficult to make new relationships and was beginning to have to pay for them.

"My God, how fat he's become—and no wonder," she said, squinting toward Leo at the dining table. His cheeks were bulging with cake and he was reaching out for more. To Louise she said ill-naturedly: "I suppose you're still gaga about him . . . I don't know how you can, Louise, a fat ugly old man like that. One has to be a little bit aesthetic." She looked up at Louise standing over her sofa: "I don't like the way you do your hair."

"But Regi! Darling! It's been this way for thirty years!" Louise pushed at the knot into which her hair was wound. It was completely gray and straggled in every direction.

"Why don't you take care of yourself like a decent person?" Regi admonished her. She herself was still a redhead though a very lacquered one, her hair sitting on her like a metal cap. She would be keeping it another five years, then it would be superseded by a wig more splendid and flaming than anything that had crowned her in her youth. "Ridiculous," she said, watching Leo bounce balloons across the table with Mark and Natasha. "He doesn't even like children."

"But he's so wonderful with them," Louise said. But it was true that he was only wonderful with them when he felt like it; on the whole children bored him, though he didn't go as far as Regi who actively disliked them. She had not had any of her own and had never felt the lack.

And what she simply couldn't understand was why Marietta should have gone out of her way to adopt one. Moreover, if one had to adopt a baby, at least it should be a pretty one and not Natasha.

"Are you sure that child's all right?" she asked Louise not for the first time, looking across at Natasha in the dining room. At that time of her life—she was four—Natasha's head was too big for her body, and—unlike Mark who hadn't been able to get started soon enough—she had learned to walk and talk very late.

For answer, Louise rushed off to the table to hug and kiss Natasha who went on eating cake; she was used to these attentions from both Louise and Marietta. Of course, it had been a long time since they had been able to take such liberties with Mark.

He didn't like them taken with Natasha either; he

frowned and said, "Leave her alone, Gran, can't you see she's enjoying her cake."

His wise, admonitory air made her laugh; she even dared ruffle his hair and laughed even more to see the way he rebuked her by smoothing it down again. "Look how cross he is," she said to Leo on the other side of the table.

"Take no notice," Leo aligned himself with Mark. "She's crazy. All women are crazy. You have to look out for them." He jerked his head toward Regi on the sofa: "What's the matter with her? Why is she not joining us? Madam!" he called. "Won't you give us the exquisite pleasure of your enchanting company?" He and Mark exchanged looks of amusement.

"You have the most horrible hideous loud voice, did you know that?" Regi complained from her sickbed. "You always sound as if you're addressing an audience. I suppose you do it so often it's impossible for you to speak like a normal human being anymore."

"A normal human being," Leo repeated. "That's an ambiguous, not to say a tricky, concept."

"There, now we're going to have a clever lecture for free," Regi said from the other room. Getting into the old game of sparring with Leo, she seemed for the moment to forget her headache.

"Would you call yourself a normal human being?" Leo inquired of Mark. "If so, where do you set up your standards? And what about her?" He pointed at Natasha and glanced at her too, but only for a moment: there was something in the way Natasha was staring at him—was it in fear? in fascination? She often looked at him like that. He turned away and said irritably, "She has chocolate in her hair."

Mark found this to be true and wiped it off, taking the opportunity of wiping the rest of her face too.

"Do you think your grandmother's normal?" Leo continued his discussion with Mark. "And your mother—where is she, by the way?—and Regi over there—"

"Come in here so I can hear all your wonderful philosophy!" Regi called in challenge.

"Yes, where is Mother?" Mark said with the frown that, even at that early age, characterized the sense of responsibility he felt toward the women in his family. "It's time to cut the cake. May I leave the table, Gran? Thank you," he answered himself while Louise was still crying out, "Bless you, little worm!"

Mark searched for his mother in various rooms—the apartment was as spacious as a house—and found her in Louise's bedroom. Marietta was on the flowered chaise longue which stood at the foot of the bed. This bed was the marital one Louise had shared with Bruno, and also Bruno's mother with his father, so it was old and heavy with primal scenes.

"We're supposed to be celebrating Gran's birthday," Mark said, looking at his mother where she lay on the chaise longue, smoking and thinking. "Everyone's waiting for you. We're going to cut the cake."

"Go away," Marietta said but corrected herself at once, calling out, "Come here, come here, darling!"

Mark continued to stand at the door: "Natasha's covered with chocolate. Someone will have to clean her up."

"I'll do it. Only just sit with me for one moment, darling."

"I haven't got time."

"Mark, give Mother a kiss."

At this familiar line, his frown deepened. "Not now," he said and retreated before any demands could be made of him. He was anxious to have the sixty candles lit—the birthday party had to be conducted along its proper lines, and he felt himself to be the only one there responsible enough to do so.

But—wouldn't you know it—by the time he returned to

the dining room, Leo and Louise had wandered away from the table, leaving the cake unlit and uncut and Natasha smearing herself with the remains of her own plate as well as Mark's. No one heard his protests, for they were busy talking around the sofa on which Regi lay. In complete disgust, he made Natasha get down from her chair and led her away to wash her in the bathroom.

Regi had really forgotten her headache now. Although her affair with Leo had ended long ago, there was still something very potent to her in his presence; or perhaps this stemmed from the weight of all their past together, hers and Louise's and his, and all their feelings for each other.

And especially Louise's for Leo: this was her sixtieth birthday; she was a tall, dignified, gray-haired figure in a burgundy silk gown and black pumps, but when he was there she still trembled. The air vibrated with her feelings for him. It astonished Regi, irritated her, and as always she couldn't keep off the subject: "What do you see in him?" she asked for the thousandth time. "It's because you never meet anyone new. You need to get out among people instead of sitting here with grandchildren—and him," she said, pointing at Leo comfortable in the deepest chair in the house. "You look terrible," she told him. "You've aged a hundred years. And what are these ridiculous baby clothes you wear?" she said, referring to his pastel-colored bib overalls. "As if it isn't perfectly obvious that you're in your second childhood."

"It's practical," Leo said, amused and unperturbed, smoking his cigar.

"I'm surprised you let him run around this way," she told Louise. "But of course you always let him do just what he likes. You've never known how to control him."

"No," Louise said. There was a big brown leather pouf which she drew up close by Leo's armchair. She sat down on it; she leaned her broad back against his leg and he let her rest there.

"It's my opinion," Regi was saying, lying opposite them on the sofa, "that a woman has to use her influence with a man. She must mold him, make him into a better person, or what's the point of a relationship?"

She felt Leo looking at her over the top of Louise's head. He had always looked at her with amusement, and she didn't know that it was a different kind of amusement now. Unconsciously, in a movement that was ancient and instinctual in her, she coquetted one hip and her legs at him. She thought this was still effectual—and why not? since her clothes and hair and jewelry were as bright as ever and her teeth even better for she had had them all capped. She was particularly proud that she had kept her figure, unaware that it was no longer svelte but completely skeletal.

"All you've done all your life," she accused Louise, "is spoil him."

"It's my birthday," Louise said cheerfully, "you can't make me quarrel with him today." He dug his leg deeper into her back and this gave her great happiness and security.

"I give you up as a bad case," Regi said. "And my head is splitting. I wish Ralph were here to give me my head massage, he's so gentle, you have no idea; when he does it, I just go to sleep like a baby."

Mark, leading a washed Natasha by the hand, came into the salon: "We want to cut the cake."

"Call your mother," Leo said.

"Mother won't come. She's in Gran's bedroom."

"*I'll* get her," Leo said. He stubbed out his cigar and withdrew his leg from behind Louise's back without warning, so that she toppled and had to steady herself.

Leo went into Louise's bedroom. He shut the door behind him. He looked down at Marietta lying on the chaise longue—a very different sight from Regi laid out in the salon. Leo ran the tip of his tongue over his lips, which were as full and moist as ever.

"Leo, please go away and leave me alone. I don't want to talk to you."

"But I want to talk to you very much."

He turned the key in the door to lock it. He lowered his great bulk on to the end of her chaise longue. He said: "Anyway, I think it's time you and I had a little chat together."

"Thank you very much. I don't need an analyst." Marietta couldn't help laughing—here she was lying on a couch and there was Leo, who had by now a reputation for his own brand of psychospiritual therapy, sitting at the foot of it.

"No," Leo said, "that's not what I was thinking of at all."

Marietta couldn't believe it: he put his big heavy hand on her, first on her ankle, and then as she watched incredulously, he let it slide upward on her calf, and then under her dress, on her thigh and next he slid it in the top of her tights. "You're crazy," she said—but she herself seemed to be, for she was still laughing.

Leo just kept on. He didn't say anything more; he couldn't, he was breathing too heavily.

"Crazy," Marietta was repeating. She too was beginning to pant a little—but with what? Here was the man she detested more than anyone else in the world—an ugly old man who was bringing his hands into her most secret places, and she didn't do anything except laugh and say "crazy." Then she said, "Not now, Leo" and "Not here." "Why not here and now," he said, and anyway things had gone too far. He lay on top of her and held her with one hand and with the other he fumbled at the placket of his ludicrous nursery suit. Marietta was in a turmoil of conflicting feelings. Principally, there was fear: supposing this delicate little chaise longue broke beneath them (he was very heavy); or if they made too loud a noise, he in his excitement or she in whatever it was she was in, and the others—Mark! Louise!—heard them and came and rattled at the door? And then there was fear of him too, on top of her and so big; and fear of herself—of what she was feeling now, more intensely, if the truth were told, than with anyone ever before, just as the hate she had for him was more intense than anything she had ever had for any other man.

Louise and Mark were lighting the candles on the cake. They had carried it into the salon and stood it on a round marble table there, near Regi, so that she could enjoy it too. But she wasn't enjoying it; she looked at them with a jaundiced eye as they lighted all those candles. And as if that weren't bad enough, there was a big sixty written in icing in the center. "There's absolutely no need to shout it out over the housetops," Regi grumbled. On her own birthday she never had more than just one candle.

They had got them all lighted now—no, there was one left, Mark saw it and lighted it, and then he said, "I'm going to get Mother." He went to Louise's bedroom, and when he found it locked, he was really annoyed and called angrily through the door.

"Yes, yes, I'm coming!" Marietta called back.

And in fact, she and Leo soon reappeared. Then all was ready. Even Regi managed to get up and they stood around the blazing cake and sang for Louise who held her hands clasped before her—one of them with a widow's two wedding rings—giving thanks in her heart for such an abundance of happiness with all her dearest ones around her.

Marietta went to India every year, and on her sixth visit she had her most meaningful encounter there, or her deepest immersion and enchantment (after that, it all went downhill). This was when, on Ahmed's recommendation, she visited a woman singer who lived in a town in a Rajasthani desert state. Her name was Sujata; she was a Hindu woman though, as happened often among musicians, with Muslim affiliations. Sujata received Marietta lavishly; at first because Ahmed had sent her and because she was a foreign guest, and then afterward for her own sake, as a friend.

Marietta had never had a friend like Sujata. She was a queen, regal in her personality and in her manner of living. She had a large, strangely assorted, ill-defined household where it was impossible to tell who was who and why they were there: except that they were there because of her, living on her bounty and in her affections. Growing up in a family of courtesans where every girl was taught to sing, dance, and be delightful to men, Sujata had turned out to be one of those jewels that every family like hers hopes and prays for—a great singer. Her fame soon spread, and she became very much in demand to sing at weddings, state and public entertainments, and former royal courts. Her fees rose and so did her status and that of her entire family. They gave up their room on the floor of a house divided up between a dozen families like theirs and rented one that was entirely their own. It became known as Sujata's house and retained the name long after her death and when the rest of her family was scattered.

Marietta never discovered where everyone slept in the house except that a great many of them slept together, crammed side by side into some little room or out in the courtyard. Marietta herself, as an honored guest, was the only one besides Sujata to be given a room of her own. It was a tiny, whitewashed cubbyhole from where she could hear and smell all that went on in the house: the instrumental and vocal music, the ankle bells and stamping dancer's feet, the smells of clarified butter and essence of jasmine, of rotting garlands and bad drains. The only time the house was silent was not in the night—something was always going on then— but during the hottest part of the day, in the early afternoon. At that time everyone sank down in the coolest corner they could find, too sleepy to eat or fight or even find work for the shriveled little servant boy who was at everyone's beck and

call. Sujata retired to her room; often she invited Marietta to
come in and lie beside her on the mattress which took up
almost the entire floor, covered with a white sheet and many
bolsters and cushions. The room was kept as cool as possible
with water sprinkled on fragrant grass screens and a noisy fan
churning from a corner, but Sujata was very large and very
hot and the scent she used gave out a pungent, hot smell. She
loved touching Marietta. She spanned her hands around
Marietta's waist, marveling that they went all the way
around; she compared Marietta's slim thighs with her own
huge ones deeply inscribed with white stretch lines; not to
speak of Marietta's little pink-nippled breasts and the brown
mountains Sujata carried. Sujata admired her and kissed her
and gave her shiny pieces of silk to wear.

They communicated in a mixture of Hindi, English, and
common feeling. Sujata told her about her beginnings as a
singer when she had been taught by her grandmother. She
remembered her grandmother as very old—though actually
she couldn't have been much older than Sujata was now. Her
voice had been too cracked for her to sing, but she had retained her sharp mind, her sharp ear, and an exquisite sensi-
bility to the finest nuances of music. This made her an
excellent though very exacting and impatient teacher, and all
the girls in the house tried to hide when it was time for their
lesson with her. Sujata also tried to hide, but her grandmother always found her and dragged her out and then those
terrible lessons began. But slowly Sujata began to realize that,
terrible though they were, full of blows, curses, and tears, she
wanted them; and once, when her grandmother had failed to
find her hiding place, she had come out on her own to have
her lesson. For there were those moments of pitch and intensity when suddenly she got something right—she never knew
how, but suddenly she was in some higher place she hadn't
suspected was there, though her grandmother seemed to
know all the time that it was: and when it happened, her

grandmother gave out a cry and pressed Sujata's head into her lap, so that forever afterward when—unexpectedly, always unexpectedly—she reached some highest moment of her art, her feelings of rapture and recognition became mixed up with the memory of her grandmother's lap and the darkness there and smell of unwashed clothes and tobacco and betel.

Marietta saw a lot of little old women around the house, former singing and dancing girls who could no longer practice their profession and had to be taken care of. One of these was Sujata's mother. Weak, silly, and pleasure-loving, she had not played much of a part in her daughter's early life—there were always plenty of others to look after children in the household—so that Sujata had hardly been aware that she *was* her mother. Until the grandmother died: then, while that frail, tough old corpse lay on her bier, smothered in flowers and with her jaw tied up, at that moment of grief and loss, Sujata's mother had remembered that she had a daughter, and clinging to Sujata, stifling her in her embrace, she had screeched that now only her daughter was left to her and all her hopes and life lay in her. And Sujata, holding the plump, aging little courtesan in her arms, had accepted the charge; and along with her, that of all the others whom her grandmother had ruled over—the light-minded girls and the equally light-minded and even more carefree little old women that they became—Sujata understood that now it was her turn to protect and provide for them.

Sujata also had a daughter—a low-spirited, discontented girl who wanted nothing to do with the family profession and was certainly unfit to learn any of its arts. Ambitious for her to have an education, Sujata had sent her away to boarding school and afterward to college. Only the girl wasn't smart enough for so much higher education, and for this she blamed her mother and Sujata also blamed herself. The daughter was the result of a relationship Sujata had had with a rich businessman who had been her protector for many years. Sujata had respected but not loved him, and now it was as if all the love she hadn't had for the father was lavished on the daughter—who looked exactly like him, with the same muddy complexion and flabby features of his merchant caste. Sujata felt she could not do enough for this girl, she wanted her to have everything in the world there was to enjoy; but the girl suffered from bad digestion and enjoyed nothing, and the more the mother tried to do for her, the more surly she became and even sometimes seemed to hate her; but that only spurred Sujata on to further feats of loving and giving and she spent much time thinking up what more she could possibly do for her to make her happy.

Love: Sujata lived for it. Not one love but many, and of many different kinds, shading off into each other so that it was difficult to know where one ended and another began. There was her son—a different story altogether from her daughter. Her son's father had been a pimp and occasionally a pickpocket, an unworthy youth in every way—but what charm, what sweetness and tenderness and delicacy! Of course he had disappeared long ago—evaporated like a drop of dew, except that here he was again in the son he didn't know existed. The boy was a replica of his father: playful, beautiful, irresponsible—Sujata hated these qualities in him and also hated herself for being nevertheless unable not to adore them in him as she had in his father. It was all just a vicious circle she had got herself into—of boundless love where she was as ready to die for this feckless boy as she had been for his father (and nearly had when he left her).

And now, what was worst of all, worse than anything, Sujata was in love again. Yes, and with a boy—her son's friend, the same age as her son—but the way she loved him was not as a son, it was with sex and everything. It was shameful, and she *was* ashamed, knowing perfectly well that the time for all that was past; and in communicating all this to Marietta, Sujata did sometimes cover her face in shame.

But when she raised it again, it was flushed with laughter that became as uncontrollable as the tears falling from her eyes in streams. Then she grew very serious and very seriously she asked Marietta, as though expecting her to have the answer, that if it was so wrong to have these feelings, then why were they sent? Why did they come to a human being—as suddenly, unexpectedly, irresistibly as those notes of perfection, those high moments of highest art that her grandmother had taught her to lie in wait for? If it was wrong, if it was shameful, then why was it there? And why was it so glorious?

In his younger days, Leo had traveled all over the country trying to establish different centers, which usually collapsed once his back was turned. He had spent many years in California and had a whole different life out there that Louise knew nothing about; all she knew was that, at unspecified intervals, he would suddenly appear in the city, in her apartment, and take over his usual bedroom there. Sometimes he stayed a day, sometimes three weeks, and would not be heard from again till he turned up the next time.

It was his habit, when he came on one of these sudden visits, to dash in, unpack, have a bath, dress, telephone, and dash out again. Louise was expected to help him in all these practical chores, and usually she loved to do it, down to scrubbing his back where he sat in the tub. Bruno was also kept busy. It was his task to answer the telephone and take down messages for Leo, and he was as meticulous, not to say fussy, in this as in everything he did. There would have been work for Marietta too, but she locked herself in her own room and practiced modern dance movements to her phonograph played very loudly.

Every now and again, Louise had her moments of rebellion. One morning, when Leo had just got in from Los Angeles and was in a great hurry to be off to a series of appointments, she remained in her bedroom and sat on the bed and brooded. When Leo called to her from the bathroom to come and scrub his back, she didn't answer but stayed where she was, one elbow supported on her knee, her brow on her clenched fist. He had to call several times more before she would go to him—and then not joyfully as she usually did but with dragging feet.

Leo liked very hot baths and the bathroom seemed to be dissolving in vapors. More hot water was running, making the tub overflow with bubbles out of which Leo emerged pink, plump and naked as a pagan god.

He urged her to hurry; he held out the loofah to her, sticking it out of the bath like a trident. She didn't take it; she said, "No, leave me alone," and put her hands behind her back. Leo stopped singing; he turned off the tap; he listened in silence and apparently with respect while she broke out: "You don't write, you don't call, you don't even know if I'm alive or dead. I don't know if you are. Weeks and months."

"I called you—when was it?—in March."

"From a phone booth, collect."

"I was on my way somewhere."

"Yes, you were in a hurry. You must have been at a gas station—"

"Right. On my way to Santa Barbara."

"—and you jumped out of your car full of other people and dashed in the phone booth and dashed out again so you could drive on and get on your way with all these other people that I don't even know who they are. I'm tired of it," Louise said; and continued: "And all the time I think, when's he coming? I want it so much that I can't understand why it's not happening. I wait for the mail—I look at the phone and it's all dead and doesn't ring and when it does it's someone else, it's never you. I can't live like that. It's not worth living like that."

"Yeah," Leo agreed. He didn't defend himself; he just sat there waiting, still holding the loofah sticking out of the bubble bath; till at last she approached the tub and sat on the edge of it and took the loofah from him. His back rippled with pleasure as she scrubbed it. She did this thoroughly, and though not sullenly, yet as a heavy duty: as something laid upon her that she couldn't escape.

It was a strange fact that the one thing Leo had always found difficult to get out of Louise was money. They had had plenty of scenes and arguments about it, starting from way back when they had first got to know each other. In fact, the subject had come up on his very first visit to Louise. This was a few days after they had been introduced at Regi's. Leo had come to follow up that introduction—not only with Louise but with several of the other ladies he had met there. Although no promises had been exchanged, each of them seemed to expect him; he had that capacity for arousing expectations. So, like the others, Louise was not in the least surprised to see him when he called. He sat with her in her huge salon, under the chandelier hanging down in clusters of swollen grapes, and unfolded his huge plans; and so excited her that she had to hold herself down by clutching the edge of her chair. He talked brilliantly, sometimes flicking his tongue over his lips; he too was excited—by his own plans (he really meant them), by her excitement, and also by her presence. In the same way that his tongue flicked over his lips, his eyes flicked over her—her strong hips and thighs pushing through her dress. They talked on one level, they felt on another. It was all beginning. At the end of a long afternoon, he got up— young, plump Adonis that he then was—and stretched himself and smiled. She too smiled and got up and gave him her hand. He took it and held it and they exchanged looks laden with promise. But when he said he needed a hundred dollars, her expression changed, and she withdrew her hand. He went on smiling.

"Come on," he said. "Don't disappoint me." He meant

don't disappoint me in the estimate of your character, but she thought he meant about the hundred dollars.

"It's a lot," she said cautiously.

That made him laugh: after all he had been saying—after all these plans he had unfolded before her that were going to shake humanity to its foundations, she balked at a paltry sum like that! He took his hat and perched it on his blond curls and then lifted it again in farewell as he turned to leave.

Of course she called him back, but grudgingly; and grudgingly she got her handbag and opened it only enough to draw out her wallet. "I can let you have twenty-five," she said.

"Fifty?" he said, watching her with amusement as she drew out the notes with cautious, counting fingers. (She was a big generous woman, physically and in every other way, except with hard cash.) She drew out two tens and a five, and when he waited—amused, tender, watching her—she added another ten and then she quickly shut her wallet and slipped it back into her bag and snapped the clasp shut, looking at him defiantly. He pocketed the money cheerfully and patted her hip with a gesture that was already proprietary. Her caution with money appealed to him; it was the same as his own and showed a good housewifely quality to be esteemed in the woman he already instinctively knew would be as much a wife to him as he would ever need.

In the ensuing years, other women opened their purses much wider to him; he took their money and despised them for their carelessness. That didn't mean he let Louise off. He was always making her give more than she wanted to—that ten dollars extra was played over and over again between them. He liked sometimes to tease, sometimes to bully it out of her. What made her madder than anything was when he got it out of Bruno. Bruno was as impressionable as she was; and having been born to money, he was much more generous with it. All Leo had to do was closet himself with him in the study and, making a very serious face, explain the details of some scheme for which he needed a sizable check. And Bruno, also very serious, would write out that check in his slow, clear hand while Louise listened outside the door. When Leo came out, she would attack him: "What did he give you? Why do you ask him?" Leo showed her the check from just far enough away for her not to be able to read it. When she came closer, he moved off farther, walking backward, and they continued that way through the apartment and out of it to the elevator. With his luck of the devil, the elevator always happened to be just there, waiting for him, and he got into it and the elevator man shut the grille while Leo kissed his fingers at Louise and sank out of sight.

Very much a city person, Bruno had learned late in life to love trees. This may have been because he had so much time and opportunity to be among them. It became his habit to go for long walks, and always in Central Park, crossing the intervening West Side streets as quickly as possible, as though they were hostile territory. But once in the park he seemed happy: he strolled, he sauntered, he sat on benches, he looked at the water. In the winter he wore spats and an overcoat with a fur collar; in the summer lightweight suits of dove-gray and a dove-gray Homburg. When Marietta was small, she sometimes accompanied him; she walked sedately, her white-gloved hand in his. When they met acquaintances—which was rarely—he raised his hat and inclined in a small bow; he encouraged her to curtsy but she felt a fool doing it, so he didn't insist. He pointed out the beauty of the trees to her, and other fine sights; they looked at the animals in the zoo but did not participate in any of the amusements such as pony rides and carousels. When she was with him, Marietta felt such things to be beneath her dignity; she didn't even want any ice cream or popcorn or anything and looked scornfully at other children eating them and spoiling their clothes.

She and Bruno had grown-up conversations. He told her about planets and stars and geological formations and other facts he had learned from books. He went often to the library and read up these facts of nature and the universe. He also read the newspapers very carefully every day and shared with her the information he had gathered there. He encouraged her to ask questions and never pretended to know the answers when he didn't; instead he said he would look it up or think about it, and he kept his promise, so that often she received an answer to her question a week or two after she had asked it.

Once she asked, "Why does he have to be there?" She was referring to Leo whom they had left at home with Louise. In fact, Marietta had a distinct impression that that was why she and her father had gone out on this walk. She had wanted to stay home and play with her new wooden menagerie, but Bruno had gently helped her into her little fur coat and buttoned up her gaiters and fastened her hat under her chin. It was snowing outside.

In the park, Bruno didn't want her to speak so that no cold snow should enter her mouth and throat. He made her hold up her muff against her face. But they enjoyed it—the cold flakes falling so evenly, and the pure glittery foamy snow that was beginning to be powdered along the paths and on their shoes and on the stark branches of the trees stretched out against the sky which shone like a dull sheet of metal. When they left the park, they got a cab on Fifth Avenue, but instead of taking her home, Bruno took her to the Old Vienna where she drank hot chocolate with whipped cream and had the cake trolley come around several times.

However, a week or two later, on another walk, Bruno talked about Leo. The snow had melted by this time, leaving the earth brown and fresh with here and there little white pools ingrained in it. The lake was frozen and people on skates were skimming over it, their cheeks pink, and colored scarves flying. Bruno said that it was a privilege to have Leo staying in the apartment; that Leo was founding an important movement to make people better; and for this he needed and deserved all the help that anyone could give him. In his own case, Bruno said, the help given was small, nothing more than making calls for him, taking messages, giving some monetary contribution and keeping a room in the apartment always prepared. Bruno was very glad to do that; and Marietta should also be glad to do any little service asked of her—as, for instance, this morning, why had she been so cross when Leo had asked her to get the apricot jam for him from the sideboard? These were all little services they should be proud to render.

"And mother?" Marietta asked.

Bruno smiled. There was always something sad about him, even—no, especially—in his smile. But what he said was upbeat, joyful: "Oh, we must be so proud of her. She is a very extraordinary person. I, unfortunately, am not an extraordinary person—no, darling, you're very kind, but I'm not. You see, if I had been an ambassador—or general—or a senator—then she could have had her rightful place. But as you know I'm just an ordinary man—husband and father." Marietta made him stand still so she could kiss his wet cheek. He continued, still smiling: "For me, of course, it's enough. I'm happy and grateful. But for her—for her sake, darling—she needs more. She is big, and so is Leo," he concluded with a sweep of his small hand in its fine leather glove.

Marietta did not mention a scene she had witnessed that very morning while he was out for his walk. She had made a play corner for herself between the Japanese screen and the wall in the salon and, engrossed in her game, gave no thought to anyone else in the apartment. She presumed her mother was at home, and since it was so quiet, she presumed that Leo had gone out. When Louise opened her bedroom door and called for her, she didn't answer, unwilling to have her game disturbed; but when she heard Leo say—also from the bedroom—"She's gone out with Bruno," it became a matter of principle with her not to answer. If Leo was around, she didn't want to be there; she hadn't actually formulated it like that, but that was how she felt.

Louise, satisfied that no one was home, didn't bother to close her bedroom door, and now Marietta heard sounds in there as though they were having a game of their own. She tried not to listen, she didn't want to, but they were so noisy they distracted her from her game. At first she heard her mother laugh out loud—and next it sounded as if she were shrieking, like someone had pinched her or something? Surely they wouldn't be playing a game like that—the way she herself sometimes played with other children, to see who would shriek first; although, of course, Marietta thought to herself, grim beyond her years, with those two who could tell? And the next moment there was a loud thump as of someone heavy falling on the floor and then another shriek from her mother—definitely of laughter, triumphant laughter— followed by a roar from Leo, vowing vengeance. Next came a thud of feet as her mother bounded along the corridor giving out cries of mock fear while Leo roared more as he pursued her. They arrived thus, hunted and hunter, in the salon. Marietta kept her eyes glued to the space left between the panels of the screen. She couldn't believe it—but Louise as she came running into the room was stark naked, and so was Leo who followed behind her. Later in the day, when Bruno said that Louise was big and so was Leo, Marietta couldn't help seeing them as she saw them at that moment, pounding and capering through the salon. They dodged in and out among the furniture—and this was no spare modern room but crammed with urns, and a marble bust of Beethoven and another of the boy taking a thorn out of his foot, and cabinets full of glass and china and Bruno's grandmother's Biedermeier doll's house: but Louise and Leo romped around there as if they were out in the open, impeded only by trees. But suddenly Louise pretended exhaustion—she held her hand between her breasts and stood by the sofa, stag at bay; and Leo, catching up with her, stood over her in menace while she murmured submission. He gave her a push that bounced her down among the needlepoint cushions on the velvet sofa. And amazing, amazing to Marietta, peeping through the hinges, what had so repelled her as he romped through the room, that large male member bouncing from thigh to thigh, changed its character completely. Swelling with a monstrous being of its own, it stood up at a right angle; and next thing he fell on top of Louise on the family sofa and these two large people coiled and looped themselves together into one person, or rather, one unknown primeval animal. Now Marietta had to keep absolutely quiet and not move till they were through —which took a long time, or so it seemed to this small girl. At last, when they got up and went back to the bedroom—like loving friends now, their arms around each other— she continued to stand behind the screen in silence, knowing she would have to be silent about this forever, for the rest of all their lives; and she was.

Every few years Louise made a resolution to break with Leo. Not only when Bruno was alive but afterward too; regularly every few years she decided on it. Regi wasn't often around in these later years—she had become more and more restless and was always planning some new trip for herself; but when she was there, Louise would confide her resolution to her and Regi always said the same thing: "And about time too."

There was the year when, having nowhere else to go, Regi joined Louise and Natasha on their annual vacation in the Hamptons. They stayed in a beach hotel that Louise and Natasha had liked in previous years; it was impeccably run

by a family in family style with every kind of home comfort.
But Regi didn't like it, she grumbled all the time, right from
breakfast on when she sent back the coffee for not being
strong enough, or found what she suspected was a spot of jam
on the tablecloth. When Louise protested at the fuss she
made, Regi said, "They're charging enough, aren't they, my
goodness." Natasha sat there with her eyes lowered in shame.
Louise whispered to her, "Don't mind Regi, she's always like
that": and it was true. Wherever Regi went, she was indignant at the service given on the one hand and at the prices
charged on the other.

The hotel, standing on an elevation above the beach,
had a porch facing the ocean, and here Louise and Regi sat
all morning on white basket chairs with their legs stretched
out on matching white footstools. Louise, who loved the sun·
and turned a healthy ruddy brown color immediately, would
have liked to go out on the beach, but Regi would only con-
sent to walk there late in the afternoon; and even then she
had a parasol and big dark glasses and covered her neck and
arms with gauze scarves against the sun, which was absolute
anathema to her. Natasha was left to walk by herself and gaze
out over the ocean. She gazed so much that it seemed her eyes
must have absorbed the color of sea and sky; but not at all—
they remained dark and strange. So did she herself. Louise
was worried by the way Natasha was always alone. There
were so many nice young people of the same age—Natasha
was fourteen at the time—all having a good time together,
swimming and throwing colored balls and burying each other
in sand; but Natasha, who was very shy, spoke to no one and
no one spoke to her. Sometimes, watching her walk there all
alone, Louise stood up on the porch and put her hands to her
mouth and shouted to her to come up and join them. "Don't
make an exhibition of yourself," Regi rebuked her. Natasha
never joined them. Actually, Louise was relieved because she
wouldn't have liked Natasha to overhear Regi's conversation.

Regi talked about *everything,* every kind of unsuitable subject, she had absolutely no reticence at all.

One morning, while they were sitting this way on the porch, Louise was called to the telephone. It was Leo. He was calling from somewhere across the country—she wasn't sure where: the last she had heard he was in Colorado, getting a group together there; but now he said he was coming to New York and was going to live in Louise's apartment. He was running a summer school in the city and there would, of course, be a number of people with him; but she wouldn't mind that, would she, especially since she wasn't there anyway but was enjoying herself by the seaside. He asked her about sheets and towels for everyone, "That sort of thing," he said, speaking in a testy, hurried manner—his usual manner when he had to discuss practical matters which he felt someone else (for instance, Louise) ought to be dealing with. She felt the same—in fact, offered: "Do you want me to come?" To which he answered at once, "Good God, no," and hung up.

She returned to Regi in a pensive mood. "Who was it?" Regi asked eagerly, hoping it was an invitation to something nice like an evening party with music. There were always so many things going on in people's houses during this season; and Regi was getting bored just sitting here looking at waves going backward and forward.

"Leo's coming to New York."

"Oh, well, Leo. I suppose you're going to pack your bags and run there. Leaving me sitting here. Naturally—Leo. He comes first."

"No," Louise said. She didn't mention that she had offered to come and he had refused her. Instead she heard herself say, unexpectedly, "I'm not going to see him anymore."

"Ha-ha-ha," Regi said—which made Louise continue more heatedly: "Ringing me from God knows where: 'I'm going to stay in your apartment with fifty people.' I should

have told him there and then definitely not. Find somewhere
else. Find yourself another big fool like me."

"There is no other big fool like you." Regi squinted ill-
humoredly toward the seashore where Natasha could be seen
wandering up and down like a lost soul. "What's that child
doing? . . . If she's not doing anything—and obviously she's
not, she never does—at least you could send her down to get
my juice. It's no use ringing the bell or anything like that
here, of course, they're all much too busy padding our bills."

"Leave her alone," Louise said. "She's thinking." She felt
it necessary to add: "Young people think all the time." Regi
didn't have to point out that there were plenty of other young
people on the beach who were not doing it. But Natasha
seemed to have less in common with these healthy youngsters
than she did with the seagulls swooping between sea and sky
as if trying to decide to which element they belonged.

"And those clothes she wears," Regi deplored.

Natasha bought her clothes herself from men selling
them out of cardboard boxes on the street. They consisted of
long dragging cotton skirts and cheesecloth blouses made in
underdeveloped countries. Natasha favored these clothes because they hung on her loosely and did not constrict her in
any way; because they were very cheap; and because by buying them she might be helping to feed a starving family in
some terrible famine-stricken part of the world.

"You don't understand her, Regi," Louise said. "The
child is an idealist. She has very high principles. You just
can't understand, so please don't talk about her anymore."

"All I'm asking is can't she get my juice? You know I
have to have it with my pill. You know very well what the
doctor said."

"You're just a selfish woman, Regi. You always have
been, you always will be. The only person you can ever think
of is yourself. Not that I'm any better," Louise went on. "Sit-

ting here like this, a grandmother, with my hands idle, not even knitting—"

"As if you can knit," Regi said.

"I'm ashamed that I can't! I'm ashamed that I'm sitting here this way! A useless old woman with useless thoughts about an old man who doesn't even want me. Well, from now on it's I who don't want him. I'm not going to think about him anymore but about myself the way you do, Regi, and about my child and my grandchildren and what I can do for them. From now on. Natasha!" she called. She stood up and put her hands around her mouth and called again.

All that day Louise was as in a fever. She was always that way when she was contemplating ridding herself of Leo. Regi, of course, could not afford to be drawn in by any of this: the taking of her pill, the eating of her lunch, the hours of rest after her lunch, her walk on the beach, her dressing up for the cocktail hour—it was all like the planets set in their course, and no wild winds whipping up Louise could cause the least ripple in that ordained rotation.

It happened to be a sultry day, and they had to pull down the shades in their rooms for their siesta. There were little warning rumbles in the air, augmenting Louise's foreboding that something momentous was about to happen. She took off her dress, she lay on her bed, but she could not sleep. Thoughts as oppressive as the weather simultaneously weighed her down and stirred her up. She felt she *had* to talk to someone. But when she went next door, Regi, who had disposed herself on her bed in her crimson kimono and with eye pads on her closed lids, was very indignant with her: she said she had never heard of such a thing, to come in and disturb a person who was lying down for her afternoon siesta. Louise quickly shut the door and went back to her own room. She lay on her bed; she shut her eyes. She tried to shut off her thoughts. Regi was right—it was the time for sleep and rest, not for vain speculation on a worn-out old passion. And at this age, she told herself in disgust. She was over seventy, and it might have been expected that by this time her only concern with her heart would be a clinical one.

In the adjoining hotel room, Natasha was writing in her diary. It was Mark who had advised her to keep a diary and had also given her the book in which to write it. Sometimes she copied passages from it and sent them to him as a letter. This was in addition to the other letters she wrote him. Just now he was traveling in Europe with a friend, and he had instructed her to send care of American Express in Paris. She didn't know when he would be there to pick up his mail, and it was frustrating for her not to be able to calculate the day when the messages she sent him—though winged, she felt, straight from her heart into his—would actually reach him. She didn't expect to hear from him, so she really had no reason to keep loitering around the reception desk at the time the mail was being sorted. She knew perfectly well that when he traveled or was with a friend, he did not want to be diverted by unnecessary thoughts of home, and that her letters could only receive his attention when he returned to Cambridge at the start of his semester. But then it would be his full attention: he corrected, commented, criticized, praised. Often she got them marked up in red like a school essay. When he was younger—just a schoolboy himself—his criticisms had tended to be negative, even destructive, but now that he was a college student he was very patient, thoughtful, and encouraging with her.

At his instigation, she had also begun to write poetry. She was writing some now, induced perhaps by the strange weather outside. She had her blinds up and her windows open: the beach was now as empty as the sea. The wind had risen and not only spurts of sand but every straw and shred of paper lying on the beach were being whirled up as into a dervish dance. The waves were mounting into giant cumulations toward the sky, which hung down low to meet them while frightened sea gulls were tumbled up and down and up again between the two. Pulses of thunder throbbed through the swollen ocean and the swollen sky. All this Natasha was trying to get down in her poem, together with the feelings in her heart which were more tumultuous than one would have suspected from such a small, plain, undeveloped girl.

After a while she saw her grandmother hurrying down the incline on which the hotel stood. Louise was barefoot and ran nimbly across the sand; seen thus from the back, she might have been a much younger woman. She went as close to the ocean as possible and stood there alone. Her loose gown billowed; her gray hair flew around her head.

Natasha followed her. As soon as she reached her, Louise fell around her neck. Natasha was used to this, Louise was always doing it in moments of high stress. Often she said nothing at all and Natasha didn't know what it was about and didn't ask but only stood there, doing her best to support Louise who was heavy. But today Louise did speak; she said, "Now he wants to have a summer school in the apartment. He wants to live there with God knows how many people; God knows what sort of people."

The rising waves sprayed them, the water lapped around their bare ankles. The edge of Natasha's cotton skirt got soaked and hung down lower. Also, she felt the first rain drops, quite different from the spray of seawater, fall on her neck like round, warm tears.

"We have to go in," Natasha murmured. "We're getting wet."

But Louise, though equally wet, only moved back a few steps. She retained her hold on Natasha so she could speak close to her ear; she had to do that because of the noise from wind and water. "If he cared for me, it'd be different—one jot

for me—but he uses me, that's all. That's all he wants from
me. I have to be fair: from anyone. He is like that. It's his
nature. Natasha, I've had enough."

"But Grandma, if it's his nature—"

"I'm going to be with you now. And Mark. And your
mother. That's it. I have to have some peace, Natasha; some
peace of mind," Louise insisted as if Natasha were denying
her right to it.

More raindrops fell and faster; lightning streaked
through the mass of clouds and waves, and thunder rolled.
Natasha gave up hope of getting her grandmother inside before they were both drenched; also she felt they had to continue talking, the subject couldn't just be dropped because of
a storm.

"I should have told him this morning on the phone. I
should have said to him there and then, that's it, good-bye."

"But Grandma, you like it when he's there. He makes
you laugh."

"He makes me *scream!*" Louise put back her head as if
she wanted to do it right there. But she didn't have to, the
storm did it for her.

"He makes you laugh too. And you run up and down
and do things for him. You like it."

"I didn't expect this from you, Natasha: taking his side."

"I said *you* like it. I'm thinking of you. Supposing he
didn't come anymore or phone or anything—"

"Fine. That's what I want."

They walked out of the range of the waves. There was
nothing they could do about the rain. It was coming down in
sheets and had drenched them both in seconds.

"And Regi says I should."

"Oh, Regi."

"She's been saying it for years. Why 'Oh, Regi'? We
could learn a lot from her."

"I wouldn't want to learn anything from Regi."

"Darling, she loves you; she's concerned for you. That's why she's critical," Louise urged.

Natasha wasn't prepared to go on standing in the rain to talk about Regi. "He doesn't come all that often," she got back to Leo.

"No, only when it suits him. He doesn't care what suits me. He doesn't care," she went on in a different tone, "that I might want to see him; or at least know where he is; when he's coming; instead of months and months passing and not a sign—"

"He comes on your birthday."

"Big deal," said Louise and made the same derogatory face she had made as a schoolgirl.

"He always comes for that."

"Now I'm going to tell him not to anymore!" Louise raised her face to the storm. Water streamed from her hair and from her clothes. She loved it. She loved the roar of the thunder and of the ocean. It made her feel very strong and ready for the most resolute action of her seventy years.

But Natasha caught flu as a result of that day's exposure, with fever and rheumatic pains, and she had to stay in bed for the remainder of their vacation. Regi was furious. A doctor was called in and altogether a tremendous fuss was made and Louise was preoccupied all the time. Regi had to sit by herself for hours on end with nothing to do except quarrel with the management.

Natasha didn't mind too much being sick. She was used to it for she was always catching something. Louise made the hotel room feel just like Natasha's usual sickroom, with lemonade and flowers on the bedside table and their favorite eau de cologne, the original from Cologne with the blue and gold label, which even Louise's mother had used. Louise sat on a chair close to the pillow and read aloud from one of the books Natasha had brought with her. These books had been selected by Mark, who always regulated Natasha's reading, so

that in a way it was as though he were there with them in his
usual supervisory capacity. Louise read everything he recom-
mended too, and she loved it and didn't know whom to praise
more, the author or Mark for recommending him. This year
it was Turgenev, and Louise went into such raptures that
often she couldn't go on but had to hide her face behind the
book and call from out of there "That man! That man! How
does he know it all?" The smell of the pages as well as the
illustrations—it was an old edition with color plates of girls in
white dresses playing the piano and moonlight coming in
through the windows—reminded her of the time she had read
the book, or perhaps some other book that had filled her with
the same emotion, all through one summer lying under the
apple tree in her father's garden. She told Natasha an anecdote of that time—how her mother had baked a cake for visitors and had put it to cool on the windowsill. It was her
mother's specialty: Louise could still smell it in her memory, a
lemon madeira. She had left Turgenev and gone to the windowsill and cut herself a big warm moist piece; she could still
taste it too. But her mother had been annoyed, having to be
ashamed before visitors for serving a cake with a slice missing.
And for Natasha, fevered, hot, yet not at all unhappy, the
book and the anecdote got mixed up forever—the girls in
white dresses stopped playing the piano and came out to join
Louise in the garden and eat hot cake with her under her
apple tree.

When the doctor came, it turned out he was German too
and very old. He was retired, really, but kept being called in
by summer visitors. He liked talking to Louise and Natasha
and didn't seem pressed for time at all. He even smoked a
cigar—"Very bad, very bad," he said. "One, for a doctor to
smoke, and two, to smoke in the sickroom; couldn't be
worse." He seemed ready to stay for hours. He and Louise
discovered that they used to go to the same place in the
mountains for their vacations and had once been there in the

same year though not in the same *pensione*. Then he said that they had better be careful, and he told the joke about the man in the railway carriage who wouldn't tell his fellow passenger the time because they might get into further conversation and then one thing would lead to another and before long they would discover that they were related. Louise and Natasha were so appreciative of this joke that the doctor at once got ready to tell them another. He had a big store of them.

But then Regi came in, very cross, and he pulled his gold watch out of his vest pocket and found it was time to visit another patient. Regi hated all sickrooms except her own. She really hated them; they did something to her, she said. And she couldn't stand the sight of Natasha in bed, her eyes full of fever, her large nose red and rheumy, and wearing nothing more attractive than Mark's old striped pajamas he had had at school.

Regi paced the room in her black cocktail gown; she always dressed up in the evening, wherever she was. "Horrible smell of medicine in here," she said. "What's he given you? Are you sure he's a proper doctor? You can't just take anything anyone gives you, you know."

"I think Regi and I will just go and sit in the lounge for our drink," Louise said. She put a bookmark in Turgenev and gave a secret wink to Natasha.

As soon as they were outside, Regi said, "I told you long ago—that child is not healthy."

"But it's because she got wet. It's my fault, Regi, completely."

But Regi had always said it about Natasha, that she wasn't healthy. To outsiders she went further: "Naturally, what do you expect when you adopt a child and don't know where it comes from. I told them at the time; I said 'You wouldn't buy a horse that way, would you?' So they can't say they haven't been warned."

Louise and Regi were the only two occupants of the hotel lounge. Everyone else was on the beach, for there was still some sun to enjoy. But although Regi loved nature as much as the next person, everything had its own time and six o'clock was cocktail time.

Her mood was bad: "We might as well go home," she said. "I don't know why we're still here, spending money uselessly." The waiter brought her drink. It was called English Rose; it was a concoction she had first tasted years and years ago, in one of the old hotels in New York, and insisted on having made up for her wherever she went. Of course, most people never got it right—certainly not here in this beach hotel where the waiter was just a philosophy student on a summer job, mostly reading a book.

"I'm not enjoying myself," Regi declared.

Louise felt guilty. Not only because of Natasha's sickness, but for bringing Regi here in the first place. The setting was wrong for her. The hotel lounge was done up simply with white wicker furniture and green cotton cushions. Regi looked a complete misfit in her elegant black. "We can't go home," Louise said, biting her lip. "Leo's there."

"You can tell him to get out." Regi tasted her English Rose and put it down again. "Horrible. They might as well poison me straight out. . . . You said you wanted to get rid of him. Now's your chance."

She looked at Louise out of the corner of her eye. When they were girls, they had often dared each other to do things: to ride a bicycle, to smoke in the street, to sing a song in a café. When she had been in a bad mood with Louise, Regi's dares became more daring: "Send a note to that officer over there, the one with the red hair, tell him you know his sister: go on, I dare you . . . Oh, I can see you're just a mealy coward." So then Louise would toss her head and do what she was dared—and more: called a coward, she would become reckless.

"Go on," Regi said now, in the hotel lounge. "You're always saying you will but you never do. It's just talk with you. You don't mean it." She continued to look sideways at Louise. She saw Louise's face working with emotion: "Oh," she said fliply, "you're just a mealy coward."

Louise tossed her head. She got up. She went over to the public phone in the lounge. Her head held high, facing Regi, she called her own number in New York, collect. A strange voice answered, there was some explaining to do, then Leo himself came on. As soon as she heard his voice, Louise turned her back on Regi.

As soon as he heard hers, he went into a flood of talk: he was so glad she had called, there was such chaos in the apartment, not to be believed—no one could find anything—and he had never, in his life—

"Leo," she said.

—in his whole life seen such a bunch of useless people.

"Leo, I don't want you to stay in the apartment."

"And I don't want to stay here. It's terrible, Louise, you can have no idea. No one can find the towels, they can't find the sheets, there's no orange juice, the dishwasher's not working—I can tell you, you can thank your lucky stars you're not here."

"I want to come home, Leo."

"Absolutely unnecessary. I appreciate it—but on no account do I want to spoil your holiday. I'll manage, don't worry. It's not the first load of shithole students I've had on my hands." He laughed bitterly, could be heard to bark out some order, than spoke back into the receiver: "There's nothing you can do. This is my problem. I've asked for it and I'm getting it. Well, don't worry. Just relax and go on enjoying yourself. I'll pull through somehow."

"There are more towels on the top shelf of the left-hand closet in Marietta's room."

"Towels. Sheets. Would you believe it? That's what you

get for setting up as a goddamn guru. Who wants it. Who needs it. . . . I suppose it's just wonderful up there. Good food, good sun—you don't know how I crave it. I tell you what, Louise: if I absolutely can't stand it here, I might come up for the day on Sunday. Well, I don't promise anything, but I'll try."

"They do a very good Sunday lunch in the hotel. Roast meat, potatoes, and some sort of English savory. Or are you still a vegetarian?"

"Good God, no. I *need* meat."

He hung up. She turned around and went back to Regi. Regi looked at her with her shaved and penciled eyebrows raised high; one pointed crimson fingernail, hard as a bird's beak, tapped the table. But Louise couldn't say anything; her upper lip trembled more. She was afraid she would burst out laughing—the way she had done after sending the note to the red-haired officer—so she turned suddenly, abruptly, and hurried out of the lounge. And once outside, she did more than hurry: she ran—up the stairs, into Natasha's room. She flung herself on Natasha's bed, her face on her pillow. She burst out laughing into that. Natasha smiled; she stroked her grandmother's hair. "You've been speaking to Leo," she said.

"He may be coming up for the day on Sunday." Louise's face was now as flushed as Natasha's, so that they both looked as if they had fever.

Mark was immensely enjoying his acquisition of the Van Kuypen house. Nothing—no one—not even Kent could stop him from his weekend expeditions to watch the progress on the place. Fortunately, the part damaged by the fire had been a later addition, and now that Mark had had it stripped away, the original dimensions of the house, simple and grand, could be clearly seen. However, although willing to restore the house to its old lines outwardly, inside, Mark was willing to sacrifice period authenticity in favor of his modern needs.

He had an exact idea of what he wanted done, and how it was going to look, and moreover what sort of a life he was going to lead there with his friends.

One weekend Kent was keen to attend a party with Mark. It was in celebration of yet another newly decorated loft, this one belonging to a dancer and his friend who was a lawyer. It had been done by another friend of theirs, a decorator, and was said to be the most attractive yet in a long line of daring and attractive lofts. Everyone anyone ever knew or had heard of was going to be at the party, and Kent felt it to be important that he and Mark should be there too. But Mark needed to go to his house.

"It'd be good for me," Kent urged. "Professionally. I'd meet people. I might get a commission to photograph the place. Listen, I thought you wanted me to get on. But all you care for is your dumb old house."

Mark left it at that, and for the next day or two Kent was alternately sulky and seductive. He said, "You've got someone up there, that's why you keep going."

"I go for my house."

"That's what you say." Kent turned away in a sulk, and he did so with a graceful swing of his hips for Mark's benefit. Mark observed and delighted in it—but he was also irritated, on two counts: he did not like to be nagged, and he did not like too many feminine seductive gestures in his friends. He was interested in boys who *were* boys—with scars on their knees and warts on their fingers from handling toads. Was Kent getting spoiled? Was he himself getting tired of Kent? These questions always came up for him in the course of his relationships, which had many ups and downs with now one person getting tired and then the other, in a seesaw of intense affections.

Meanwhile, Mark was getting used to going away by himself on the weekend. After his usual business session with Leo at the Academy, he and Natasha would drive over to the house. Sometimes Stephanie and Jeff joined them, and while Mark was busy with the architect and the contractor, the other three lay in the grass, drowsy and drunk with the fragrant scents brought out by the sun. Natasha did her best to explain Mark's plans for restoring the house, but she must have done it badly, for all Jeff ever said, from under the battered straw hat tilted over his eyes and with a blade of grass between his teeth, was "What's he want it for?" Natasha was willing to start again, but perhaps it was hopeless; perhaps she would never get it right. It was strange—when she was here alone with Mark, she saw the house as he did: as a beautiful mansion, an immensely desirable possession, but when she was with the other two, she saw it the way they did, as just an old dump.

But they were all glad to get away from the Academy for a while. Even Stephanie, though still involved in her work there, felt she needed an occasional rest from Leo. He kept on sending for her at night and had also begun to follow her around in the day. Sometimes when she looked around, she found him loping behind her like some great bear; or he would jump out at her from behind a tree, crying "Boo!" and laugh till he choked over the shock he imagined he had given her.

All this, although a nuisance, did not undermine her faith in her work with him. She studied his doctrine and ardently followed the exercises and felt herself becoming a truly more integrated person (or, as they put it at the Academy, a more *become* person). As for Leo's odd behavior, she took it as an additional incentive to her faith. Yes, it would be very nice, wouldn't it, she said scornfully, if he were a stereotype saint with a long beard and kindly eyes and all of that; very easy to believe in him then—but to believe in lecherous Leo in his dirty monk's habit, that was something else again. When she talked like that Jeff appeared to be asleep under his straw hat; until suddenly he jumped up and ran through the grass which sloped from the house down into the lake and he dived straight in the water with his clothes on and thrashed around there, making a lot of noise as though wishing not to hear anymore.

The fact was, Jeff was getting ready to move on. That was his life, moving on: he didn't really know anything else. This may have been because from his father's side he came from a long, long line of prospectors, moving from place to place in a hunger for wealth and adventure, and on his mother's side from migrant workers who had also moved in hunger, but only for food. Jeff had never known his mother who had run off when he was a baby; he hardly knew his father either, for like Jeff himself he had been constantly moving on. He had worked when he had to—on the railroads, in construction, in auto plants, as a short-order cook—and when he could afford to lay off and just spend, he did that. There had been no place for Jeff in this scheme, so he had been mostly in foster homes. No one family ever seemed to want to keep him for long, and as he grew older he grew wilder and got into trouble and spent some time in the reformatory. Here he found a library and read a lot and also wondered a lot, including why it was that no one wanted him. Later, when he grew up and began to move around the country, it was not like his father only in search of pleasurable survival but also of what he had read in those books or had thought for himself. He took the same sort of jobs as his father—whatever came to hand—but ranged farther and met up with people who were thoughtful like himself. He traveled with them and tried out different ways of living with them in communes and different ways of being in drugs and religions.

When Mark had finished with his people in the house, he came to join the others lying in the grass and to listen to their conversation. But often Natasha saw that he was not so much listening to as looking at Jeff; and she also saw that Jeff was aware of this and that he did not seem to find it unusual. Jeff was a nice-looking boy, blond and sunburned with flat hips and rounded buttocks in very tight jeans. And when Mark's eyes lingered on him, Jeff could be seen to arrange himself in attractive attitudes. Natasha tried not to notice all this, but where Mark was concerned she noticed everything, whether she wanted to or not.

In this instance, Stephanie also noticed, for one night up in the attic, she said, "I think he's getting really hot for Jeff."

Although she spoke casually, Natasha, lying in the lower bunk, became alert. She longed to ask questions but felt shy about doing so. There were so many things she didn't understand that everyone else seemed to take for granted.

Stephanie went on musing as casually as before: "Jeff wouldn't mind. He does it with men sometimes; he's still sort of free-lance. He told me about an actor he was doing it with, out on the coast. He said he did it for the money but you could see that wasn't a hundred percent true. It's fantastic the things you can see when you know what to look for." Now she stopped speaking casually and became engrossed in giving Natasha a rundown on the techniques of lie-detecting, in oneself and in others, that Leo was teaching them. She talked till she fell asleep, which happened very suddenly.

Jeff could be seen to wander over more and more frequently to Mark's house. This may have been because he was getting tired of what went on at the Academy, and of the Academy itself. Mark's house was in the greatest possible contrast to it. Leo's house and grounds were as Gothic, convoluted, inward-looking as the psychic activities that went on inside it; whereas Mark's house was simple and classical, standing on an eminence which commanded a clear view over the surrounding countryside. It was a long drive up to the house, and though the gates were missing, the gatekeeper's cottage was still there, a sturdy little one-room stone house of the same period as the main building. One day Jeff asked Mark: "What are you going to do with it?"

"I guess I'll need a caretaker," Mark said.

After a longish silence and probably much thinking on both sides, Jeff said, "That's right." With that, an understanding seemed to have been reached between them, so that they didn't need to talk about it again.

Leo had once confessed to Mark that he too had at one period of his life tried to love men—as indeed he had tried, experimented with everything (one had to if one was, as he put it, "into human nature"). "It was quite fun, Mark," he said, "but it wasn't the same thing." He then went into the sort of rapture over the luxurious intricacies of the female body that he liked to indulge in, especially with Mark whom he knew to be bored and irritated by the subject. "No," he concluded, "you see, Mark, once you've been into all that"— he roared for a moment at the accidental ambiguity—"you can't be satisfied with some little boy's backside. . . . By the way, I understand you're taking Jeff away from me."

"He's going to be my caretaker."

"So that's what you call it." Leo never could resist that kind of joke nor laughing at it inordinately himself. But this time he sobered up more quickly than usual; he raised a warning forefinger: "Don't expect much from him, Mark, in your line. He may be willing to play a little bit here and there, but once you like girls you like girls, even when it's the thing not to." And then he sighed in real deep human concern: "It's all just fucking around, body and mind—except that fucking is too good a word for it. No one's serious," he lamented, very serious himself, even grave, and in despair of a generation so light-minded that it didn't even know which sex it wanted to belong to.

But Mark found Jeff to be serious—certainly about moving into the gatekeeper's cottage. While work on the main house proceeded under contract, Jeff fixed his own little place up himself. Wearing nothing but a pair of cut-off jeans, he worked from morning to night, whistling cheerfully. It turned out he could strip and solder and plaster and carpenter and put in sanitary and electrical fittings. He didn't seem to think anything of knowing all these crafts. He couldn't even tell how he had picked them up. He had often worked on construction sites, all over the country, months at a time, doing every kind of work; but then, he had worked at many other kinds of jobs too, anything that came to hand, skilled or unskilled, he didn't care as long as he could earn enough money to live on. That was the only reason he did it.

Now he was on Mark's payroll, and while getting the cottage ready, he camped out in the big house. Dinnertime, he sat with the men working there, eating pastrami leaking out from huge rolls and drinking Pepsi or beer. At night he was alone and cooked and slept either in those lofty rooms or, on very warm nights, he stayed out on the grounds, rolled up in a sleeping bag and smeared with mosquito repellent. Natasha and Stephanie came to visit him, and on weekends Mark came too. Mark still checked into the fancy local inn, but he spent all day and slept most nights with Jeff in the unfinished house, or out on the grounds. This was very idyllic for him. He felt himself to be really taking possession of his property. He also incidentally took possession of Jeff, but this was just part of the pleasant summer nights, which were always astir and alive with passionate insects.

Mark's relationship with Kent was far more complicated. All week in the city Mark kept long office hours and had meetings and site inspections and all sorts of business to attend to, and during that time he could only hope that Kent was, if not profitably, then at least innocently, employed. Of course he called frequently—and it was remarkable how often Kent was at home, so that it was really unreasonable for Mark to be so agitated when he was out. Whenever that happened, Mark called again and again, every ten minutes sometimes, in between all his business, and when Kent at last answered, Mark couldn't stop himself from saying first thing: "Where *were* you?" Kent didn't answer that question, and when Mark held out an excuse for him—"Were you out taking pictures?"—he didn't take it up, too proud or too indifferent either to account for himself or to tell a lie.

For his own social pleasure, Mark wouldn't have gone anywhere near the Old Vienna. But he sometimes took out-of-town people there—businessmen from Oregon or Oklahoma with whom he had property dealings. Some of them brought their wives, eager to see exciting aspects of New York, and with them the Old Vienna was always a great success. They didn't realize that they were mainly excited by people like themselves who had been brought there for the same purpose. In vastly increasing its popularity, the Old Vienna had changed its character. While in earlier years—in Leo and Louise and Regi's heyday—it had been a gathering place for theatrical and other well-heeled bohemian circles, now only the audience of this former clientele remained. If people connected with the arts came in, they were mainly agents or publicity managers. But these were certainly impressive enough to give full satisfaction to Mark's guests: they dressed very stylishly, ordered lavishly on expense accounts, and spoke famous names often and loudly. The management had, over all these years, not only maintained the standard of its performance but brought it up to a higher pitch. Chandeliers, mirrors, and blue velvet were there in such profusion that they were almost a parody; the dishes on the menu had retained their exaggeratedly Viennese quality; and while the cooking was nothing to write home about—who came to the Old Vienna to eat, anyway, except Leo—there were some wonderful drinks. Made up of a basis of vodka or brandy mixed with fruit juice and liqueurs, these were sweet, pungent, and unexpectedly potent.

One day, when Mark came in with a couple from Portland, Oregon, Mr. and Mrs. Cross, the first person he saw sitting there was Kent. He was with an older man, who wore a pink shirt and had gray hair beautifully modeled in a boy's haircut. They had one of the tables for two down the center—as it happened, Regi and Louise's table—so that Mark, whose party was in an alcove at the side, had a good view of them. Although electrically aware of Kent's presence, Mark in no way neglected his guests. After ordering the house specialties for them, he casually mentioned some of the interesting people who had figured there in the past. He pointed out Leo's table; he explained the signed photographs of other celebrities which could be glimpsed through the potted lemon trees; he greeted people here and there and murmured their connections; he drew their attention to the hatcheck girl—into her fifties now—who had once been slapped at her post by a famous actress. It did not take much of this to enchant his guests—especially Mrs. Cross (Alice) who sat next to Mark on the velvet banquette; her husband faced them, overflowing his little gilt Viennese chair.

Mark liked Mrs. Cross, and it seemed she liked him. She had pressed her leg against his, and he good-naturedly left it there. It didn't make any difference to him though probably a lot to her, reminding her of much earlier days when she had sat with her leg pressed against the young man who was taking her out. Mark was used to this; it often happened to him with the middle-aged matrons whom he had to entertain in the course of business along with their middle-aged husbands. He had worked it out that it was being around these social scenes that excited them and brought back the time, full of possibilities, when they had been pretty girls. They tended to recall scenes from that time—at this very moment Mrs. Cross was talking about the party her parents had given for her and some of her friends at the country club on their high school graduation. She had worn a dress of lemon-yellow net over silk and had petted in the rose arbor with a youth called Philip whom she had liked all through senior year but until that night had thought to be more interested in her friend Lynn. The party had been less successful for Lynn—in aqua net over silk—and in the early hours of the morning she had had some sort of crisis in the changing room by the pool. Alice talked about all this with a tender, nostalgic smile on her pretty, wrinkled face. Mark found her delightful—he loved these wives—and so did her husband. Mr. Cross was a big, bearlike, ugly man, self-made and rich, but as he listened to his wife he wore an adoring, utterly weak and tolerant expression. While pressing her thigh against Mark's, she also exchanged smiles with her husband and their eyes spoke to each other in a way that moved Mark and made him glad to be with them.

Meanwhile, something within him keen as a hunter was poised in Kent's direction. He saw that Kent's companion was really putting himself out. He was a man considerably older than Mark, and much older than Kent. But he had kept himself together pretty well and presented a distinguished appearance with his gray suit matching his gray hair and the ensemble lightly relieved by his pastel shirt. He appeared to be a successful professional man—an actor's agent? a show business lawyer?—and with his good manners and pleasant life-style supported by easy means, he would make an excellent, not to say delightful, friend: this would be the aspect of himself that he was just then presenting to Kent. Mark guessed their acquaintance to be in its earliest stage, for Kent's companion was making conversation with him in that rather formal, mannered way—weaving his hands in stylized gestures—that showed he was going through the introductory passages in which he would be trying both to impress Kent and to test him out.

Kent was listening in the impassive manner that Mark knew well. He also knew that this manner would be as exciting to Kent's companion as it used to be to himself. It always suggested that Kent was thinking of something else—that in spirit he *was* somewhere else, somewhere more beautiful and pure like in a meadow or by a stream. In fact, however, Mark reflected rather sadly, Kent wasn't there at all nor did he want to be. In spite of his faraway look, he was very much here in the Old Vienna, with waiters running around to serve little drinks and leaning sideways under trays of hors d'oeuvres; and moreover, though appearing to ignore them, he was perfectly attuned to the meaning of his companion's gestures and knew how to respond or, if he so chose, not respond to them.

Alice Cross, smiling at the recollection, wondered what had happened to Philip, the brightest boy in the class of— (well, never mind, she said, with a wink at her husband, not giving any dates away). He had been really something—all the girls had had a thing for him, and he had been voted not only "Most Likely to Succeed" but also "Most Stylish Man of the Year."

Mr. Cross had information: "He failed in the air-conditioner business and, as far as I know, moved to Roseburg."

"You never know with people, do you?" mused Alice. She told Mark, "You remind me of him, a bit. It's the way your hair grows." And she touched it at the temple, in a manner that was partly maternal and partly not so.

"You look out now," her husband warned him, twinkling at the two of them across the table. "She was the belle of Beaverton High, the rangers' mascot and all of that."

"That was just kid stuff," smiled Alice, touching up her hair a little.

"I had competition, I can tell you."

Mark entered into their smiling good mood; he pressed his knee against hers lightly, like a friendly, reassuring, almost paternal pressure of the hand.

Kent never glanced toward Mark's table. He sat there in lordly abstraction—one long leg stretched out along the carpet, a hand resting on his hip. Nevertheless, Mark knew that

Kent was as aware of him as he was of Kent: each feeling the other's presence more intensely than anything else that went on in that crowded place.

"The one thing I don't like in the Fifty-fourth Street lot is that crappy little house bang center," Mr. Cross said.

"He'll sell, don't worry," Mark assured. "He's already offered air rights."

"Oh, please, must you, you two?" Alice said. "Spoil my evening?" She pouted in the way wives are supposed to pout when their husbands talk business on social occasions.

Mr. Cross humored her: "Someone has to pay the bills on all that shopping. Can you believe it?" he appealed to Mark. "The whole morning in Lord and Taylor's."

"And you know very well what for," she replied. Her leg still snug against Mark's, she too appealed to him: "I had to get his mother one of those warm robes with fleecy lining—you know how old people feel the cold."

"Like we have no stores back home," Mr. Cross pretended to grumble.

"Yes, and Norleen? Girls want something different from what everyone is wearing. . . . I got her the cutest little outfit you ever saw—cerise, with a darling row of buttons here and its own little blue blouse to go. She'll love it. She'll have it on her in a minute and call everyone to see."

Mr. Cross turned red with pride: "I've never met a girl like that Norleen for going crazy over clothes. Except," he twinkled across the table, "her mother here."

"There he goes," said Alice.

But Mr. Cross's attention was back on the Fifty-fourth Street lot, and Mark, always entirely alert when it came to business, responded. In the ensuing discussion, both of them forgot about Alice. She was used to that, and was sensible about it; this trip to New York was business-*cum*-pleasure, and she knew the business came first. And it was a privilege for her to have been brought to this place where famous people

came and to be sitting there in the company of a good-looking young man. Strange, the way his leg rested against hers;
strange but nice, stirring up nice memories. As her eyes roved
around the restaurant, she smiled a little to herself: she loved
her life in Portland—her family, her lovely home, her reading
group, her work with dyslectic children—but of course she did
like glitter; she always had. Norleen was the same; her mother
saw it every time she caught her looking at herself in the
mirror—wondering, no doubt, if she could be a fashion model
or something of that sort. It was silly, a dream, but one that
never entirely faded, so that whenever Alice was anywhere
really nice, like this place, glamorous, or even when she just
heard a tune she liked from way back, suddenly it would be
there again, filling her with strong, sweet feelings. And overcome by these, she pressed her thigh closer to Mark's: but was
shocked, bewildered by the way he withdrew it as though he
had been stung.

And for a moment that was just what it felt like to him.
Engrossed in his business talk, he had as completely forgotten
about her leg attached to his under the table as he had about
her sitting beside him. Next moment he was sorry; he saw the
look on her face and interpreted it exactly. He had lived close
to women all his life and knew about their feelings. Not only
that, but he had these feelings himself. He only needed to
look across to where Kent sat with the other man to be aware
of that.

Kent appeared to be in a deep reverie. He had his head
back as though he were lying in a field looking up at the blue
sky instead of at the chandeliers of the Old Vienna. But the
more abstracted he became, the more intensely determined
was his companion to hold him. The older man was talking
volubly now, his hand gestures had become both more stylized and more frenzied; he frequently patted his hair and his
fine necktie. Their table was too far away for Mark to see the

expression on his face, but he knew what this would be. He had often seen it on the faces of middle-aged men like Kent's companion: and the more sensitive they were, the more intelligent, the finer their nature, the more marked this expression of—what was it? Desire was one word for it, but desire in so poignant, so refined a form that it reached to what Leo, in his later teaching, had characterized as The Point.

Mr. Cross was weighing the pros and cons of various types of mortgage. Mark nodded intelligently; at the same time he placed his hand on Alice's knee under the table and smiled at her over it. He wanted to make it up to her for his momentary forgetfulness. He felt a bond with her as he did with Kent and Kent's companion. Only Mr. Cross—successful male, husband, father, Elk—was out of it.

Marietta insisted that Natasha be brought back to the city because it was time for her checkup with the dentist. Natasha had terrible teeth, but it was always a struggle to get her to keep her dentist's appointments. In earlier years, she would argue for days: "Supposing I was poor. Supposing we couldn't afford a dentist." "You're not. We can," they had answered her. But nowadays they didn't go into any of that with her. Mark just told her to get in the car, so she apologetically took leave from Leo and told him she would be back in a day or two. "Hm," Leo said; he was listening to Wagner on his stereo and may not have heard what she said.

But if Leo didn't care whether she came or went, Marietta did. She wanted Natasha to stay with her, and when Mark came to take her back, she was reluctant to let her go.

"She has to go," Mark argued. "She's got a job."

"She doesn't need a job. And specially not with Leo."

"Well," Mark said, "so far he's been the only person willing to keep her. *And* he actually pays her."

"It's you," Marietta, who was a lot shrewder than Nata-

sha, said. "You made him. Probably you're paying her salary
too. Isn't that something?" she said when he couldn't contradict. "I need her, and you pay her to go away."

She was sitting on her sofa; she put back her head and
shut her eyes. Mark gazed into her face and saw that the skin,
stretched taut over her fine small features, was beginning to
crack into many lines; he saw the pulse twitching in her cheek
like a live thing.

Natasha came in, ready to leave. When she saw Marietta
sitting there like that, she exchanged a look with Mark. There
was a silence during which Marietta remained with her eyes
shut.

"Why don't you come with us?" Natasha said at last.
"You'll like it. I mean, the country and everything."

"I don't like the country. I never have liked the country.
And I can't stand Leo." She opened her eyes, she got up, she
took out a cigarette and forgot to light it. "I know I've got to
the age where I'm supposed to be susceptible to Leo; where
I'm supposed to need him. Well, I don't. I never will. He's
never going to be the answer to my problem."

Natasha said, "I wouldn't want him to be." They were
surprised, for she spoke more vehemently than they were used
to from her. But she was thinking of Marietta up in the attic
of the Academy, or in a workshop working on herself like the
others; and that was what she didn't want. Not for Marietta,
not for herself, not for Mark, though she was willing to grant
that it might do other people good.

Not only did Natasha fail to take part in the Academy
workshops, she didn't even attend Leo's famous Saturday
night lectures or the party that followed them. She preferred
to be by herself up in the attic with her own thoughts and
feelings, which were not lonely but on the contrary deeply
and strangely fulfilling. However, she was never alone for as
long as she would have liked to be, for sooner or later one of
the others would turn up there, in some sort of psychological

trouble. Leo's Saturday night lectures might be compared to the Sunday morning sermons the original owners of the house had gone to hear in the white clapboard church that was still extant, half a mile down the main road. But whereas these original late-nineteenth-century owners may have yawned and fidgeted through their pastor's exposition, Leo's students listened to Leo with the same high seriousness, the same intense concentration as the earliest settlers to their preacher's message. For just as that preacher's message was directly connected with the lives of his congregation at the deepest level, so Leo had what he called a "hot line" right into his students' souls (or psyches). And in the same way as the preacher had the means to bring the sinner to repentance, so Leo brought his listeners to an awareness of their maladjustments: and it happened every time that some of them were so deeply affected by what he said that they had to withdraw to think about themselves.

One Saturday night it was a woman called Shirley who, overcome by his lecture, had to come and be in the attic with Natasha. She sat on her little narrow bunk under a light bulb dangling from the rafters. When she lifted her face, Natasha could see it was puffed with tears. She looked like someone's grandmother. As a matter of fact, Natasha knew she *was* someone's grandmother: she had a son who was married and lived with his wife and two children in a Hare Krishna community. Shirley was not on good terms with them; whenever she visited the community, the atmosphere there depressed her so much that she began to quarrel with the son and the daughter-in-law and almost succeeded in stirring them back into the anger that they had cast out of their hearts. She also got sick from the vegetarian messes they ate, and their carrot juice.

"Can you imagine," Shirley said to Natasha, "my great-grandfather was a famous rabbi in Zlotchov, and so was his father. Can you imagine: *rabbis?* I wake up at night and think,

my God, what would they have said if they saw Trevor now
with his little shaved head? He isn't even called Trevor any
more. He's called Prem Dass. It means 'servant of love' or
some such screwy thing in their Hare Krishna language. The
great-great-grandson of a line of famous rabbis and he's
called Prem Dass."

"Maybe that's why," Natasha suggested.

"My parents would have had a fit too. They were so
proud of being liberal agnostics. Well, of course, my parents—
that's another chapter."

Natasha had heard part of it. Parents featured large in
the workshops and were always being recalled, like spirits at
séances. Sometimes these spirits were invited to speak through
the living person—"Be your mother"—and that way Natasha
had actually heard Shirley's mother talk through Shirley.

Of course, like all mothers she had damaged Shirley and
had been the first person she had to cut loose from. The second person had been her husband, Norman, a dentist—"A
damn good one," Shirley said, "a real provider and ready to
spend on his family. That's all he cared about, his family,
Trevor and me. I guess he thought he loved me—but he didn't
know me, Natasha, and I didn't know he didn't till I started
going to Dr. Koenig for my depression and nervous indigestion. Can you imagine? Nervous indigestion—me! That
just shows how desperate things were; I mean, if I couldn't
even *eat.*"

Everyone knew Shirley to be a great eater; and always
with such relish, it was a pleasure to watch her. Leo said
about her "You don't *have* an appetite; you *are* one." She gave
the impression of a very healthy woman, short and compact
with a tight bust (she said she hadn't seen her feet since she
was fourteen) and a shock of healthy curly gray hair and a
florid face: the sort of woman whose senses are not diminished
but vitalized by menopause.

She stood by the dormer window of Leo's attic and

peered down into the garden hazy in the summer dusk. She saw the girls with their long hair in the ankle-length flounced skirts they had stitched for themselves. Leo didn't like girls who cut their hair and he couldn't abide them in pants; he said women who weren't women didn't turn him on, and what were they there for, he joked, except to turn him on?

"I got married when I was nineteen," Shirley said. "I didn't even finish college, just got married like an animal. So it took me till I was thirty-five to wake up and know what I'd missed. And then, will you believe it, Trevor goes and does the same damn thing. I warned him, I told him, but no, on his nineteenth birthday his guru said he had to. It was a mass ceremony, eight couples all married under Hindu rites walking around in a circle throwing puffed rice. I wanted him to be a marine biologist, but he was more interested in selling packets of joss sticks in the subway. Nothing turns out the way you plan it, nothing, nothing, nothing . . . Are you sure you want to be sitting up here with me, Natasha? I mean, when everyone's having such a good time down there."

But Natasha preferred to be with Shirley in the attic. She knew she wasn't very helpful and she couldn't ever really think of anything to say to make people feel better when they were low. But she was prepared just to sit there with them, and if they wanted to touch her, hold her hand, that was all right too.

Shirley took her hand now and brought it up to her cheek. How warm Shirley's cheek was, how cold Natasha's hand. Shirley was surprised. She dropped it and said, "If this is how you are in the summer, what are you like in the winter?"

"The same," Natasha smiled. She was always cold. For years she had thought everyone felt that way, and she couldn't understand it when Louise would fling off her dress and stand there in her petticoat with naked shoulders fanning herself.

"Norman's got married again," Shirley said. "To a much younger girl. They live in the identical same home in Tarry-town we used to have in Briarcliff Manor. They've got two great kids, Edgar and Mary Beth. He's crazy about them. He's got what he wants, I guess, at sixty, poor guy. I'm glad for him, I really am. He's been through hell. . . . Norman used to come to the apartment I'd taken for me and Trevor in the Village. He'd just sit there and cry. He's a big guy with a long face and the tears would just roll down this long face, very slowly like they were taking forever to get from his eyes down into his collar. It was terrible. I had to tell him not to come anymore in the end. And Dr. Koenig said it was bad for me to see him. Dr. Koenig!" she said in outrage, for her psychiatrist was another person she had had to cut herself loose from. For five years she had gone to his office which wasn't really an office but just a room in the apartment he shared with a big Swedish blonde. "He didn't even have a couch," Shirley said, "just this chair you had to sit on telling him all these things. When I said I was leaving, he was worse than my mother. First he made his profound face and said we'd have to live this decision through again; then he said I was destroying myself; in the end he got really aggressive because I was ruin-ing five years' work he'd put in on me. Have you ever been in analysis?"

"They wanted to send me to someone from school, but my grandmother wouldn't allow it. She said if there was any-thing wrong with my psyche, Leo would see to it."

"And did he?"

"He said I didn't have one. Leo's never been interested in me," Natasha admitted.

"There he is—just look at him." Shirley clapped her hand before her mouth, laughing at the sight she saw from the attic window. Leo was chasing Stephanie through the grass while other students got out of their way fast or set off running behind them. It was Leo in his playful mood, acting out an impulse the way he said one had to. Maybe it was in illustration of something he had been telling them in his lecture. He often used such actual illustrations, and it could be embarrassing. For instance, when he said, "Now here is Robin. I would like to take Robin's nose and twist it." And he would do this, explaining, "Why do I want to do it? I don't know. What does it satisfy in me? I don't know. Only I know it satisfies me." He would continue to twist Robin's nose, and even though tears would come into the unfortunate student's eyes, he had to keep still because he was being used as an illustration. When he had finished, Leo would say, "Sorry about that." And Robin, sitting there with a flaming nose, would have to smile and say, "That's okay, Leo. My pleasure."

Now Leo was acting out his drive toward satisfaction by chasing Stephanie. He had hitched his monk's robe above his ankles in order to run better, but of course she was much too quick for him. Her slim, bare feet hardly touched the ground as she ran, her hair flew behind her; she was so confident of her superior agility that every time she reached a tree, she swung round it—once, twice—and laughed at him lumbering behind her.

"At least he has fun," Shirley said, watching them from above. "Look at him—an old man like that having a good time. He must be right somewhere."

But Natasha had turned away from the window. She lay down on her bunk. Now she could only see a fragment of sky, which was dark and calm; she folded her arms behind her head and kept on looking at it, and when she shut her eyes it was as if she were enfolded by it.

"Oh, you're asleep?" Shirley said. She herself didn't feel like sleeping—not at all, she was wide awake and hungry to join in the fun that was going on outside. She went down the attic stairs and then down the main staircase through the completely deserted house and out into the garden. Leo had caught up with Stephanie now, or she had let him catch her, and he was dancing with her. Although the record was of a very modern jazz group, Leo was hopping around in an old-fashioned polka. Others also joined in, doing whatever dance they felt like, regardless of the music. Shirley walked through the grass, looking for a partner, and bumped against Janet, another middle-aged woman, on the same mission. They danced with each other but it didn't matter, for each had her eyes shut and was doing a dance of her own. The overgrown lawn in front of the house was turned into a ballroom, and no one looked back at the somber old mansion looming behind them with only Natasha inside it high up in the attic.

On Marietta's last visit to India, she had taken Mark with her. He was sixteen at the time and very responsive to everything he saw. They traveled around together and she took him to all the places she knew. He enjoyed them with her but also wandered off frequently by himself and made contacts of his own. Like herself, he was entirely open to the place and made friends everywhere—with a railway booking clerk, with the son of a textile millionaire, with a young monk at the Ramakrishna Mission. But his greatest friendship was with Sujata's son and with her lover, Ravi.

These two were college boys and spoke English and were eager to learn more English and anything else that Mark could teach them. Even though he was several years younger than they were, they looked on him as a guide to more sophisticated areas of living. Mark accepted this role without misgiving—he was used to guiding and took it for granted that he always knew best. He also at this time made it a point of honor not to be impressed by anything and to remain cool and impassive about everything they showed him. One night they took him to a brothel where the singing girls paddled their fingers in the back of his white boy's neck; but even when one of them perched herself in his lap and, fumbling at his fly, breathed garlic and betel and essence of roses all over him, he managed to keep absolutely still and not give in to his overwhelming desire to rush out of there and throw up.

Sujata loved it that the three boys were such wonderful friends together, staying out all night while the women sat at home and talked and cooked till they fell asleep on a bed or a mat, with a child curled up beside them. But Marietta lay awake in her hotel room and waited for Mark to come in. Beneath the sound of her air conditioner, she imagined she heard all sorts of noises seeping in from the streets; and while on previous visits she had been thrilled to think of everything that went on, now she could only think of Mark out there and was frightened. When he came back at last—sometimes it was dawn—he didn't like it that she was awake; waiting to trap him, it seemed to him, and he answered her questions laconically or not at all. He was soon asleep in the twin bed next to hers. It was one of the things she loved about traveling with him, that they always shared a room the way they had done when he was a little boy. While he slept, she could look her fill into his face, and it seemed to her as tender and pure as the dawn light by which it was illumined.

By noon next day, and before he was up, his friends came surging into the hotel suite. They walked through the outer room, past Marietta—whom they greeted politely, even obsequiously—and straight into the bedroom. She heard jovial shouts and sometimes playful thumps as they tried to get Mark out of bed; and then jokes and laughter as they talked about what they had done the night before and what they were going to do the night following. When Marietta, feeling indignant, left out, superseded, went in there, she saw Mark sitting up in bed in his pajamas with his hair tousled, his face rosy, his eyes clear; and the other boys sat around him, on his bed and on hers, and once when she came in she saw Ravi

with his arm around Mark's shoulder and the hand of that
arm playing with Mark's ear; and Mark, so freshly awake,
keeping quite still and apparently liking it.

Of course, she had got used to seeing boys and men
everywhere strolling around with their hands intertwined,
and interpreted it as a friendship more high and lofty than
anything known in the West. Besides, Ravi was not in the
least inclined that way, as Marietta well knew from her conversations with Sujata. Sujata loved to confess everything,
and what she confessed was astonishing to Marietta, especially as she never saw the least flicker of anything between
her and Ravi—who indeed called her Auntie and comported
himself toward her with the respect due to the mother of his
friend. But when Sujata spoke of him to Marietta, she was
sometimes sly and sometimes shy, and she looked down to
play with her bangles and then up again to laugh. She managed to make Marietta understand that, in spite of his youth,
Ravi was a cunning and a daring lover. Sujata thought that
she would probably burn in hell for what she did with him,
but for the time being it was worth it.

Marietta told Mark that they were leaving, that she had
to go to New Delhi on a business trip. (She had begun to
export Indian materials for her fashion house.) As she had
expected, Mark protested, but he didn't say, as she had
feared, that he would stay behind. For at that time—in spite
of his considerable independence and show of strength—some
childishness remained in him, some dependency; and also,
though he was struggling hard against it and by the next year
would have overcome it, she was at that time still first with
him. So he went with her to New Delhi and was even cheerful
about it, and as soon as they arrived he contacted friends
he had made there and began his usual round of activities
with them.

She, meanwhile, had business appointments with offi-
cials of the Ministry of Commerce and with the directors of

textile mills. But for the first time, after all these years and all these visits, she suffered some of the irritations that India holds for its visitors. She didn't even have the excuse of heat, for it was winter and the days were cool with a mountain freshness infused into the mild Delhi sunshine. One day she was invited to lunch at one of the luxury hotels by a business contact. Her host was a rich mill owner, not self-made but second generation, had studied at Berkeley and went abroad several times a year. His interests were music and films, and they discussed these while he tried to caress her thigh and was not inhibited from continuing their conversation when she shook him off. The setting was brilliant. The hotel specialized in outdoor buffet lunches for which little white tables and chairs were set up all over lawns kept emerald-green by a team of gardeners using gallons of scarce water. The sky formed a wonderful canopy of unmarred November blue with the bulbous dome of a fifteenth-century mausoleum rising against it. Apart from a scattering of foreign tourists, the company assembled on the lawn consisted of upper-class Indians and their ladies in gorgeous saris. Everyone was enjoying their meal, the ladies as much as the men, tearing the legs off skinny oven-baked chickens and bringing their heads forward to bite into them. They talked and laughed a lot, opening their mouths wide and showing the food and their healthy teeth within.

Above this scene, birds floated in the crystal air like lazy swimmers letting themselves be carried on their backs in water. An erroneous impression, Marietta discovered—as one of these birds swooped down and tore a piece of chapati out of her hand. She gave a cry, both of fright and of pain, for the kite's beak had scratched her. Her companion got to his feet and flapped his napkin in the direction of the birds so far above him. People at the other tables turned around, frozen in surprise with their chicken legs held in the air. Marietta brought the scratch to her mouth, but next moment spat in horror as she thought of what disease the bird might have transmitted into her blood. "Do I have to have shots?" were her first words. "No, no, no," and "Let me see," said her companion. She gave him her wrist to hold and look at, only to snatch it away again at once as though his touch filled her with the same horror she felt for the bird. Waiters and the headwaiter came hurrying up, all full of protestations, all wanting to examine her wrist, so that she held it behind her back. She felt a rising hysteria, and everyone else felt it too. They gave her strange, guarded looks, and her companion became distant, a stranger disowning her. "I'll get rabies," she kept on saying. "Are you sure I won't get rabies?" When she wouldn't be reassured but looked around at their faces with scared eyes—the people at the other tables were saying things about her now to each other with amusement—her host gave some curt Hindi command to the headwaiter. Medicine was brought; it was one of the waiters and not her host nor even the headwaiter who had to dab red Mercurochrome on the scratch. He did this very gingerly with a piece of cotton, taking the best possible care not to touch her with his fingers, not for her sake but his own.

Her companion was now only anxious to get rid of her. They were to have done business together, and although she did later place orders from his mills, he never again made any personal approach; and even on his visits to New York, he carefully kept their contacts to the telephone. He had no time or taste for hysterical women. That day, he dropped her off in the street of open stalls which sold Tibetan jewelry and monks' robes converted into housecoats. She had planned a shopping tour after lunch, and not wanting to admit how upset she was, she stuck to it. She continually looked at her wrist, now bright red with Mercurochrome; she fought down her thoughts of where that bird's beak had been, what rotting carcasses it had torn before it grazed her skin. She made her purchases in quick, nervous agitation, ending up with a great many little parcels. While she was looking for a taxi to take her to her hotel, two little boys descended on her, shouting cheerfully how they were hungry—starving—hadn't eaten since Tuesday. Marietta managed to fumble out a note to give them but they asked for more, making a sport of it as if they had bet each other how much they could get. Other little boys came running, and a somewhat bigger girl with a very old face and someone's baby on her hip. They pressed Marietta so close that she began to run; and running, she dropped some parcels and stooped to pick them up again. When she did that, they pushed against her and laughed the way the people in the hotel holding chicken legs had laughed. Only the girl with the baby kept right on whining in a grown-up way how hungry she was, and the baby, which had a growth on its shaved head, looked on with great beautiful eyes full of solemnity.

A taxi drew up, and its driver, a Sikh, strong, bearded, and turbaned, got out to put the children to flight. They stood laughing and watching from a safe distance while he deposited Marietta and her parcels into the taxi. She quickly put up the window, for the girl with the baby was still standing there, repeating her whine with imperturbable monotony; and when Marietta could not bear to look in her direction but only at the sturdy neck of the driver, the girl let out a stream of spittle on the taxi window before turning away in search of another client. The spittle trickled very slowly down the glass. The driver didn't notice—he was telling Marietta how these children were no good, that they had been trained to beg and make a nuisance of themselves to nice people. The hotel was not far off and soon they were driving up under its portico, and there was the doorman, dear old Muta Singh, so beloved of all the guests with his stately figure and his scarlet uniform modeled on that of the President's bodyguard. Muta Singh helped her out—he helped her with her parcels—how well he knew to do all that without ever touching her. She was already feeling much better as she went up in the elevator to her suite; all she needed now, she felt, was a shower and a long hot bath to wash everything off her and out of her.

"Mark!" she called as she entered, but the living room was empty. He was off on one of his excursions—well, let him make the most of it, for in a day or two she was going to take them both back to New York. She was even glad he wasn't there so she could get herself clean, hygienic again before he returned and came near her. But when she opened the bedroom door, he was there and Ravi was with him. They were both on the bed, sitting up rather stiffly as if they had just shot up from a different position.

"Surprise!" cried Ravi, smiling at her with his bold charm. "Auntie sent me, she said go to Delhi and have a nice time with your friend Mark. And with his mother," he added politely, and politely doubled his charm; while Mark, his eyes lowered, his hands in his lap, sat dangling his feet over the side of the bed.

Marietta's relationship with her son reached its lowest ebb when he was in his early twenties. This was the time when he was always taking off on trips and was even absent on important occasions such as Louise's birthday and Louise's Christmas. So was Regi—especially at Christmastime when she chose to be in a warmer climate. Mark didn't necessarily depart to a warmer place but just anywhere he felt like going. It might be Texas, it might be Italy. He was always accompanied by friends—or perhaps only one friend, they none of them really knew. He managed to telephone on Christmas Day, but that was as far as it went. Leo didn't even do that. He had no regard for Christmas at all, in fact, it irritated him.

One year Mark was there unexpectedly. He arrived on Christmas Eve with all the suitcases with which he had set out the day before. Louise, who was at the climax of her Christmas preparations, embraced him with ardor. She could make out with one glance into his loved face that something was wrong, but she kept her own counsel. So did Natasha, but she could not refrain from throwing constant anxious looks at him. She hovered near him though she knew he wanted to be left alone; she suffered because he did; and it was only his coolness toward her, his stiff silence acting as a warning not to ask questions, that kept her quiet.

Marietta arrived with her current young man, but she completely forgot about him in her delight and amazement at seeing Mark. Fortunately, the young man had too good an opinion of himself to feel neglected. He attached himself to Louise and followed her around while she moved between her kitchen and dining room. The apartment blazed with lights and festivity and was saturated with rich cooking smells. While Louise opened her oven door to baste her oozing goose, the young man, who was a surgeon, told her about a kidney transplant he had helped perform on an oil sheikh.

But by the time Louise was ready to serve, Mark had locked himself in his bedroom and Marietta was trying to get him out. "Can you believe it?" she said to Natasha who had been sent to call them both. "Locking himself in on Christmas Eve." She knocked imperiously.

"He's talking on the phone," Natasha said. She could hear his voice, though she could also hear that he was trying to keep it low.

"Who's he talking to? Come on, Natasha, you must know. He must have told you *some*thing. People don't just come back after you've said good-bye to them and not say *any*thing."

"He didn't," Natasha pleaded. She was trying not to listen to sounds from inside, but nevertheless it was clear to her that he was arguing painfully with someone he loved.

"He's had a fight with someone," Marietta went on re-
lentlessly. "Whoever it was he went with. Whom *did* he go
with? Some girl, I suppose." She shot a probing glance at
Natasha—entirely unnecessary, Natasha's face needed no
probing, each emotion she had was displayed there in full,
flagrant view.

"Oh, surely you know he's got a girl friend," Marietta
said. "What else could it be, all those phone calls and sulks
and all the rest of it?" She shrugged: "I don't know why
everyone has to be so secretive. As if it's some great and unusual thing to have an affair. I seem to be the only one who's
open and aboveboard—I mean, look at me, bringing him to
Mother's Christmas Eve." She made a face toward the dining
room. Now that Mark had come, she had no need of her
lover's company and heartily wished he would disappear.

But he was a large and solid presence and was there to
enjoy a good family meal. He was leaning back in his chair,
anticipating this pleasure, and still entertaining Louise with
the story of the transplanted kidney while the two of them sat
alone at the sumptuously laid table. Louise was listening to
him with a strained smile, her attention on the door, waiting for them to appear. But only Natasha entered, and
she slipped silently into her chair, avoiding her grandmother's eye.

Louise said, "I'm ready with my goose, but I need Mark
to carve."

"I guess I can do that better than anyone," the young
doctor said with a jokey wink. Of course he realized that
something was wrong, but regarded it as the price to be paid
for partaking of these wonderfully well-cooked family meals.
As long as it wasn't his own family, he wasn't perturbed and
was even good-naturedly willing to help keep everything
going. He had spent last Thanksgiving in an even tenser situ-
ation with a family in Connecticut, and then too he had

helped out with stories taken from his professional experience. He found that people were always interested in learning about what went on behind the scenes.

But here things were getting more serious. They heard Marietta begin to pound on her son's door, and then that door opened and shut again. Louise jumped up to get her goose. The doctor heard Marietta's hysterical voice mingling with her son's. The young man felt sorry for her and would have liked to intervene. She was at least ten years older than he was, but he felt protective of her. Her nervousness—the sense she gave of exposed nerves—made him want to give her the support of his manly strength. There didn't seem to be anyone else around to give her any. That daughter of hers sitting opposite him at the table—by the way, how could such a good-looking mother have such a homely daughter?—just sat there playing with a knife, which she then dropped; and the old mother came in from the kitchen carrying her god-damn goose, which was so outsized that her face was scarlet from exertion. As for the son—well, one look at that boy and the doctor had known what he was all about: amply confirmed now, for his voice could be heard as shrill and high as his mother's and as hysterical.

And indeed—if the doctor could have seen them—Mark and Marietta did at that moment look like two women locked together in a fight. Or rather, two girls, for both were slim and fair and almost the same height (Marietta was slightly taller). They stood face to face and glared into each other's beautiful light-green eyes—he with his hands clutching her upper arms, she pounding her fists against his chest. Both were yelling, but each so loud that neither could hear the other. He was calling her bitch and she—irrationally but instinctively—used the same word for him. Their contorted faces mirrored each other. At the exact same moment they both realized what they were doing and stopped doing it, but

continued to stand there, frozen in an embrace and still looking into each other's eyes. He let go first and turned away and
muttered, "Now will you leave me alone?" And she did; she
let herself out—she didn't even slam the door—and went quietly into her room.

Now it was Natasha standing outside his door and
urgently whispering through it, "You have to let me in." She
went in anyway and found him weeping on his bed. She sat
near him, frowning over his head at the chart on his wall and
holding her hands clasped tightly in her lap, determined not
to touch him.

"Why couldn't she leave me alone?" he said at last.

"She was upset."

"Oh, when isn't she."

"She only wanted to know—"

"Whom I went with?" he quickly took her up. "I'd
gladly tell her, if only she weren't so hysterical. . . . The big
joke is, she'd be equally hysterical if it were a girl." He
laughed drily, then wiped his eyes—but next moment they
brimmed again, with other thoughts. "Like a fool, I fought
with him at the airport. It was my fault, entirely. It was just
the stupidest thing—about who had the tickets—and now he's
sulking and alone on Christmas Eve when we should have
been in London together. We've never been there together.
He's never been at all—he's hardly been out of Oklahoma; it
was to have been his big treat, from me. He's only seventeen
and so dumb, so *sweet* . . ."

Smiling through his tears, he wanted to say more—but
not wanting her to hear more, he went into the bathroom to
wash his face. After a while he called her in there: "How do I
look?" he asked, lifting his face to the light so she could see it
better and make sure he had wiped away all trace of tears.

"How do I look?" Marietta was at the same moment
asking her young doctor. He had followed her into her room
and was surprised not to find her prostrate on her bed and in

need of his comfort but vigorously repairing her makeup. She said, "I hope you didn't hear anything."

"Not one thing, sweetheart," he assured her with a wise, grave face.

"It was my fault, entirely. All he asked was to be left alone for five minutes—" She caught sight of the doctor's knowing expression in the mirror and said: "You don't understand a thing. You don't know what he's like. You can't judge us—"

"Who's judging? Who's judging?"

"Mark's very responsible. He always has been. Sometimes I feel like it's the other way around with us—that *he's* the parent. What's the use? I can't explain and you'll never understand."

"Don't forget I'm a doctor."

"What's that got to do with it?"

"We have to know about people."

"About sick people. Mark's not sick. He's the sanest, strongest, manliest man I know. You only think people are sane and strong if they have football muscles like you do."

"Want to see?" he said, proudly flexing them inside his jacket and holding them out for her to feel. As she did so, he bent down to kiss her, but though his lips were young and hygienic, they didn't make her feel any better.

After her last visit to India, Marietta did not see or hear from Ahmed for over five years. Then one day he telephoned her from New York, where he had come again as part of a troupe of Indian musicians. She was astonished and delighted and insisted that he move in immediately. So within an hour he was at her door, with his sarod and his modest, battered little suitcase, looking up at her—grizzled, wry, and amused. Automatically, he went to put his luggage in her bedroom where it had always been; smiling apologetically, she diverted him to one of the other bedrooms. So then he too smiled and was perfectly happy to carry his suitcase into the guest room. She began to explain at once, in a rush, that there was this young doctor who sometimes came to stay with her, but although he kept his pajamas under her pillow and a razor in her bathroom, it wasn't anything much. "He's just a boy," she said—she was in her early forties and didn't like older men anymore.

But she still liked Ahmed. He sat in her raw-silk armchair with his shoes placed on her rug and his feet tucked under him. He drank Scotch and chain-smoked. He appeared pleased to be there again. He had narrow, shrewd eyes—there was a touch of Tartar in him—and she was aware that with these he gave her a few quick glances. It made her self-conscious and she put her hand to her face: "What do you think? How do I look?" Instead of answering, he asked more questions about the children, and she brought out photographs of Mark and Natasha.

As on his first visit, when the other musicians returned to India, Ahmed stayed behind with Marietta. She called the young doctor and told him it wouldn't be convenient for him to visit her at this time; and she packed up his few belongings and met him for a drink one evening to give them to him. She was irritated by the way he made out that the break which this meeting signified was his idea: he was kind, even patronizing, and patted her sleeve to show how much he still liked her. But she forgot about him the moment she left him. That night, when she went into her bedroom, she called to Ahmed from the door: "You can sleep in here now, if you like"; and he assented as cheerfully as he had before taken up his quarters in another room.

There was something of Bruno, her father, about Ahmed. Perhaps because they were both spare and small and patient; both were a head shorter than Marietta, both had had a soothing effect on her. But if in the past she had tended to see Ahmed as a father figure, he had never got things mixed up that way. He had made love to her quite lustily, whenever he felt like it, which was surprisingly often for a man his age. He also had a surprisingly large male organ— when she pointed out the disproportion of it to the rest of him, he looked down and raised his eyebrows at it with amusement and pride.

However, on this last visit it was different. Now he fell asleep as soon as he got into her big double bed. He even snored a bit, lying very still and straight on his back with his mouth open, catching air. Sometimes she couldn't stand it and woke him up again. "Ahmed! Ahmed!" she called him. Then he would wake up at once with a cry of shock as for a fire or some other disaster. One night when he did that she went around the bedroom turning on all the lights so that the crystal bottles and their silver stoppers and the orange silk cushions and the shaded lamps glowed and shimmered, once in the room and twice in the mirrors; and it was a very bright scene except that its centerpiece, in the center of the bed, was this little old man in a white *kurta*, sitting up with the shock of his sudden awakening.

But once fully awake, he seemed to know what it was all about and waited patiently for her to be sufficiently calm; then he said, "What can I do, Marietta, I'm an old man."

"How can you just *say* that!"

"But it's true." He laughed and laughing made him cough as it always did—as it did Leo too, both of them because of smoking too much. There was no doubt about it, he *was* an old man. She sat down on the bed by him. "Even my grandson has a son," he said. She laughed and hid her face in her hands, as though he had said something shaming. "Six months old," he said.

"But, Ahmed, you're hardly sixty!"

He drew his finger along her face until, to hide it from him, she buried it against his chest. Then he patted her back: "You're too thin," he noticed while he did this. "You're not eating. You must eat. Women must eat. They have to be strong." He pushed out his elbows to show how strong. "You should see in my house how they eat, the *food* they put in themselves each day. And they're big, big women. When they walk—everything shakes, they shake, the house shakes, it's like an elephant walking. And when they laugh or, God forbid, when they get angry—oh, oh, oh, thunder from heaven. And all because they eat good food." He patted her back again. "Tomorrow I'll cook for you. Will you eat it? Proper food like pilao, dhal, meat."

She got up and turned off all the lights again and then she lay side by side with him, both of them on their backs, and she held his hand. "Don't go to sleep yet," she begged. "Talk to me. You're yawning. Say something. How's Sujata?"

After a tiny pause in the dark, he said, "Oh, you don't know. Sujata's gone. It was an accident with a motorcycle rickshaw. The driver had taken something and drove like a crazy man and they went straight into some metal pipes on a bullock cart. Sujata's mother was with her and nothing happened to her, though she is very old, eighty years old: not even one bruise. They took Sujata to the hospital but she was finished that same day. Everyone came to the funeral, and the weeping and crying was not to be believed. And her mother, eighty-ninety years old, showed everyone how she didn't have one bruise and she kept crying, 'Why her and not me?' This was in everyone's mind, especially the people who lived in the house. Now everything is sold and they have gone to live in different places, whoever would take them. I met one of her old men, Sohan Lal, he played the *tabla*—he was crying, not even money for betel, can you imagine, an old man like that in need of little comforts. And after so much luxury she provided. All gone, just like that."

When anyone accused Leo of having a bad effect on people, he stretched his pale eyes wide open in surprise: "But I only want to do them good!" It was true, from his point of view. He thought he knew what was good for people better than they did themselves; and he did have a kind of insight that enabled him to see through a person's complexities and diagnose whatever might be wrong there. He was, in that respect, like a really gifted physician—though whether he had such a physician's healing powers was something else again.

His followers believed he had and wanted to put themselves entirely in his charge. But he resisted them: "no hang-ups, please," he said. He wanted to do them good, lead them along the right way—but not in the one-to-one relationship they craved from him. The only person with whom he was willing to stand in such a relationship was himself. As he explained it, he needed himself as a laboratory in which to experiment on human nature. He was prepared to share the results of these experiments with others, but he had to be left free, unhampered, unentangled. "Don't fence me in," he would say—he would even sing it. He had made up this song for himself:

Don't fence me in. Don't pin me down.
I'll flutter my wings, you flutter yours. Let's see
who'll make it first, up to the sky.
That's where I'm heading for: look out, brother,
I'm flying high!

While he sang, a student accompanied him on the guitar, and at the end they were all invited to join in the refrain: "Look out, I'm flying high!" It could be quite stirring when they were all together and expressing their longing for freedom and expansion in this united cry.

During the summer months there was a big get-together every Saturday night on the grounds of the Academy. It was open house and all sorts of people came—friends of the students, followers of Leo's from the city, neighbors, anyone interested—and they were all welcome to help themselves from the long trestle tables set up on the circular lawn in front of the house. There were various health-food dishes prepared in the Academy kitchen and also a very strong punch made of California white wine, orange juice, and Christian Brothers brandy into which they all dipped their plastic cups freely. It put everyone in a good mood and made them more expansive—took them out of themselves, or, in the idiom of the Academy, out of the prison of their own selves. They drifted around the grounds, sat by the stream, the grotto, in the overgrown orchards, had various experiences, formed or unformed some relationships; but sooner or later everyone ended up in the sunken garden.

The sunken garden was the only part of the grounds to have been cultivated. Surrounded by a high hedge with four arched entrances, a radial of paved paths converged, between grass and flower beds, toward a stone pool in which stood a stone nymph squeezing water out of her nipple. But although this fountain was geometrically the center of the sunken garden, the real focus lay elsewhere. Between two of the arched entrances, an arbor had been formed out of white wooden lattices: and here Leo sat with a few favorites on a Victorian wrought-iron bench. This lovers' seat became the magnet to draw everyone from the rest of the grounds. Not that anything intense was going on—on the contrary, the atmosphere was easy, unforced, just a nice time being had by all. Music played from a hi-fi. It was the latest dance music played very loudly, and although for his own pleasure Leo listened to Wagner and Mahler, he enjoyed this too: so much that he snapped his fingers and made dancing motions and said "Terrific." But there was always someone waiting with a guitar, and when the order was given to take the needle off the record, it was time for live music. This was always original music composed to words based on what they were learning and experiencing: a summary of the week's work expressed musically and always ending up with Leo's own song followed by the chorus of "I'm flying high!"

It was the prelude to Leo's weekly address—which he never wanted to give, disclaimed the right to make. "Come on," he said, "a bit more music, let's swing, okay? I'm in the mood." "Leo, Leo, talk to us!" "Ach, talk. Who wants to talk when they can sing?" And he sang again—by himself this time, with a lot of swing and uplift, snapping his fingers, swaying his body in the monk's robe so that his silver pendant swung to and fro. Everyone was silent—all crowded along the paths and around the flower beds and the rim of the pool into which water continued to drip from the goddess's nipple; and then, when there was absolutely no sound except for this dripping—and the unseen secret night life of insects in the tangled gardens all around—then at last Leo said "Okay." And he talked.

He talked about The Point. This was the summit of his philosophy—at least the summit he had so far reached: though, as he always said, "While there's life there's hope," and he still had life in him—plenty!—and might yet ascend higher, as human beings are supposed to do. He had never drawn back from that, from striking off into new directions in order to reach a new summit. But so far, here and now, at the Academy, this summit was The Point. It was where he had got to over all these years and had taken anyone who cared to follow him. Here was the climax of all his various experiences and experiments: his theater group, his psychological encounter group, his quasi-psychiatric practice, his study of Eastern philosophies, his absorption in Ahmed's music, his travels up and down America, his years of residence in California, the drugs he tried, the religions, and the love affairs with women, with girls, sometimes ("just for fun") with boys, his mental and physical exercises, everything he was and thought and felt—it was all summed up, for now, in The Point. This was, for him, and by extension for everyone, what it was all about.

The Point had a double meaning: it was both the point
of human life—its goal—and also the point of intersection
where its highest attainment, by which he meant its highest
experiences, met. And what were these highest experiences?
They were twofold, he explained: one on the physical plane,
the other on the—what do you want to call it?—the psychic,
the spiritual? Whatever. "Now, what would you call the highest human experience on the physical plane?" he asked his
audience on these Saturday nights in the sunken garden. No
answer, a hushed stillness except for the incessant plash from
the fountain, and the insects shrieking (sometimes a bird
woke up and sang by mistake from the depths of some dark
tree). "What, no one knows? You don't even know that?
What have I done to deserve this bunch of dummies?" And
then he supplied the answer himself: "The orgasm, of
course—isn't that it? Isn't that the Point of our highest physical experience?" It was, there was no question of it. Yes, Soc-
rates. "Okay. Now: and what, may I ask, is the highest
human experience on the spiritual—the psychic—the you-
name-it plane? . . . Give up? Well, I must say, you're for the
birds. It's a wonder I don't pack up and get out right this
minute. The answer is—of course—again the orgasm! My
God, any child knows that. What's your problem? Don't you
know that there's an orgasm of the soul just as of the body?
Haven't you heard of the frisson that takes place there and is
every bit as delicious as that of the body? And some say, if
you can believe it, even more delicious—a thousand times
more delicious—but we won't get into that. We haven't got
there yet. We can't say. But what we can say—what we do
say—what *I* say—is that there is a Point to be reached. A Point
of intersection for both our highest points, and that's what it's
all about! That's The Point. To be reached. By all of us. Play,
brother, play and sing." And the follower with the guitar
strummed up again and he sang and everyone joined in while

Leo refreshed his throat with another plastic cup of his Saturday night punch.

Whenever Leo sent for Stephanie, the same thing happened as the first time: only now they both expected it, and she wasn't the only one who laughed, he did too—a bit ruefully but still, amused. And after that he put himself out to entertain her in other ways. He played her his Wagner records and sang all the parts himself—Isolde and everything, rising on tiptoe and with his hands laid on his heart: or he declaimed and translated German love poems to her that he hadn't thought of in years. If it got too hot for her in his den— it was stifling in there, he had to have the heat on high all the time—he allowed her to open the window a fraction on condition that she keep him warm. So then she lay very close to him while he held her and breathed and snuffled in her hair. When, overcome with heat and fatigue, she fell asleep, he tried to rouse her, begging her not to leave him alone, thinking up some joke he hadn't yet told her. To oblige him, she laughed but in the wrong place and before he finished and then she went to sleep again. He shook her chin between his fingers, he called her—"Hey! Hey!"—but when he couldn't wake her, he smiled with a tenderness and indulgence he had never before shown to anyone.

Jeff still stole up to the attic sometimes, or Stephanie and Natasha went to visit him in his gatekeeper's cottage at Mark's house. Stephanie and Jeff were completely free with Natasha, not only in making love when she was there, but also in talking about their deepest, most private concerns. Of course that was nothing new—everyone at the Academy was talking about those, it was what they were there for. But it wasn't always or even often interesting. The students got really deep into themselves: they analyzed their own motives, and interpreted their own actions or, rather, reactions—there didn't seem to be much action—or, most boring of all, their dreams. Natasha always had difficulty pretending she was listening. But when Stephanie said "Shall I wash my hair?" or "Should I wear my pink T-shirt?"—that was a degree of intimacy that Natasha really cherished.

Leo didn't like their excursions to Mark's house, but he was powerless to prevent them. Yes, for the first time in his life, Leo was powerless: and this when he was at the height of his career, was absolute master of his house and all its inmates! But when he told Stephanie not to go to Mark's house, she promised she wouldn't—and went nevertheless as often as she pleased.

Natasha was surprised by the casual way in which Stephanie deceived Leo. She didn't seem to think anything of it. One day Leo, who suspected these visits, was standing in wait for them when Jeff brought them back in the old pickup Mark had given him to drive around in. As soon as Jeff saw Leo standing on the front steps, he dropped off the two girls and backed his truck out through the gates, just waving his arm out the window in farewell.

"Oh, hi, Leo," Stephanie said, skipping up the steps, shaking her long hair and her small hips, and evidently terribly pleased to see him.

Natasha was coming up behind, and it was she whom Leo asked: "Where did you go?" He spoke mildly, though at the same time fixing her with his uncomfortably flat porcelain eyes.

There was need for a lie, but Natasha had no experience in telling one. Stephanie, however, didn't waste a second: "Jeff took us over to Great Barrington to do some shopping."

"What did you buy?" asked Leo, still mild as milk.

"Oh, shit—we left it in the truck!" cried Stephanie, stamping her foot at herself and shaking back her hair again, in temper this time.

"Hm," Leo said. He gave them both another of his looks,

but when Stephanie met it with a pout at her own carelessness, he turned and shambled off, in his monk's robe like an
elephant's loose skin.

Later, Leo called Natasha to his den. She was embarrassed, fearing she would have to tell lies to protect Stephanie.
But Leo asked for nothing like that. He was gentle and reasonable. He told Natasha that Stephanie was there to work
on herself and that it was his responsibility to see that she did.
Left to herself, she would just go off again into every kind of
wrong direction. All his students were like that.

"Why do you think these people come to me?" asked this
gentle, reasonable Leo, looking straight at Natasha perched
uncomfortably in one of his old-uncle armchairs. When she
raised her eyes, she saw that he was looking at her not in any
of the ways in which he looked at people—always in some
superior capacity—but as at an equal; and he spoke to her as
to an equal. "Because they've made a mess of themselves and
can't deal with it. Psychologically, they're all waifs and strays.
Not like you," he said, smiling his small teeth at Natasha—she
who, physically, was the epitome of all waifs and strays.
"You're strong," he said. "You know what you want. You've
found your Point."

Natasha was amazed. She didn't know what he meant.
In fact, she never did know what he meant when he talked
about The Point. She couldn't understand about the division
between the physical and the other part and had come to the
conclusion that she was lacking in one or the other or maybe
both. In a way, her life was simpler than other people's: she
had few attachments, and these were strong, unquestioned,
and had never changed. When she was small, the most unhappy moments she knew were when Mark had no time for
her. He had gone to school six years before she did, and every
day she would run from window to window in her grandmother's apartment to watch him walk away with his school
bag on his back. Sometimes he was joined by other boys, and

though the street was far below and they were tiny figures, she could easily make out how lively and interested he was with them. Of course, he never knew she was there watching so he didn't look up to wave; but Louise came and knelt behind her and put her arms around her and said "Never mind, worm, soon you'll go to school too." But when Natasha did go, she wasn't interested at all and only waited for it to be time to return home.

So then Louise and Marietta decided that the only way was for her to grow up and develop and form new attachments. They told her about the changes in a girl's body, and she was informed about sex in detail by both of them in two differing versions. But her breasts hardly grew, and she was sixteen before she had her first period and after that it only came very haphazardly, as if she had been forgotten about in some evolutionary cycle. Regi asked more often "Are you sure she's all right?" But Natasha never missed anything—having dates, or being whistled at down the street—she hardly noticed that it happened to other girls and not to her.

When Jeff came to the Academy at night, he threw handfuls of gravel up at the attic window. He had pretty good aim, but the window was too high and he missed frequently, so that his missiles fell in spurts to the ground. Natasha had learned to listen for them. She woke up Stephanie who cursed a bit at first, but then—tousled, warm, and fragrant from sleep—she stole down the stairs, rubbing her eyes.

On nights when Stephanie was with Leo, Natasha had to go down and tell Jeff. He was angry and disappointed and he cursed Leo. So one night when Jeff said, "You come along, then," Natasha agreed, just to put him in a better humor. He took her back to Mark's house, driving her in his truck through country lanes so narrow that the hedges lining them swept the car roof and tapped the glass as with ghostly fingers. But then the land cleared, and Mark's house, standing on its hill, rose from out of the black trees. Jeff parked his truck inside the gate and invited Natasha into his one-room stone house. It was bare and masculine inside, with a wood stove in the middle and the old bedstead he had found somewhere and his clothes hanging from nails he had hammered into the wall. His shoes stood under the bed, including a pair of battered hiking boots, and also under the bed was his knapsack, which was all he traveled with. He didn't have much else except his transistor and an oval stone that looked as if it held magical properties, for him at any rate. There was nothing there that couldn't be packed up in a moment and stuffed back into the knapsack and carried away on his back.

Natasha stood around like an awkward guest, not knowing what was expected of her. But also like a guest she was eager to oblige her host, so that when Jeff asked her to take her clothes off, she did so at once. It was quickly done, anyway—she only had to step out of her Indian cotton skirt and slip her cheesecloth blouse over her head, and there she stood—inadequate, but bare and willing. Jeff looked her up and down; he was surprised both by what he saw—he was used to girls who were girls—and by her attitude. He couldn't make out whether this was indifferent, experimental, or sacrificial. But there were the two of them alone in the night and he would have considered it unnatural not to get together.

Matching her politeness with some of his own, he inquired: "You sure you want to?"

She nodded and smiled, and he said, "Okay" with what was almost a sigh. He asked her to lie on the bed and she did so. They resembled doctor and patient. He stepped out of his clothes. She didn't look at him—he had a perfect boy's body, but she wouldn't have been able to appreciate that. She lay flat on her back with her arms by her sides and looked up at the light bulb. It was so bare and bright that it was like looking into the sun, but she forced herself to; she was bracing herself to feel pain and not cry out. But nothing happened except that Jeff grew heavier on top of her and wet with perspiration like he was really working hard. "Relax, for Christ's sake," he panted. She thought she *was* relaxed. She was prepared to continue lying still for as long as required. But this was not very long. He tumbled off her and fell beside her on the bed and lay there, exhausted and amazed.

She turned her eyes to look at him; she wondered if she had done something wrong but didn't like to ask. He looked back at her. It was strange, this meeting of their eyes—hers so dark and deep they seemed to reach down into caverns way beneath the earth and his blue and clear as a lake into which the sun could shine all the way to the bottom.

"You remind me of someone," he said. "Someone I knew as a kid. Myrtle her name was—she was half Indian and living with her mom in this shack in the Great Smokies. Her old lady didn't like it, her playing with me, on account I had a bad name around there. But we didn't do anything bad—we had nice games, a bit sexual but clean." He raised his hand to the switch he had fixed up so he could turn the light off without getting out of bed. He said: "It's like that with you; like we're both ten years old."

It was peaceful and good to be in the dark. He was asleep before she was. Through the bare window she could look straight up to Mark's house glimmering on its hill, a heavenly vision.

It wasn't only physically that Natasha felt herself to be inadequate. She also failed to come up to other people's emotional intensities—especially at the Academy where every word, gesture, and detail of daily life was invested with a deep charge. There was the question of bedrooms. These were situated on the second and third floors of the house, and their occupation was a matter of finely graded prestige. The second-floor bedrooms were kept up the way they must have been by the original owners, with canopied beds, mahogany wardrobes, dressers, fine lawn curtains, quilts and counter-panes, Brussels carpets. The third-floor bedrooms were bare except for utilities; the wooden floors had no carpets, many of the rooms had two beds in them, and one of them three. Still, they were more prestigious than the attic where most of the students were housed.

Newcomers were always made comfortable on the second floor, but before long they were moved up to the third to make room for other newcomers or for guests. There was considerable shuffling to and fro between this third floor and the attic. Some students were allowed to stay in the third-floor bedrooms indefinitely—there was one elderly Englishwoman, a Miss Kettlebury, who had never been asked to vacate. Some, moved up to the attic, were allowed to move down again, changing places with others who, for no reason apparent to them, were told overnight to pack up and go to the attic. These arrangements and rearrangements generated considerable feeling.

One day Natasha was on kitchen duty with a woman called Janet, who had just been relegated to the attic from the third floor. The kitchen was as gloomy and cumbersome as the rest of the house, and since Leo did not believe in spending on laborsaving devices, it still had many of the inconveniences of a Victorian kitchen. It was below ground level, and the sunlight was filtered through burdocks before entering by way of the barred rectangular windows. Natasha was cutting onions, and Janet was washing spinach; a big cauldron of stew simmered on the stove, giving out pleasant smells of fresh vegetables, herbs, and cloves.

Janet had the tap on over the sink, so it took some time before Natasha realized that the sounds she heard were not only of water running but also of Janet sobbing. Sobbing was not unusual at the Academy, but Natasha never could get used to it. "Oh, gee, Janet," she said. Tears were running down her own cheeks, from the onions she was cutting.

"Leo's right!" Janet broke out at last. "I *deserve* to be in the attic."

"But, Janet, it's only that they needed your room."

"Then why me? Why not Shirley? How is she. better than I am?" Irresistibly, she went off into Shirley's bad qualities—emotional dependency, and inability to sustain a relationship—also, a particular incident where Shirley had made free with Janet's organic night cream. Halfway, she pulled herself up: "There you are, you see, there you have a good example of me; what sort of a beast I am."

"Janet, no," Natasha said. "You're upset, that's all; you're not a bad person." It was what she usually said to people—the Academy constantly rang with self-accusation— and they always refuted her with a list of their character delinquencies.

Janet went right back to her childhood when she had often been mean to others and had been noted for her neurotic behavior. At school she had had crushes—searing attachments—on teachers and other girls, and she understood now that this was to make up for the terrible lack in her childhood when her mother failed to love her. Janet had adored her mother, and had longed to be like her when she grew up, but instead she took after her father's family where the men and women tended to look alike, all retaining the heavy features of their family portraits. It seemed to Janet that her mother disliked her for her disappointing appearance, so was it any wonder that from loving her Janet grew to resent her and even worse. But all her life after that—it had long been made clear to her by a series of psychiatric and other healers—she had been in search of love and beauty and, in the course of this quest, had recklessly entangled herself in one harmful relationship after another.

The last of these, just before she had come to Leo, had been with an Iranian—or was she an Iraqi?—girl who claimed to be a princess and certainly looked like one. They had met at a benefit performance that Janet had helped organize. Janet had often involved herself in good causes but never for long, because she couldn't stand the internal politics or the people who sat on the committees with her. The Princess, who was a singer, a chanteuse, had donated her services for one such performance—actually, it was a good opportunity for her because the committee members and the people who bought the tickets were the sort to help further her career. The Princess was very single-minded about her career. Janet admired her for it, how she made it her business to get information about every single person she met, who they were, what sort of family, what sort of contacts they had.

"She was amazing," Janet said, "the way she'd find out everything, and often about people who couldn't possibly ever be any use to her at all. But if I said that, she'd get mad at me. She said I didn't know what it was like to be on your own and have to make your own way—and I'd say 'But you're a *princess*,' and then she'd get really mad at me."

The fact was she was often so irritated with Janet that she couldn't stand to have her around. Janet was sad but understanding; she knew she did have an irritating effect on people. During the days that the Princess banished her, Janet would just stay in the room she had taken in a women's hotel in Manhattan and wait to be called. She knew that sooner or later—usually it wasn't more than a day or two—her friend would telephone and be very sweet and forgiving. On these occasions, she always had some task for Janet—one that was mainly symbolical, signifying reconciliation, but also practical, such as buying provisions and cooking for a party the Princess was giving in the evening. Janet ran around happily, tirelessly, and arrived on the Princess's doorstep dragging a little shopping cart piled high behind her, and after hastily collecting her kiss of forgiveness, she rushed into the kitchen to start cooking.

The Princess had installed herself in someone's pent-

house apartment—Janet never knew whose it was—a brand-
new place in a flashy glass block that wasn't quite finished
yet. There was practically no furniture, so it was very good for
giving big parties and all sorts of people came. Janet did not
know any of them, and anyway most of them were younger
than she was. She went helplessly from group to group, not
finding anyone to talk to or who wanted to talk to her. She
knew herself entirely unfit to be there—and worse, understood
that the Princess knew it too, that she saw her wandering
around, large, dowdy, and awkward, and felt ashamed to
have her there. Nevertheless, in her kindness, she tried to
draw Janet out, introduced her to people and urged her
to talk about herself—or rather, about her family connections
—she gave her such a good start on that, so that the other
guests would know who Janet was, in spite of her unpromis-
ing appearance. But Janet could never carry it any further;
she was left tongue-tied, wringing her hands—a cook's hands,
a gardener's—and shifting from one large foot to the other, so
that the Princess could not bear the sight and turned away.

All this was painful, but a thousand times worse was the
jealousy Janet felt toward the Princess's lovers. She had absolutely no right to feel like that, for there was nothing of that
sort between her and the Princess. And, moreover, her friend
made no secret of her lovers before Janet; she was completely
open and aboveboard. She would even call Janet in while she
was in bed with someone—in the big onyx and brass bed,
which was the only piece of furniture in the room—and she
would ask Janet would she be very sweet and make some
coffee? She always explained to her companion that there was
no one in the world who could make coffee like Janet, so fresh
and fragrant. And Janet would make this coffee and bring it—
but not with good grace, not with a quiet heart, not with
satisfaction in being able to serve the person she loved—no,
but burning with torment and fury. And once—the last time—
it had been so bad she could not control herself. She had gone

into the bathroom and, taking the razor with which the Princess shaved her legs, she had begun to slash at her wrists—so wildly and clumsily that the blood had spurted up on the mirror and over the Princess's towels. Then she had swept a shelf of glass vials to smash on the floor so that they would hear the noise and come running. Well, of course, the Princess had been furious; but also calm and cool, and she had phoned for an ambulance and then she had called Janet's brother in Wellesley, Massachusetts, to tell him what hospital Janet was going to be taken to, and that he had better get himself down there and take care of her.

"That's the sort of person I am," Janet told Natasha with a shudder at herself. "I still wake up at night thinking I'm in that bathroom again, smashing the glass and cutting at my wrists—and all the time, what I really wanted to do was run in that bedroom and murder and kill them. So don't you ever say to me again that I'm not a terrible person, because I'm worse than anyone you'll ever know." She dropped the spinach she was washing and sobbed into her wet, raw hands.

Natasha regarded her with wonder and some admiration: so much strength of love! Her own feelings—for instance, for Mark—seemed in comparison a very small, still pool.

While everyone else at the Academy was busy looking into themselves, Natasha spent long hours looking out the attic window. Up till now she had lived only in the city and her awareness of the changing seasons had been confined to the spindly trees that lined the streets and put out frail tufts of green in the spring. But from the attic she looked out over summer trees and ripened fields and hills; and watched it all changing—first blazing, then fading, and falling and sleeping under snow. Then the trees and the hills were black, the river and lakes frozen, and everything just lay there waiting for the whole process to start again.

All this time Mark's house was progressing. Much of it

was still obscured by scaffolding and building materials; the windows gaped, the interior was ripped open: but by the time one cycle of the seasons had gone round and it was the second summer of Mark's occupancy, the house, rearing above the shimmering trees, was no longer a corpse sinking into the earth but new growth pushing out of it.

Jeff remained in his gatekeeper's cottage. Mark still came every weekend, although after that first summer he and Jeff had ceased their activity in the grass. Never more than an extension of what the insects did through the warm nights, it had died away with them. On a human level, they remained good friends. But by the second autumn Jeff was getting restless, for by then the house had reached a stage that didn't interest him. The rough construction work was over; the painters and decorators were moving in, and Mark was beginning to drive around to auctions to bid for pieces of furniture dating from the period of his house.

One day when Natasha was with her friends in Jeff's cottage, Stephanie told her that Jeff wanted to leave. She and Jeff were on the bed and Natasha on a velvet armchair that Jeff had salvaged out of an abandoned house. It was smelly with age, dirt, and damp, but Natasha felt comfortable. Jeff had stuffed his wood stove with kindling and it blazed away and made the little stone room warm and snug. While waiting for the giant on the hill to awaken, the entire life of the estate appeared to have contracted into the space of its gatekeeper's cottage.

"He wants me to go with him," Stephanie went on. Although he sat next to her on the bed, she spoke as though Jeff weren't there—which in a way he wasn't. He was engrossed in figuring out an astrological chart.

"Where's he going?" Natasha said.

"Where are you going?" Stephanie asked but had to answer Natasha herself: "To Arizona. He's got a friend there who's started a stone-crushing plant." Stephanie swept her hair up to the top of her head and twisted it into a new style. "I wouldn't mind going to Arizona," she reflected, but after that she didn't seem to want to talk about it any further. Natasha had noticed this about both Jeff and Stephanie: they broached ideas and plans and then dropped them—not out of lack of interest but as if to let them germinate in regions deeper than their conscious minds. Meanwhile, outside, a chill wind blew through the layers of dead leaves on the ground and crackled them, and also through those still left on the trees, so that they sighed and dropped like tears.

Was it the season that was making Natasha feel sad? She longed for things to stay as they were, and above all for people to stay where they were: for a permanence that she imagined to have been there in the past. One only had to look at the furniture of the past—those heavy beds and sideboards—to know that it belonged to people who expected not to have to move. Only permanence wasn't the right word: she had no word for what she meant—what she longed for—and only knew that it was something other than this cottage Jeff had fixed up and was already planning to abandon, and those loosely attached leaves out there ready to fall at a touch of the wind.

The door opened, letting the wind in, and Mark stood there stamping mud off his shoes. His eyes met Natasha's and for a moment they looked at each other fully. This look between them was a lifelong one, as were the feelings it engendered in her. Through the open door she could see the wind whirling the leaves around and it was treating the clouds in the same way, driving them across the sky like sheep to be penned in for the winter. But with Mark's entrance her feeling of shiftlessness and impermanence vanished and did not return as long as he was there.

She had other moments very different from these and yet an extension of them. This was when she was by herself up in the attic. Hours passed, and she really couldn't have said what she was thinking, if anything. She sat with her hands folded in her lap, her eyes fixed on the landscape outside though usually without seeing it. If anyone came in, she often failed to notice. She felt reluctant to move, as if in moving she might be displacing, disturbing something. There was a peculiar sensation of being attentive and waiting and yet at the same time having already received what she was waiting for. The feeling in her heart was the same she experienced in Mark's presence: a fullness—as of a very full cup—which came to the point of being a physical sensation. That was why she was afraid of moving: as if she really did hold such a cup in danger of overflowing and spilling some drops of its precious contents.

III

One day Louise had a call from a young man whom she didn't know. He said he was speaking from Regi's apartment and would it be convenient for her to come over? No, no emergency, he said to Louise's anxious inquiry—but he hesitated somewhat, so she realized she had better get herself over there as fast as she could. And fortunately Louise, though now in her eighties, could still move fast. Her hat askew, her coat flying open, her handbag bulging with spare glasses and wrong keys, she arrived at Regi's Park Avenue apartment house. All the way there she kept muttering to herself: "I thought she was in Florida"—she said it over and over. She tried to remember when she had last seen Regi: no, Regi hadn't come to this year's birthday party (the eighty-fourth) nor the one before nor the one before that. It must be three years, four years, five—Louise muttered and muttered—the years were like the days now, both infinitely short and infinitely long as they shaded off into the nights and slipped into a big black hole and were forgotten. How luminous the past was by comparison, how each figure there glowed and moved and was alive, vibrant, real.

"I thought she was in Florida," Louise muttered to the doorman at Regi's apartment house, and again to the elevator man who took her up. She didn't know them—she had been coming to this building for over fifty years and had been known by name to every doorman who had ever worked there; but the ones today, though old men themselves, were new to her.

And, "I thought she was in Florida," she repeated to the stranger who opened Regi's door—she didn't look at but only past him to see where was Regi. What was wrong? Was something wrong?

"Who is it, why are you opening the door, what have I told you a hundred thousand times?"

That was Regi, all right. Louise followed the voice and found her in her bedroom, sitting in the middle of the bed in her fur coat. "Oh, it's you," Regi said. "Where have you been, keeping me waiting like this?"

"But I thought you were in Florida!"

"Ridiculous," Regi said.

Yes, it was Regi—and yet there was something strange. Louise looked around her at Regi's familiar bedroom with the white bed shaped like a shell and curling around her pink eiderdown (like a vagina, Leo used to say). The place was dusty, and the floors had lost their shine. In the past, Regi had been fanatical, firing maid after maid for not looking after her floors properly; but now the apartment lay unused for months and even years at a time, so its air of neglect was to be expected. The blinds were down, but that wasn't strange either because Regi never had liked strong light. As for the smell in her bedroom, the cloud of stale perfumes—it was the ambience of her latter years, as of a shuttered, shut-up beauty salon: and yet, piercing through it, there *was* something else—what was it? A strange smell, acrid, sweetish, foul.

The young man had followed Louise, and seeing him, Regi cried out: "Who's that—why are you letting people in?"

"It's me," he said. "Remember me?"

"It's Ralph," Louise said. He looked at her strangely, so she asked, "Aren't you Ralph?" "No, I'm Eric," he said. And then Louise remembered—Ralph had been more than twenty years ago.

"She calls me Ralph too sometimes," Eric said. "Or Billie. Or Chuck. She gets mixed up."

"Naturally, anybody'd get mixed up with all these people running in and out," Regi complained. To Louise she said: "There was an Eric. Erich, not Eric. We went out in a boat and he jumped in too late and got his leg in the water. When he pulled it out—ugh, ugh—it had all dirty filthy weedy things on it. On his white trousers. He *was* upset, his whole day was spoiled." She chuckled.

"But why are you wearing your fur coat?" Louise said, but that made Regi hug it closer around herself.

"I told her," Eric said. "I laid out all her pretty things I found—her nighties and robes—but she won't wear them. She says she's cold. Cold!" he exclaimed, for the heat was up so high that it was stifling in there; and then that *smell,* all mixed up with the heat.

Regi told him, "You can get my juice instead of hanging around here talking your head off. You have to watch them," she told Louise when he had gone. "Come here, come closer, I have to tell you something." Louise approached the bed, and Regi grabbed her and pulled her down to whisper in her ear: "He steals. He's after everything. Why do you think I have to wear my mink?"

Bent over Regi, Louise could look down into that mink and see that Regi had nothing on underneath; her spavined, breastless body was completely naked.

"Where's your jewelry?" Louise whispered back, her eyes on the door.

"I've hidden it. It's under my panties. He's been looking everywhere but he won't know to look there. In the third drawer, go and see. Count it."

Louise opened the drawer. There were Regi's peach-colored, lace-trimmed panties and camisoles, and tumbled in among them, glittering amid the shiny, slippery silk, was a pirate's hoard of necklaces, bracelets, brooches, bangles, watches, pendants, rings. When she heard a noise, Louise quickly shut the drawer.

"I've been trying to get her to lock them up," Eric said, "but every time I go near there she blows her top. She thinks I'm after them," he said simply. "Go on, take your juice," he told Regi. "You said you wanted it."

"This is not my English Rose. I want my English Rose."

"Oh, you've done it again!" he exclaimed. "I told you to tell me when you have to go."

"It's cold," Regi said. "It's wet." She began to cry, and so did Louise.

Louise went to sit on a tubular chair in the living room with the white wolf rugs. Eric came and joined her there. When he found her crying, he was as apologetic as if it were all his fault. He said he had first met Regi about two weeks ago, in the dance studio where he worked. He thought she had come to dance, so he offered himself a few times, but it seemed she only wanted to sit and talk. That wasn't un-usual—many of the ladies came there just for the company; it was only natural with no one home except the TV. Once he sat with her, Regi wouldn't let him go, and when he tried to, she held on to him so tight her nails dug into him. Well, he didn't mind, but there were other ladies waiting to dance and he was there on a job. Regi went on and on, she got involved in a long story about a ball she had been to with her friend Louise who had worn a white dress with a big yellow sun-flower embroidered right on her bosom: no doubt to draw attention to it, Regi had commented. It all made good sense—

until he realized it had happened sixty-five years ago. And then suddenly, when he tried to disengage himself from her again, she threw a tantrum just like a little child, balling her fists and drumming her heels on the floor. He had no idea what to do, but fortunately Vivera, the owner of the studio, was there that night and he came over straightaway and knew what it was all about. He even knew Regi—she used to come there regularly, though he hadn't seen her for a long time, maybe as long as ten years. Vivera had run this place for thirty years and he was a real gentleman, not only very nice in his manners but also in his feelings toward people. He told Eric to stay right where he was, and then he took Regi's handbag—it was amazing the way she trusted Vivera, just like he was her father—and he found her address in there and her keys, and he told Eric to take her on home. And because it was Vivera who said so, she went as good as gold, though once Eric had got her upstairs and was trying to make her go to bed so he could return to the studio and earn some bread, she locked them both in and chained the door.

"That was two weeks ago," Eric told Louise.

"You mean you've been with her—you've been looking after her—for two weeks?"

Eric confessed that at first he didn't want to. He had managed to put her to bed, and then he got out as fast as he could and went back to the studio and danced with the customers. Vivera had asked him how he had got on and he said okay and Vivera said who's looking after her now and Eric said no one and went back to dancing with another lady, though Vivera raised his eyebrows right up into his bald head and said, "No one?" When the studio closed—around three in the morning, it was amazing the number of customers suffering from insomnia—Eric went back to his own place and lay in bed, and then he found he was thinking of Regi. He remembered the way she lifted up her poor little skinny arms so he could pull her frock off, and it was just like when he had undressed his little sister to put her to bed when she was three and he seven (this was before they had been put in different foster homes); and Regi's panties were wet too, just like his sister's used to be, and when he reproached her she looked both guilty and sly. So next night when he was at the studio and Vivera asked him about Regi, he said, "I think I'll just stop by and see how she's doing," and Vivera said, "Why don't you?" it being Monday anyway, which was always slow. But after that he went every day and even over the weekend, which was his busiest time, and it seemed like Regi was expecting him, like he had been coming there forever, and the first thing she always did was bawl him out for being late.

He had been hunting around in her old address books and he had called a number of people listed there before he got Louise. Some of the numbers were disconnected, and at those that weren't no one had ever heard of the people he asked for; twice it happened that when he asked for a name a woman shrieked, "My God, he passed away twenty years ago; who *are* you?" So he was very glad to find Louise still—and he caught himself but she took him up, "Yes, yes, I'm still here."

Eric said, "She talks about you more than anyone: all the things you did together, she tells it like it was yesterday." When Louise began to cry again, he turned his face away discreetly. "I can't always understand on account of she says it in German. She talks a lot in German," he said, and indeed at that moment Regi called out in German, "Louise"—and she pronounced it in the German way—*"Luise! Da ist jemand hier—ich glaub ein Dieb! Komm schnell!"*

Later it was decided that they would try to get a German-speaking nurse. But when such a person was located—it was Mark who did all that, having had to take charge of all Regi's financial and other affairs—Regi took one look at her and said to throw her out immediately. She did the same with everyone else they brought. In fact, she became very suspicious and wouldn't let them in without checking to see whether they had brought anyone. She put the chain on the door and peered through the peephole to make sure they were alone. She might be like a little child in many ways, but she was also strong in her will and cunning in getting it enforced.

Every day Louise took the bus across town and she bought food for Regi and cooked it for her and fed her and tried to clean her and keep her happy. But it was not easy—the harder Louise tried, the more discontented and demanding Regi became, so that Louise's exertions were both physically and emotionally exhausting to her. Mark knew he could not let her carry on this way. Unfortunately, Marietta was going through one of her bad times just then and was not sympathetic to the problem of Regi. It struck Mark that the older she got the less sympathetic Marietta was to any problems except her own. Perhaps because the latter were so overwhelming to her—so overwhelmed her—that she couldn't take in anything else: she who had wanted to take in everything! When Mark as much as mentioned Regi to her, she put her hands before her face and begged him not to. "There's nothing I can do," she said. "Nothing anyone can do. She needs professional care. Leave me alone, Mark." She added, as if this were an excuse: "I never could stand her, you know that." It almost made him laugh—and yet at the same time he did excuse her. He put his arms around her and felt her shake with nerves; how different it was when he put his arms around Louise who, whatever happened to her, remained like some rooted old tree.

The only other person Regi would admit was Eric. She was always cross with him, but she did allow him to do things for her, of the most intimate nature. Mark had already tried to repay Eric for his kindness and services when there had been no one else, and he now approached him with the offer of a more permanent position with Regi. He went to seek him out at home and found him living in a neighborhood of grim turn-of-the-century houses. These would have sunk into decay long ago if people desperate for living space hadn't shored them up: amid broken stoops, dirty gutters, and boarded-up windows, each tenant had tried to scratch out a nice home. Mark groped his way up a dank stone staircase and took a few wrong turnings in unlit corridors before reaching Eric's door; but then, when all the safety locks and bolts had been uncreaked from within, he found himself in a very cozy nest. Eric had painted each wall in a different color and put up large framed photographs of movie actresses of the sixties; he displayed a variety of artistic objects such as crystal ashtrays and silk flowers in a blue vase shaped like a shell; and concealed everything that wasn't artistic—like the old sofa and a couple of armchairs discarded generations since from more prosperous homes—by smothering it with cushions coverd in suede and fur.

Eric served tea with some ceremony in a flowered set, and when his preparations were complete, he settled himself to face Mark in a chair on the other side of the boarded-up fireplace. They were genteel and polite with each other. When Mark tried to thank Eric again for what he had done for Regi, Eric waved it aside: "You'd have done the same. Anyone would." He poured tea through a strainer and smiled: "You get fond of the ladies you meet at Vivera's and they get fond of you. Too fond, some of them. They want you day and night then, they're never off the phone calling you. You can't blame them. I mean, they're *lonely*," he said, pronouncing this word with deep personal feeling. "You should see them coming to the studio, sitting there on the chairs waiting to dance. While they still can dance: oh, I've seen some of them go down pretty fast. All the same, they can carry on long past their time—isn't it funny the way women are so tough? But then they start falling, or with some of them it's their minds going—it's always one or the other—and that's it. That's curtains—I shouldn't be talking so morbid," he said, giving himself a little shake and picking up the teapot to replenish Mark's cup. He put milk and sugar in for him too, and even stirred it like a good mother. "But sometimes you can't help having morbid thoughts. When you've seen what I have. I don't always go to the studio. Only to help out when I'm not working. I'm an actor," he said, looking at Mark straight; and Mark nodded respectfully. "I really go there to help Vivera out. The way that man spends himself, it's just incredible. Can you believe it, seven days a week, every day till three A.M. Because they can't sleep, you see. And they're scared going home and no one there and not being able to sleep. So he has to keep open. 'Eric,' he's said to me, and he's said it fifty times if he's said it once, 'wouldn't it be great to close this place down and go to bed every night at ten?' But where would they go if there was no Vivera's? Another cup? Sure?" Eric slid down from the chair and sat on the woven rug before the fireplace. He put his arms around his knees and his back against the chair and said, "I'm comfy this way; I love it. I only wish I could have a real fire to look into and make my dreams." He looked up at Mark and smiled an invitation to come and join him on the floor; but didn't mind at all when Mark remained where he was.

"She's in a bad way," Mark said, reverting to Regi, the object of his visit.

"Yes, but she's got money." Mark had heard others speak the word money the way Eric did: with longing and bitterness, as of a cruel lover. Mark guessed that this might be a good point at which to introduce his financial proposition with regard to Regi; but in his embarrassment and fear of offending his host, he did it badly: "My grandmother says she would love to see you again, that perhaps you would come and have tea with her. She says to tell you that she would really love and appreciate it, and so would I, Eric," he ended, sincerely but somewhat breathlessly.

He found himself misinterpreted: "I'd love it too, Mark,"

Eric said. Still sitting on the floor, he looked up at Mark and put his hand on his knee.

Mark returned Eric's soft look with one he tried to make friendly and manly; and in a friendly, manly, but businesslike voice he said, "My grandmother was also asking if you'd be free anytime—convenient to yourself, of course—to come and help out with Regi."

Eric let his hand lie there a moment longer; then he withdrew it. "Sure," he said with a little laugh. "Why not? It'll pay the rent." He shook the hair out of his eyes: "You can call me anytime you like," as friendly and businesslike as Mark. "I'm busy Tuesdays and Thursdays in the afternoons but okay in the evenings and vice versa Wednesday and Friday."

"Fine," Mark said. "We'll work it out. Thank you. It's really good of you."

Eric shrugged a little bit and smiled a little bit. Probably this was the gesture with which he met every little humiliation that life offered him. It touched Mark. Although he was already on his way out in the corridor, he turned back to where Eric stood in the door. He put his arm around Eric and hugged him and said, "I'll be seeing you," his voice full and warm with feeling.

"Thanks, dear," Eric said, returning both the hug and the feeling.

Eric was very conscientious in carrying out his new duties. His first concern was to clean out Regi's apartment, and soon he had the glass-and-chrome furniture shining as it used to, and the wolf rugs lying there white and shampooed. But his best efforts were expended on Regi herself. He took great pains to dress her up, and if he didn't like one outfit on her, he would start over and try another. He also did such a beautiful job of makeup on her that Louise wanted him to go professional and had already decided to send him to a beautician's course. Regi was very good when he made her up; she lifted her face to him and sat absolutely still for as long as he wanted. The end result was always splendid, and Regi sat enthroned like a mannequin, glittering with all her jewelry hung about her and her eyelids painted to match her dress. She had taken on an amazing resemblance to the expressionist portrait hanging on the wall above her, with its skeletal outlines and one eye glaring green and baleful from its center.

Propped up on a piece of Art Deco furniture, she was usually happy in her thoughts while her two companions played cards. But sometimes she clamored for their attention—as on the day when she suddenly exclaimed: "But where is he?"

"Who, darling?" Louise said, holding her cards tight against her chest so that Eric wouldn't see them.

"That one! Where is he? Why hasn't he come to visit us?"

"What's she saying?" Eric asked, for all this was in German; at the same time, he said to Louise, "Now what's that you're hiding under your skirt? Don't think I don't know what you're up to."

Louise slipped the hidden card farther under herself and said, "You're imagining things."

"Where's the fat one? The great big fat one?" Regi demanded.

"What's she want?" Eric asked again, and when Louise translated for him: "Who's the fat one?"

"An old friend of ours," Louise said—but just then the card she was hiding slipped from under her, so she threw down the rest and said she was tired of playing. "I hear he's got a new girl friend up there . . . Leo's got a new girl friend!" she shouted to Regi.

"Don't shout," Regi said. "I can hear you." It was true that Louise usually shouted at Regi—not to get past bad hear-

ing but to penetrate into her jangled, crowded mind. But
sometimes, as now, Regi understood perfectly the first time.
"It's always some horrible little blonde with red cheeks," she
said, making her disdainful Regi face.

"We should go there and see," Louise said. She laughed
at the idea but was also taken with it. She told Eric: "It's her
birthday on the fourth; we must do something. We could take
her to the Academy—a day in the country, it'll do us all good.
You need a change too. What is it to be locked up with two
old women. I wonder you can stand us."

"I wonder too," Eric said, gathering up the cards she had
scattered. "The way you cheat."

"We'll have an outing!" she called to Regi. "In the country—like we used to. Wandering, and a picnic with a big
hamper. You'll like that, won't you, darling? On your
birthday."

"I'm not inviting him to my birthday," Regi said, pointing at Eric. "Not Hofbrau."

"Who's Hofbrau?" Eric said.

"You're Hofbrau!" Regi shouted. "Don't think I don't
know. Hofbrau the swindler."

There was a pause. Then Louise said: "Oh, my goodness." She got up and stood behind Regi's chair and stroked
her wig. "The things she remembers," she said, smiling and
stroking while Regi smirked like a child praised for its clev-
erness.

Hofbrau really had been a swindler, but they hadn't
known it till he was arrested. Up till then he had been a very
welcome addition to their circle in D——. He had joined all
their excursions, had gone boating and bicycling with them,
and of course to the opera and theater. He had been a fine
amateur actor himself and such a wonderful mimic that he
had made them laugh till they cried. Regi had been very
taken with him, for in addition to everything else he was a
stylish dresser, and Regi had always judged people by their

clothes. (It was a joke among them that the man who had the best chance with her was the one with the sharpest crease down his trousers.) Anyway, they were all beginning to think there was something happening between her and Hofbrau—especially when at her seventeenth birthday party they disappeared during a game of hide-and-seek and couldn't be found till they came out by themselves. Regi's high pale cheekbones had two pretty red spots on them which were definitely not rouge. But on the very next day, he was arrested for embezzling funds from the insurance company where he held a responsible position, and it was later discovered that there was also a case against him in another town. Regi had never mentioned his name again, from that day to this.

Louise began to pay more attention when Regi sat there talking to herself. Mostly she only caught odd German words, half sentences, fragments of meaning here and there. But sometimes, suddenly, Regi's background babble became crystal-clear: ". . . the day I wore my white hat with the cherries for the first time," Regi said, and Louise could see the day exactly: in summer, a table laid under the apple tree in her father's garden, her mother in a long skirt sitting with her knees apart while she held the tall, blue-sprigged coffeepot; and Regi, coming to visit them, had stepped through the glass doors and walked toward them, knowing herself to be looking ultrachic in this new hat with one side of the brim turned down against her cheek and the other turned up with a cluster of glass cherries. But when Louise exclaimed, Regi pretended she didn't know what at, and then she smiled and said, "Oh, you mean my *hat?*" lightly touching it with her fingertips as though she had forgotten she was wearing it.

Marietta, whenever she came to visit them, couldn't understand their cheerfulness. She had to force herself to come; it was an effort each time. One day she happened to drop in while Regi was being given her bath. The giggling in there

and the splashing reached such a pitch that she had to go and
see: she came in just as Louise and Eric were coaxing Regi to
let herself be lifted out of the water and she was playfully
resisting them. When they got her out, it was a triumph for
all three of them: Louise laughed with relief as she enfolded
Regi in the towel, and Regi laughed when Eric, also relieved,
gave her a little pat on her pitiful shrunken behind. Marietta
turned away.

While Eric was putting Regi to bed, Louise joined Marietta in the living room. Louise kissed her daughter, at the
same time looking at her with that secret glance of worry that
everyone who loved Marietta had for her those days. "Why
aren't you taking your coat off?" she asked, for Marietta was
stalking around the room in it as though in the street.

"No, no, I have to go," Marietta said.

"To the showroom?"

Marietta nodded—not liking to admit that she didn't
spend much time there now. She would get up in the morning, intending to go, but then decide to call her manageress
and say she would be in later. And when she did go, she never
stayed long but perched on her chair, often still with her coat
on, smoking and thinking of something else, only to depart as
suddenly and aimlessly as she had arrived.

"What's he doing in there?" she asked Louise, hearing
sounds of wheedling and argument from Regi's bedroom.

Louise smiled: "He's putting her to bed. She hates going to bed. She holds out for the last good-night kiss as long as
she can."

Marietta took a deep breath. There was a silence. Then
she said, "Why don't you get a woman for her? It's so . . .
indecent with a man. A boy."

"You don't know anything!" Louise exclaimed. "You
don't know what he's done for her! How lucky we are."

"You're right," Marietta said. After a while she said,
"It's his black leather jacket. I always think of the Angel of

Death in one of those—yes, yes, I'm crazy!" She pecked her mother's cheek, and her coat flying open, she let herself out of the apartment, out of the building, into the street.

At one time Marietta had loved these city streets, striding down them as if she owned them: her hair swung, and her skirt; she swung her handbag in the air. People looked at her and she expected them to; she felt exuberant. But now it was all different. She herself had changed—she was no longer open but as if closed up within herself. And it seemed to her that the streets had changed too: when she came out of Regi's apartment building onto Park Avenue, she felt herself to be walking into an unending vista of towering buildings, repeating themselves over and over as in ice mirrors. What was left of the sky in this tall arctic landscape was also sparkling cold. Marietta got into a cab. It seemed to her that she had spent years and years, a lifetime, in one of these city cabs, cowering inside it with her fears while the driver—a Korean, a Pakistani, an Irishman, his name and number and convict photo nailed to the dashboard—presented his anonymous back to her on the other side of the safety screen inserted between them in case she should, in the course of their ride, go crazy and shoot him.

When she reached home, she called Mark. She didn't get the answering machine but Kent. This had happened before but, like other youths in the past who had answered Mark's phone, he always said Mark wasn't home and hung up without identifying himself. But today, after saying Mark wasn't home, he added, "I'm Kent."

So then for the first time Marietta also had to identify herself, and how strangely her heart beat as she did so.

"Hi," said Kent. At once a strange intimacy flowed between them—the result not of what Mark had told each about the other but the very silence he had maintained with both of them. And perhaps because of this silence, Kent's next remark had a guilty tinge: "I guess I'd like to meet you."

"Yes," Marietta said, gulping like an adolescent, "I guess I'd like it too."

And indeed, the way each got ready for this rendezvous was like two adolescents getting ready for a first date. Mark saw Kent change his belt not once but twice and asked suspiciously, "Whom are you seeing?"

Kent, after carefully straightening the belt within several loops at the back, answered with another question: "Who's Eric? . . . He's been calling. Said you'd be calling him."

"Yes, of course," Mark said.

"Of course," said Kent sarcastically.

Mark half smiled at his tone and said, in a tone of his own, "You still haven't told me who you're tarting yourself up for."

Kent was not good at repartee, but he didn't have to be. There was an abrasiveness between them now that didn't need words. They had been living together for almost two years, and although Kent often stormed out of the loft and stayed away for several days, he always turned up again; and though sometimes Mark wished he wouldn't, if Kent stayed away longer than usual, Mark set out to find him.

Marietta and Kent met in the Old Vienna. It was a very public place for so secret an assignation, and it was Kent who had suggested it. He didn't have much—he didn't have any—experience of going on a rendezvous with anyone's mother, but the Old Vienna with its mixture of coziness and glamour seemed to him the right place for it. And Marietta was amused to find herself right there, in that family place where as a child she had eaten such quantities of Sacher Torte, with this youth who was Mark's friend; his best friend, Kent told her straightaway.

And because he was his best friend and she his mother, they had no difficulty in sustaining the tone of intimacy they had fallen into over the telephone. They talked, as a matter of course and without preliminaries, about Mark. They talked as if they were his parents—yes, even Kent who was at least twelve years younger than Mark. But he spoke with the grave responsibility of a father as he told Marietta that Mark was extending himself over too many projects and too may people. And Marietta agreed with the same gravity, and united in their care for him, they deplored him together. At the same time, they excited each other strangely. Talking about the loved person was of course exciting in itself, but so was the silent speculation each made about the role the other played in that person's life. They put out tentacles toward one another's personalities. Kent felt Marietta's nervousness—he watched her hands fidgeting over the ashtray, the spoon in a saucer, the way she unnecessarily twirled the little stick around in her drink again and again. And she too was watching his hands, which were large and masculine, and from there her eyes traveled up to his chest, also broad and masculine, and from there, shyly and only for seconds at a time, to his face: manly in formation but feminine in expression.

Besides speaking about Mark, they also spoke about themselves. Or rather, he spoke about himself (what could there be to say about her? he tacitly assumed). He told her how he was a photographer: not a very good one yet, he admitted, but he was working at it and Mark was helping him. It was one of the reasons he so much valued Mark's friendship. Kent became, for him, remarkably voluble, even animated: Mark would have been surprised if he could have seen and heard him speaking to his mother. But that was just what Kent loved—not only speaking to Mark's mother but also to *a* mother. As a child, he had loved his mother inordinately and had thrust himself on her for attention in every way he could. There had been no father, and she had had to work hard at various jobs—as a taxi dispatcher, in a cookie factory—to support them both. He had resented the fact that every moment of hers wasn't his, that she was thinking about money when she should have been thinking about him. And then, as he grew older, and into the snobberies of adolescence, he resented other things about her. He began to feel that his love for her was ill-bestowed because she didn't have the pretty clothes he craved for her nor the leisure to look after her appearance the way she, and he, deserved. All this was amply corrected in Mark's mother; and not only in her but also in the place in which they sat together under chandeliers. That too was what he had dreamed of as a child—to go out to such a place with his mother for whom even the local diner had been out of reach.

Around this time of her first acquaintance with Kent, Marietta had a letter from Ahmed. She was surprised, for it was almost ten years since she had heard from him. She didn't expect to, for she knew that keeping up contact by correspondence was not something that would occur to him. He was resigned to the fact that life swept people apart irresistibly and forever. However, this letter was for a specific purpose. Cast in traditional form, it began and ended with formal, flowery phrases directly translated from Urdu: "By the grace of God we are enjoying health and happiness," it started off, and immediately launched into a recital of events that spoke of everything but health and happiness. Someone called Abida, whom Marietta could not remember, had left for the heavenly abode; another called Sayyida had been left paralyzed from an attack of polio (was she a daughter or a granddaughter?—so many years had passed since she had last seen them that Marietta had lost track of the generations). Ahmed himself was suffering from a swelling of the ankles that made it impossible for him to walk, so that he had to be carried like a child from place to place; one courtyard wall had collapsed in the last monsoon and no means had yet been found to repair it; and kindly to send one thousand rupees at earliest convenience. This request was made without circumlocution halfway through the letter, which continued with

more news, mainly of the weather and the inflated price of all
food and other commodities.

She sat with the letter in her hand. It was an aerogram
form and had grease stains on it; to get everything in, the
writing was cramped like the narrow rooms they lived in. It
seemed to her that it held the same smells too, of spices, pick-
les, and perfume essences, of mangoes, tobacco, and drains.
She tried to visualize Ahmed as he was now, old and sick and
being carried from room to room; except for his swollen ankles, he would be very thin and dried-up, shriveled away. He
was over seventy years old now! Hawking and spitting—he
had always done a lot of that; he smoked too much. She
thought about him having to write to her to ask for money.
He would be quite matter-of-fact about it. He had been that
way when they lived together. He had hardly earned anything—he taught a few pupils, and gave a concert every now
and again, with the impresario usually cheating him. But he
didn't need much, living in her apartment, taking all his
meals there except every afternoon he drank tea in an Indian
restaurant with friends; and for his cigarettes. She always
kept money in a drawer and he took what he needed; it was
very little. He wasn't shy about taking it, though; nor when
he had to send money home—he would tell her the exact
amount and whom to make it out to.

She thought of him with affection. He had always been
so tolerant, even of what he didn't understand, so accepting
of everything, including her. He made jokes about what
couldn't be helped—for instance, when the impresario
wouldn't pay him. He would turn up his eyes and one palm
to heaven as if appealing to higher powers to share the joke.
When he had bad news, he didn't speak and smoked more
than ever; then he got over it by himself, without further
comment or complaint. It saddened her to think how far
away he was in space and time—irrecoverable, irrevocable.
She could still see him so clearly: the way he smoked with

relish, enjoying every puff, the cigarette so close to the end that it almost burned the two fingers between which he held it and brought it up to his lips. His eyes were half closed against the smoke, and he looked calm, pleased, placid like a Buddha, though a skinny one.

Marietta and Kent met again, and more than once, and he even began to visit her in her apartment. With his feline instinct for adopting nice homes, he made himself easy on her raw-silk sofa. He was much larger than anyone she had ever had in there, and altogether—in his designer cowboy clothes—consorted strangely with her very light furniture and her gold-framed miniatures. He had stopped talking to her by now; they were in agreement—about Mark, that is—and there wasn't anything else he had to say. At first his habitual deep silences bothered her, but then she got used to them and talked her way through them.

Once when he was there, Mark called. It was a routine call—he was usually on the phone to her at least once a day, often more—but very strange for her, with Kent sprawled there, gazing into the distance. "Yes, yes," she said while Mark was giving her instructions—he always gave her instructions in the course of his calls, with regard to her financial affairs, or her health—there was really no area of her life with which he was not in the closest touch. And of course he knew every tremor, every inflection. "What's up?" he said. "No, no, nothing"—playing with a little gold pencil by the phone, trying not to laugh—"No, really, nothing." She knew he didn't believe her, but what could she tell him?

"What did he want?" Kent asked. The casual familiarity with which he spoke—and Mark's voice still in her ear—made her stop smiling. She said, "I think we ought to tell him, about us meeting."

"Why," Kent said, not as a question but as a negative.

"We ought to. It's stupid not to." She found herself getting excited. Kent sat staring out the window, and his immovability excited her further. She began to pace the room, her arms crossed and her nails digging into her silk sleeves. She talked—she said things that came into her mind about how they shouldn't be meeting—then she contradicted them. He just sat there, with his tremendous capacity for just sitting. His physical presence overwhelmed her in a way that was strange to her. Even in her younger days, with lovers, she had never really been shaken by their physical presence; sex was always secondary. But now with Kent it loomed, it was as huge as he was.

"He wouldn't like it," she was trying to explain herself.

"There are a lot of things he doesn't like," Kent said with a grim sort of proprietorship; and at the same time he glanced at her with his clear and youthful eyes of beauty. When he did that, she stopped before a mirror and saw her face: how old it was, and ravaged, and what was that little pulse twitching in her cheek? She put up her hand to cover it, and noticed that this hand, veined and thin, was also twitching.

"You're worked up for nothing," Kent said, absolutely calm and paternal. "Mark gets like that. I guess you're alike."

"Naturally we're alike. He's my son, after all, good heavens." She laughed—and could hear it come out hysterically. That was the way she was beginning to feel. She dared not look at Kent. The strange thing was that the sensation his presence evoked in her was not for herself but for Mark: the thought of what Kent was to Mark—what they did together—penetrated her as no physical relation of her own ever had done.

She continued—she couldn't stop herself—"And who are you to say who he's like? I should think I know him better than you do. It would be strange if I didn't."

"There are a lot of things you don't know," Kent said.

"You didn't know about me. And don't think I'm the only one—"

"The only one what?"

"The only friend he has."

Why am I quarreling with this boy? Marietta thought; but also, *What is he trying to tell me?* And next: *If he is going to say more, I won't listen.*

Kent didn't say more. Instead, he got up. He had slow and deliberate movements always, so it seemed a long time before he was actually on his feet. It was like hoisting up a large stone statue—and Marietta felt that if she were to hit him, it would be like hitting against stone. And actually, she did feel like hitting him and trembled from head to foot with the effort of holding herself back. The only other person who ever made her feel that way—tempted her that way—was Mark himself; and as if she were talking to Mark himself, she said, "Sit down. Why are you going now? Why do you say these things—throw out these hints—and then go away?"

"I'm not getting in a fight with you," he said. He let himself sink down again. "Bad enough I have to fight with him. I'm not going to start with you."

His rough familiarity was the way a lover might speak to his mistress, or a son to his mother, but no one else in between. Marietta didn't know how they had got to that stage, but there they were.

He had said he didn't want to fight with her, but that was what he went on to do—continuing his fight with Mark, drawing her into it, to get her on his side or to hold her responsible: "What's he want a house in the country *for?* I keep telling him; and running off there every weekend when he should be at home . . . But of course we all know why." He waited for her to ask, and when she did—"Oh," he said, "you don't mean to say he hasn't *told* you?"

Marietta wasn't sure whom she was defending, herself or Mark: "He wants a place down there because it's where his father's family came from. And he wants somewhere for Natasha other than Leo's . . ."

"Oh, yes, Natasha," Kent said.

"He's very fond of her. They're very, very close."

"I guess he hasn't told you about his other friends he has down there." Kent pouted, but next moment he said: "And who's Eric? Do *you* know?"

"No. No, I don't." Marietta put her hands to her temples; really, she wanted to put them over her ears and to say, please, no more, I don't want to hear any more; let me be. She who had so longed to be privy to all the secrets of Mark's life!

Kent wasn't through yet: "We have this fight every weekend. I want to stay in town; it's the one chance I have to be with him when he's not rushing off to his office or wherever. And I want to work on my photography. I really like to. It's what I do. I'm doing a lot of portrait studies now—here, want to see?"

Out of a manila envelope he drew some recent examples of his work. When she looked at the pictures, she saw that they were all of Mark—but as she had not seen him for a long time. Lit by sunlight filtered through white curtains, Mark lay stark naked on a brass bed. There was something very familiar to her in the expression on his face: wasn't it just the way he had once looked at her, years and years ago, when he was her own little boy and no one else's? This was the way he had lain on her bed after his bath, waiting for her to put his nightclothes on, looking at her with just those eyes with which he now looked into Kent's camera—full of flirtatious love. Some of Kent's studies, and these too were heartbreakingly familiar to her, were of Mark in back view. He hadn't changed at all—he was over thirty now but she saw that his back was still slender, long, and boyish, ending up in buttocks as sweetly rounded as a girl's.

* * *

Kent had his hair cut and it did not suit him at all. It made his ears and neck emerge naked and raw and also revealed a rash of small pimples on the back of his neck. He looked sullen and unattractive. "Why, he's just a lout," Mark thought; he repeated the word in his mind, looking at Kent as with eyes newly opened.

He felt that it had been a long time since he had met anyone new, and now he was eager to go through all that again—to part from a new partner at daybreak and to come home, slightly reeling with drink and satisfaction, at that point of dawn where the light from the street lamps and the light of the morning are equally frail. He began to go around the usual places and to make some new assignations; but his pleasure in them was marred by the thought that he might meet Kent there. Once he thought he did see him—it was in a dimly lit bar, and through the crowd of bodies pressed together, through the smoke and noise, he thought for a moment he glimpsed at a little table for two against a pillar an older man entertaining a young man who might be Kent. Mark strained backward a bit so as not to be seen (he too was entertaining a young man, a boy really, very sweet, English but hoping to get a green card and work in the theater). But he kept wondering—was it Kent?—and couldn't refrain from leaning forward again in that direction to see if it was. It wasn't, and Mark leaned back, exhaling, he thought, with relief; and yet for the rest of the evening he was distraught, so that his companion was disappointed in him and pouted in a terribly attractive way and said, "You don't actually really care for me."

When he did meet Kent, it was again in the Old Vienna and with the same elegant gray-haired man as before, at one of the tables for two down the center. Mark, entertaining an exceptionally dull out-of-town client, watched them. It was clear to him at once that their relationship had in the meantime considerably progressed. Although the older man was no longer as nervously on display as the last time—fidgeting with his tie, his hair, talking in a high-pitched manner in order to amuse and hold the attention—he still appeared to be under strain: in fact, even more so, and in a deeper way. Now there were silences between them filled with covert glances from the older man and broken by him with a desperate spurt of talk that died away into another quivering silence. Kent, his broad back to Mark, was as always a rock against which others had to break themselves.

Besides being bored by his companion, who was telling him about different girls he had made it with in Hong Kong and Singapore, Mark was also aware that their projected business deal would come to nothing: so his attention was entirely on the other table. He silently considered what to do. Several possibilities were open to him. One of these was to do something he had never done himself but had on several occasions been a witness to. This was to get up, go over, and make a scene. The idea, especially under the influence of the potent little drinks in which the Old Vienna specialized, was enticing to him. He imagined all sorts of possibilities, a variety of three-way emotions. But, in fact, such a public scene was not within his character, and when he did go over, it was in the cool, friendly manner of an acquaintance. Kent did not see him till Mark came and laid his hand on his shoulder; then he looked up and Mark was gratified at the tremor that passed over his impassive features. The other man, so intent on him, saw it too. Mark felt at an advantage. He even drew up a chair for a moment and perched on it and asked to be introduced to Kent's companion. When Kent unwillingly muttered a name, Mark cupped his ear and made him repeat it; it was Anthony.

One leg tucked under him, his elbow on the table, his chin cupped in his hand, Mark continued to regard Kent with a teasing look: "I wish your hair'd grow back," he said after a moment. "You shouldn't have it cut that way, it

doesn't suit you at all." He turned his eyes, slowly and deliberately, toward Anthony: "Don't you agree?" he said lightly.

The other tried to answer him in the same tone. But his
hand was shaking, so that he had to put down the glass he
held in it. Mark saw that he was a good deal older than he
appeared from a distance; also that his eyes, when they met
Mark's, were pale and drained of color as though washed by
nights of tears. They were also full of fear—not only present
fear but fear of everything that had happened to him in the
past. Mark's jauntiness left him. He got up and said good-bye
and went away. He wound his way gracefully between tables
and gilt chairs, not looking back but knowing Anthony's eyes
to be following him. Nor did he again glance over at their
table but listened to, and apparently greatly appreciated, his
companion's racy humor.

Later, when questioned by Mark, Kent was dismissive:
"Just a guy I met."

"Where?"

". . . He's an agent."

"What sort of an agent?"

"He could be useful." Kent stretched and yawned and
appeared too tired to answer any more questions. When
Mark persisted, Kent became absorbed in studying some contact sheets. Mark tore them out of his hand, and from there
on their fight took its usual course, reaching its climax when
Kent pulled out his fine leather bag (a present from Mark on
his last birthday) and began to stuff some shirts and underclothes in it. He packed with great determination—waiting all
the time for Mark's pleas and protests. These were not as
fervent as they used to be. Mark lay on his bed, with his arms
folded behind his head, saying nothing beyond, "Now don't
be stupid, Kent," so that Kent grimly shut his bag and
dragged it to the outer door. Having got that far, he had no
alternative but to go out and slam it. Mark raised himself on
his elbow at the sound: he vibrated to it, and also to the silent

cry he felt coming to him from Kent waiting to be called back. But Mark lay down again and continued to look at the ceiling, taking his time.

After less than five minutes, he was surprised to hear a key unlock the outer door. Kent had returned. He was very quiet now. He put down his bag and sat on the side of Mark's bed. He clasped his hands and looked down at the space between his feet. Mark, watching him, thought that perhaps his haircut suited him after all; it made him look very young and defenseless, like a boy of twelve in reform school.

"He's down there."

"Who?"

"Anthony."

Kent's Adam's apple went up and down: "He often does it," he said. "Stands out there half the night. Waiting. He says it's just so he might get a look at me coming in or going out . . . He doesn't leave me alone," Kent said in mounting desperation. "Calling me. Writing me letters. And he *cries*. It's weird. Says he'll kill himself and all of that. Sometimes I think he'll kill *me*, he's that crazy. Or you. He might try that. I'm scared to look out the window in case he's there . . . I'm sorry for him—I mean, he's a nice guy. But he's gotten so intense. You'd think he'd have better sense, but he's worse than anyone, worse than any crazy kid. He's *old*, Mark—that's what's so weird—how can you get like that when you're *old?*"

"That's when," Mark said. He remembered Anthony's eyes, and a sense of his own future passed through him in a shudder. But he shook it off and decided at once what to do.

Jeff was getting really restless. He had been about as long in this place as he ever stayed anywhere; and besides, he didn't like the setup in the house. By this he meant mainly, even solely, Kent: for, in order to get Kent away from Anthony, Mark had installed him in his house. Now that it had begun to take on the look of an elegant country residence,

Kent liked it. He stalked around with his camera and took pictures from all sorts of angles. Once, while he was perched in the cleft of a tree to frame a very interesting composition of the gatehouse, Jeff unexpectedly opened the door and came out holding a tooth mug. He was trying out a new mouthwash he had concocted out of various herbs boiled together. Kent shouted for him to get out of the way. It took Jeff some time to locate him, and when he did, he went on standing there and watched him gesturing more furiously; and then, when he got tired of that, and also cold—he was wearing only a pair of cut-off jeans and his chest was bare in the autumn air—he spurted out his mouthwash in Kent's direction with a horrid grimace, partly at the taste of the concoction, partly at Kent.

"I can't stand having that creep up there," Jeff said to Stephanie and Natasha when they came to visit him. He closed the green shutters of his cottage and stoked up his wood stove and they huddled around it, but it was impossible to forget the house looking down on them with Kent inside it, like a giant in his keep.

The reason Jeff was delaying his departure was that he was waiting for Stephanie to make up her mind to go with him. At night, in her bunk above Natasha, Stephanie tried to get at her own motives and to decide whether it would be more meaningful to stay with Leo or to go off with Jeff. Although she had not yet come to a conclusion, Natasha noticed that every day when they went off to see Jeff, she took some little bundle of her possessions along. "What is it?" Natasha asked, and Stephanie said "Oh, just some crummy old jeans . . . And those blue sneakers I don't wear anymore? They may be in there too. And my Book of the Dead." Gradually, everything she had kept in her trunk in the attic found its way to Jeff's cottage.

*   *   *

In the past, when Marietta had come to visit her mother, she had always given two short rings and one long so that Louise would know who it was. Mark and Natasha had used the same signal, and when she heard it, Louise would call from inside "Which worm is that?" in a voice full of elation. But now, of course, she was mostly at Regi's so that Marietta had to use her own key to let herself in.

It had always been a dark apartment because the buildings outside tended to block the light and the German furniture inside to absorb it. The first thing Louise had done in the mornings was to go from window to window to pull aside the velvet curtains—in a grand gesture, flourish almost, at the same time taking a deep breath as though welcoming streams of sunlight into her house.

But now, when Marietta tried to pull the cord of the salon curtains, she wondered how Louise had managed to make them fly open that way: for they were so heavy that she herself could only get them to creak apart slowly and stiffly. In any case, she gave up after she had parted them only a little way, for the chink of light falling through them lit up a desolate scene. It wasn't that Louise, especially in these latter years, had always been meticulous in keeping the place dusted and tidy. But now the room had an air of utter neglect, with dust ingrained and settled into each crevice of the carved and convoluted furniture and on the clustered grapes of the chandelier. Inside Louise's bedroom, Marietta found the bed unmade and Louise's old-fashioned flannel nightgown abandoned on the floor. When she stooped to pick it up, she saw some more clothes lying on the carpet—old-woman underclothes that Louise must have stepped out of and left there. A pair of stockings had rolled under the bed too far for Louise to retrieve. Marietta had to stretch out to reach it, and when she did, she found it covered with fluff like something lost long ago and overgrown.

When she went into Mark's room, she found it not only neglected but superseded. It still had his baize bulletin board onto which he used to pin reminders to himself; some remained, drooping from rusty tacks. There was the brand-new tennis racket he had never used—a present from a friend he had cherished—and an exercise bicycle that was another present he valued for the sake of the giver but had not had any use for. (He had never been addicted to sport or exercise, though admiring those who were.) Marietta sat on his bed and decided that her parents' apartment must be given up and the furniture either sold or put in storage. As for Louise, she must come and live with Marietta—that was the way it had to be now.

She wasted no time. Mark was in his house in the country, so Marietta got her car out of the garage and drove herself up there. But on the way she surprised herself by taking a detour to Tim's. She hadn't been there since Mark was born— in fact, the last time was when she was pregnant with him, thirty-four years ago. The house had been sold long since and had changed ownership more than once in between. Mark had told her that the present owners used it only for weekends and vacations. She got out of the car. The place was completely deserted—she called a few times but no one came, so she went up to try to peer into a window. And then she couldn't tear herself away but went from window to window: now she got a glimpse of the hallway, now a corner of the front parlor; from the rear window she saw the breakfront bookcase and the Martha Washington chair. She was astonished: it was almost an exact reproduction of what the house had been in Tim's family's time. Even the bought pictures resembled the ancestors! Evidently the present owners—a corporation lawyer and his wife who was something in television—loved and revered the place to such a degree that they kept it up like a museum. Marietta felt that, if they could have bought Tim's mother and sisters, they would have propped them up with loving care in appropriate positions inside the house; even Tim himself, quietly sozzled in his chair in the front parlor. Marietta knocked on the glass of a window, she rang the bell, but no one came. She was almost tempted to break in—it looked so easy except that she knew the burglar alarms would begin to shriek the moment she tried anything of the sort.

She didn't need to go in—she knew exactly what it would be like, down to the characteristic smell of furniture polish mixed with potpourri. It was strange the way there had never been any cooking smells in that house. Not even on Thanksgiving—which was the last time she had ever visited there. By that time she and Tim had separated and she was living with her parents in the city; but as a gesture of goodwill she had driven herself down to participate in the family's Thanksgiving dinner. She was pregnant with Mark at the time. She found herself alone with Tim's mother and his sisters. Tim failed to show up. At first Marietta was indignant, then she became anxious: she thought that he might have been drinking somewhere and have wrecked his car on the way home. If anyone else shared these not illegitimate fears, they didn't show it. They would have considered it bad form to brood about possible disasters—news of them reached soon enough if it had to, and until such time one carried on as if such possibilities did not exist. They were joined by Tim's mother's mother who had driven over from her house farther upstate to join them for this family meal. She looked very much like Tim's mother, as tall and raw-boned; they even appeared to be the same age—but then so did Mary, Tim's eldest sister. The tomboy of the family, Mary was always stamping around the house engaged in manual labor such as digging or fixing drainage pipes, or carrying heavy objects in and out of her pickup.

It was Mary who insisted that they start dinner, even though Tim hadn't arrived. She said she was starving and could eat a horse: "I'm not waiting another minute. Now then, where's Evie?"

"Yes, where is she?" said the grandmother. "She hasn't even said hello to Granny yet."

"I'll get her," Marietta said. As she went upstairs, Mark turned and kicked inside her. She was glad to have him do that, it was like having him share her indignation at his father's absence.

She knocked on Evie's door, but Evie cried out: "No! No! I'm not through yet!" Marietta didn't even wonder what it was she wasn't through with. Evie had strange solitary habits: sometimes she rolled bandages—who knew for what dead army—or she copied out recipes from some moldering cookbook. As far as Marietta could judge, her occupations were silent and harmless, but Tim had hinted how sometimes, after telephone calls, she had to be brought back in the middle of the night in her nightdress, having been found pounding on the doors of young carpenters living in the village.

When Marietta went in, she found Evie sitting on her bed with her legs drawn up, knitting furiously at a long gray shape. "Just let me finish this," she begged.

"They're calling for dinner, and look, you're not even dressed yet . . . I'll help you," Marietta said. She always wanted to help Evie who, tall and big-boned, looked as capable as her mother and sister but was far from being so.

But as soon as Marietta opened the dresser to try to find Evie's clothes—it was as tangled in there as a bird's nest—Evie cried out, "Don't touch!" She swung herself off the bed and dived into the open drawer and pulled out what she needed. She began to dress; it was a slow, laborious process. In putting on her stockings, Evie lifted each of her heavy legs in turn as if they belonged to someone else; she even muttered like a nurse at a difficult patient. When she got to putting on her wine-colored long dress, her head and arms got stuck and she struggled from in there till Marietta came to her rescue.

Marietta also helped her do herself up at the back and for this Evie was so deeply, touchingly grateful that Marietta felt ashamed of letting her fingers shrink from touching Evie's thick, cold flesh.

"Tim's not back yet," Marietta said, expecting more sympathy from Evie than the others.

"He's probably in the barn, making a fuss over Periwinkle. You know how crazy he is about that horse." When they were children, there had been horses in the stable, but it was years since it had been converted into a garage. Marietta realized that Evie was beginning to go into her bad period again. Although lucid and reasonable for long intervals, she tended to slip every now and again out of present reality; they took no notice until this process was speeded up and then they knew that it was time for her to go back in the hospital. She knew it herself and packed up her suitcase and carried it downstairs, waiting to be taken there.

"He'll be here soon, don't fret," Evie said, sensing Marietta's unease. Suddenly—perhaps to comfort her—she kissed Marietta: but at the touch of her sister-in-law's lips, Marietta let out a cry and her hands flew to protect her womb. Evie drew back and smiled sheepishly, apologetically. Marietta too began to apologize—"I guess I'm nervous, Evie, being this much pregnant and Tim not showing up"—but she was more than nervous, she was trembling with fright and wanted to run away and protect herself and her baby and not have to go down and sit with the women in the dining room and go through that Thanksgiving meal.

Of course she did it finally, the same way Evie got herself together and went downstairs to her appointed place at the oval table. There was something in that house that made everyone go through with their duty. It may have been the rigidity of their routine that held them all up as in an iron framework. Even their conversation had a routine—as when they commented on the stuffing, the cranberry sauce, and the

pumpkin pie. It was a tradition with them that these items
were prepared by the grandmother at home, and every year
they commented on how good they were and how Granny
had done it again. And every year, while carving the turkey—
Mary was always the one to do that, even when Tim was
there—Mary asked Evie: "Are you going to kick me to bits
again tonight?"

"Oh, I'm sorry, it's all Granny's fault," chuckled the
grandmother, who was the cause of Mary having to share
with Evie. This too was one of their traditions: Mary would
never have given up her room for anyone except her grandmother—and for her only on Thanksgiving and Christmas,
and again in the summer when Granny came to visit for a
week, bringing two bottles of cranberry jelly made from her
own berries growing in her yard.

Marietta drove on to Mark's house, past the unpromis-
ing approach—the service station, the lumber yard, the home-
produce store, the realty office—and turned inside the gate,
past Jeff's stone cottage; and then she saw the house on its
hill, and her first thought was, *What's he want with a house this
size?* And her second thought: *Well, since he's got it, he can take
Mother's furniture.*

The doors were open, and she walked in, through the
hallway, through those lofty oval rooms. She was as amazed
as when she had peered through the windows of Tim's house:
for just as the new owners of that had attempted to pickle its
ambience, so Mark too had reverted in style to his father's
family. His paternal grandmother would have been pleased
to see the care and respect he had lavished on the pieces he
had inherited from her; and to supplement them, he had
selected only those—drink table, gentleman's secretary, lyre-
back armchair—that exactly matched them in period and
style. But although everything there was at least 150 years
old, it had all been so polished and refurbished—gleaming

mahogany and rosewood with gilt bronze mountings—that it might as well have been entirely new. The floors too had been stripped and restored to their pristine pinewood planks; the walls and ceilings with their cornices and moldings were painted stark white; the carvings on the wooden mantels had also been carefully restored and repainted in white, and within them the huge fireplaces gaped, swept and empty.

Marietta shivered—literally with cold, for the heating was on too low to penetrate those high rooms. Besides, they were cold and damp with new paint, and entirely unlived-in. Yet there were people in the house—she could hear footsteps upstairs and the voices of two men. Both were unmistakable to her: Mark's somewhat high-pitched voice, and Kent's boyish growl. Her first instinct was to leave without making her presence known; but instead she went resolutely to the foot of the stairs and called Mark in a loud, brave voice.

She recognized the silence that immediately fell upstairs as one of consternation. But she kept right on standing there, and after a while she called again. Mark appeared from out of one of the upstairs rooms; he came running down the stairs, simulating pleased surprise. Kent kept very still in the upper room as if he weren't there; but both of them were very much aware that he was.

Fortunately, Marietta had come for a definite purpose and had a lot to say. She told him that she wanted to sell Louise's apartment and have her move into her own. Mark agreed, and they discussed practical details. At the same time, he walked her around his house—the downstairs rooms only—and identified for her the pieces he had newly bought and those that had belonged to his paternal grandmother. But of course she knew these latter better than he did. In the dining room she recognized the portraits of the senator, the judge, and the abolitionist; also on the sideboard the silver-handled carving set which Mary had wielded on the Thanksgiving turkey

Marietta looked around: "Well, I guess you can have Mother's dining-room furniture now. At least it'll fit in here."

"Oh, but can't you see—it's the wrong period!" Mark exclaimed, truly shocked. When she walked out and stood at the bottom of the staircase, he followed her rather quickly. He said, "Grandma's furniture is really only right for Leo's house. In size, in period, that's the only place it would fit."

"I'd rather give it away," Marietta said. She looked up: "What's upstairs?"

"Just some bedrooms." When she walked the first step up, he preceded her and stood facing her on the second, so that she could walk no farther. It was an impasse, and both were silent, wondering how to get around it. And upstairs, Kent too was very, very silent.

It was Marietta who spoke first—not in calculation but spontaneously, and what she said now was as unexpected to herself as to him: "Aren't you ever going to get married, darling?" she asked—for the very first time in all their life, so that he couldn't help looking astonished. That made her laugh: "You're thirty-four, you might have thought of it by now."

"Yes, and I can just see *you* with a daughter-in-law," he came back quickly.

She laughed again though shakily: "That's true, I'd hate her—but it's better than having you turn into one of those jaunty old boys pretending they're not lonely."

Mark thought, *She means old queens; she knows perfectly well.* Standing on the stairs, he one step above her, they looked into each other's eyes that seemed to hold no secrets, they were both so light and clear: but both mother and son had secret thoughts at that very moment. He thought, *Is she going to ask me now?* And she thought, *Is he going to tell me now?*

But it was she who didn't want it. She walked up one step so that she stood beside him. She leaned against him and began to cry, and he stood quite still and let her do that.

From out of his shoulder, she said, "I love you so terribly."

"Well, of course," he said. "Naturally. I expect you to."

Kent had got tired of keeping still, and he deliberately began to move around so that his footsteps echoed through the house; but the two of them kept right on standing on the stairs and pretended they didn't hear him.

When Louise called Leo to tell him that she was planning to celebrate Regi's birthday at the Academy, he was not enthusiastic. "Can't you keep her at home?" he said. "Our poor Regi," Louise urged—but he had never wanted to know about Regi's condition. He hated sickness, and sick women were worse than anything. "Too bad," he said. It was the end of the conversation. He put down the phone—he was in his den—and lay back on his leather couch. He pressed his call bell, and when the person on duty answered, he sent for Stephanie. While waiting for her, he lay on his couch and thought about her, with his arms folded behind his head. He didn't even have to try to forget Louise and Regi, there was simply no room for them in his thoughts.

Stephanie, meanwhile, was still trying to decide whether to go off with Jeff. When he talked about how they would travel across the country—he had done this more than half a dozen times, she only once—Stephanie got all excited and wanted to go; but afterward, when she and Natasha got back to the Academy, she had second thoughts. She said how could she leave when her work with Leo wasn't finished yet? when she hadn't yet found herself? or—as they put it at the Academy—hadn't yet reached her Point?

As always, Stephanie was tireless in discussing herself and her possibilities. Of course, so was everyone else at the Academy, but with Stephanie it was different from most of the others because she considered herself still very open to possibilities. While they were reaching into themselves to get at their own failures, she was doing so with a view to choosing among a variety of options. Up till now, these options had mainly been concerned with what sort of a person she could choose to be—but now there was a very definite, practical one: whether to stay with Leo or go off with Jeff.

During the workshops, in which she continued enthusiastically to participate, she disguised her options in the usual psychospiritual terms. But it was just as well that Leo was too damn bored with workshops—as he quite openly said—to attend them, or he would have caught on very quickly what the alternatives were that Stephanie was considering. As it was, she managed to fool him into believing that she was entirely fulfilled in her role as his favorite disciple. Or perhaps he just let himself be fooled because he needed her so. He kept her as close to him as he could and even stopped her from attending workshops, shocking her by saying, "What do you want with all that garbage?" It became difficult for her to get out of the Academy without telling lies; but as she was always cheerfully prepared to do this, and always had quite a number of them ready, she did manage to see Jeff whenever she wanted to. It was uncertain whether Leo believed her when she said she had to go into town to get a new supply of sanitary tampons—"How refreshing!" he would say. "No one else around here seems to need them anymore"—or to go to the post office, or whatever she made up when she went to Mark's house. When she got back, he was always on the steps waiting for her, looking at the big Mickey Mouse wristwatch that one of his students had playfully presented to him.

Once, when he called for her and was told she wasn't there, he sent for Natasha instead. As always, she entered the den with trepidation, and she positively jumped when he barked at her: "Where is she? . . . Gone to Mark's house, I expect, to be with that boy Jeff. You needn't lie to me." He shot a glance at her from under his eyebrows which stuck out like promontories over his glassy eyes. "That's what she's left you behind for, isn't it—to tell me lies; as if I'd believe them for a second. As if you could even tell them. But don't go and pride yourself on your truthfulness: it's a purely negative quality in you—nothing but an inability to lie." But next moment he sank back on his couch, tired of analyzing Natasha, tired of the whole exercise—not only with Natasha but with everyone, it was all not worth it anymore. Something quite other engaged him now.

"I don't know why she goes there," he said querulously. "When she knows I need her near me every moment of the day; *need* her," he said, "need her, need her . . . What do you make of it all, Natasha?" He turned toward her, supporting himself on his elbow to look at her as if he were really interested in what she might have to say. "I suppose you tell Stephanie to leave that old fool to stew in his own juice." He wouldn't give Natasha time to defend herself but went on, "You think I'm old and disgusting and that no young girl—no young swallow, no young blossom, no young beauty like her—would want to stay with me. Only let me tell you, you don't know a thing! Not a thing! Nothing!" he shouted and grew apoplectic in the face.

"Let me go, Leo," Natasha pleaded. "I'm just upsetting you."

"First I want to upset you a little bit. I'm going to do you a big favor, Natasha: I'm going to give you an analysis free of charge. Just think how lucky you are, getting something for nothing that other people would pay hundreds and thousands for. The idiots." Tired of leaning on his elbow, and perhaps also tired of talking and thinking, and just generally old and tired, he sank onto his back. He groaned: "If only they'd all go away and take their problems with them, instead of dumping it all on me. I'm sick of them. I'm tired. I want to get out and enjoy myself."

He lay there, hugely panting, looking as if he would

never get up again, let alone go out and enjoy himself. Natasha thought, *Suppose he were to die now?* She found herself
taking this possibility quite calmly.

"Come here," he said and made an angry sound when
she didn't do so fast enough. She approached warily, and
when she got close enough, he snatched at her hand so that
with a cry she snatched it back again. That made him laugh
and heave: "What did you think—I was making a pass at
you? I haven't come to that yet, not with you. I want you to
feel my heart, that's all." When she gingerly gave him her
hand, he guided it to his chest and held it there. At the same
time, he looked into her face—triumphant at her astonish-
ment: for though he appeared to be a disintegrating old man
at the last gasp, the heart he made her feel was thumping and
pumping inside him with a young bullock's strength. "Not
finished yet, you see; still some way to go," he whispered. But
he had to shut his eyes, too weary to speak or feel or be for a
while, as though worn out by his own strong heart.

Natasha was very anxious to get away. She was so afraid
he was going to keep his promise and give her a free analysis.
That was a privilege she was glad to do without—in fact, for
her the privilege was to be allowed to stay at the Academy
without having to submit to its principal function; to get off,
as she secretly put it to herself, scot-free.

He said, still with his eyes shut: "Sit down . . . There, at
the table."

The den had one small table in its center, and on it was a
red plush cloth with a fringe of little plush balls. Over the
table hung an old china gas mantel converted into an electric
lamp. But although Natasha sat there, at the table under the
lamp, in the middle of Leo's smoky, stifling den, she managed
not to be there. It was a habit she had evolved—a safety de-
vice—so that whenever she didn't care to be in a place, she
simply absented herself from it. She did this by staring hard

at whatever was ahead of her—in the present case, it was Leo
lying on his leather couch. But though she had her eyes fixed
on him, she seemed nevertheless to be seeing right through
him: gazing into an inner landscape, wider, more magical,
more full of light than the most glorious summer landscape
she had ever beheld.

But Leo, who knew all about this trick of hers, snapped
his fingers in the air with a loud report. He had to do so
several times before she unfocused her eyes from what she was
seeing and rested them, mildly, on him.

"Your grandmother called," he said. "She wants to come
here for a birthday party with Regi. My God, they're still on
birthday parties, those two." But next moment his exasperation changed into something completely different. He smiled:
"You know what? . . . Your grandmother used to have the
sweetest dimples in the most unusual place. Two of them, two
little hollows—never seen anything like it—" He began to
wheeze and cough again, so that Natasha said, "Maybe you
shouldn't smoke so much, Leo, it's bad for you."

That made him laugh as well as wheeze, and the result-
ing upheaval was frightful. Again she thought, with some
detachment, *Suppose he were to die now?* But he recovered—as he
did ten times a day—and when he could speak he said, still
laughing: "Don't worry, I'm still here; smoking or not, I'm
still around for a while. Now, if I were the old phony you take
me for, wouldn't I be saying I *have* to stay, you all need me, I
have work to do in the world and can't leave for the better
place I long for?" This he said in a saintly voice and also
folded his hands over his chest to make him look like a saint;
but next moment he unfolded them and said, "Balls! I'm
staying because I like it here. It's too good to leave." And now
he sounded wistful and sincere.

After a long silence, which he spent in wheezing con-
templation and she in wondering how much longer he was

going to keep her there, he swiveled his eyes in her direction
and gave a deep sigh which he did his best to make a mock
one: "I really feel sorry for you, Natasha. You're deprived.
There's one whole side missing for you—and what a side, God,
Christ in heaven, what shall I tell you, what a side!" And he
gave another sigh, and this one pushed up from the depths of
his being with such force that his whole frame shook with the
impact.

Although Natasha would have liked to tell him that she
wasn't missing a thing, she was afraid of exciting him, with
terrible results. Anyway, he was off on his own again: "You
don't know anything," he told her. "You can't know: it's not
even your fault. I'll prove it to you. Now, you think you love
Mark—hey, wait! I haven't finished—you think you love him
so much that you don't care what he does, whom he loves and
what he does with them and all the rest of it. And you think
because you don't care that's the height of love. I'll tell you
different: it's not the height, it's the opposite. And I can't
even teach you anything—if I could, believe me, I'd do my
best to bring you up to standard."

"Up to whose standard?"

"Nature's." Although she said nothing, he gave out
warning noises and shook his finger in the air: "Careful now—
don't underestimate Nature. You can't reach anything higher
without going through it—right through it—from top to bottom—through Louise's little dimples—"

"—You be careful now," she warned as he cackled and
cracked up—

"Ah, those two poor old women—when I think of what
they were. But I don't have to: just see how prodigal Nature
is—one Louise after another—one Regi after another—and
then in the end, at the top of the tree, there is the sweetest
little, hard little, juiciest little apple—where is she? why don't
you tell me?" But meeting Natasha's blank stare, he waved
her away: "You're really getting on my nerves now—clear out

of here, before I lose my temper. One," he began to count"—if you're not out by three—two—"

She shut the door behind her just on his count of three.

When Marietta asked Louise what she thought about giving up her apartment, she was surprised at how readily her mother agreed. Louise said, "Yes, yes, of course, what a good idea"; and went on at once to talk about Regi's birthday celebration, which had been her principal interest for the past few weeks.

Regi's birthday had never been celebrated among them as regularly as Louise's. There were years when Regi was out of sight and often out of reach, so that Louise was not even sure where to send her birthday gift; and other years when, though in the city, Regi chose to spend the day with new friends, or even chose not to be on speaking terms. However, nothing like that this year. It was Louise who ordered the birthday cake that they were to take with them to the Academy. She had been going to the same place—Blauberg's—for over fifty years, and one of the assistants, a Mrs. Weintraub, had been there for the last thirty of these, though complaining more and more about her feet and not knowing how much longer she would be able to carry on. When Mrs. Weintraub took the order for Regi's cake, she automatically wrote down mocha, which was the invariable flavor of Louise's birthday cake. But Louise changed it to strawberry—strawberry-pink—for Regi loved bright colors.

And when she went to collect it, she was glad she had done that. The cake was as beautiful as a palace—tall, shining, and pink, outlined with balconies and battlements of white frosting. While Louise was waiting for it to be packed, trays of pastries were carried in fresh from the ovens, so she bought some more—there were so many to buy for: coffee éclairs for Leo, chocolate ones for Natasha, napoleons for Mark, meringues for Eric, cheese straws for Marietta who did not like sweets, and then another steaming fragrant tray of cookies came out which Louise could not resist. Mrs. Weintraub took and packed these purchases in her usual phlegmatic, low-spirited manner; all this was nothing new for her—every day of her life an unending stream of fresh baked goods came out from the back premises to be bought and eaten by an unending stream of customers. But her packing was very efficient so that her hands seemed to be working independently of the rest of her; and all the time she told Louise about her latest complaint—this year, besides her feet, there was something wrong with her kidneys—as well as about the misfortunes that had befallen her family in the course of the year. Every time she came here, Louise was kept up on the latest in Mrs. Weintraub's family—one year her brother-in-law was in a car accident, another year her sister had to have a mastectomy, and then there was the year of her own hysterectomy. For Louise, all these events had become part of the ambience of Blauberg's, and a preliminary to every celebration. And when Mrs. Weintraub—having packed all the boxes and dispatched a younger assistant to help Louise put them in her cab—wished her joy of the occasion and to eat in happiness and good health, concluding with her usual, "Who knows where we'll all be next year": then Louise wasn't in the least worried abut Mrs. Weintraub, because in spite of all that happened, all the disasters, the next year she never was not there.

One day—this was the day Louise was expected with Regi—Stephanie took the last few possessions out of her trunk; and when they arrived at Jeff's cottage, Natasha found that he had packed up too and that they were leaving. She didn't know whether they had decided on this verbally, or whether their agreement was as instinctive as that of birds when they make off for the winter. All Stephanie said was, "Where's my stuff?" He pointed out a bulging trunk tied with rope which was already in his pickup; she made him open it again to add her last little bundle.

"You could come too," she said to Natasha.

"Sure you could," Jeff said—he meant it: there was plenty of room in his pickup.

"I can't," Natasha said. "My grandmother's coming."

All three of them went back into the cottage to make sure nothing had been forgotten. But Jeff had done a good job of clearing up: only the old armchair was left and his bed stripped down to a stained mattress. He had let the wood stove go out and the cold wind blew in through the open door, making a shutter swing and creak on its hinges. They went out and quickly shut the door behind them, so the snow wouldn't get in. Stephanie and Natasha tried to embrace, but they couldn't get near each other because of the wadded coats they both wore. That made them laugh, though they had tears in their eyes. At the same time, Stephanie's eyes were sparkling and her cheeks were flushed with cold and excitement, while Jeff was already calling impatiently from the driver's seat; so that Natasha could not feel too sad at this parting from the only friends she had ever had.

Jeff had given her the key of the cottage to give back to Mark. She locked the door without returning inside; but as she did so, she remembered she had no way of getting back to the Academy and would have to go up to the house and ask Kent to drive her. She walked the ascending path toward Mark's house. She thrust her hands deep into her pockets— tearing these a bit farther—and stamped through the first layer of snow. The trunks of the trees reared black out of the ground, but their branches were already white with the fragile, crumbly, newly falling snow. The wind drove the flakes along the frozen lake and blew them up from the ground and into Natasha's face. The sky hung down gray and swollen. And the house, shining with new paint whiter than the new snow, stood like an ice palace aloof on its hill.

Natasha let herself in. As always, and especially since Kent had taken up his quarters there, she felt like an intruder—unnecessarily, for it was too cold and impersonal to be anyone's house yet. She could hear Kent moving around in the upstairs front bedroom. This was the room in which Mark slept when he stayed overnight. Kent too had installed himself there and had laid out some of his developed prints over one of the twin beds. He was studying them and hardly looked up when Natasha came in.

It seemed polite to her to study them with him. She stood beside him, but it was strange and difficult for her to be there with him. Although the clothes flung about and the shoes half pushed under the bed were Kent's, basically the room was Mark's: Natasha recognized the bedcovers he had bought in Italy, and the rug with baskets of flowers and fruits woven into it; also the three-sided leather frame which stood on one of the bedside tables. It held the three photographs that Mark carried with him and put up everywhere like household idols—Louise's, Marietta's (taken in India), and her own.

She glanced nervously up—way up—at Kent. He was frowning with concentration as he studied his work and appeared totally unaware of her. If only she could have been so of him. Over the years, she had met several of Mark's lovers, and they had all evoked the same sensation in her. She recognized it now as she stood beside Kent: that strange, strange visceral distaste, like the tugging of her infrequent but always painful menstrual periods. It was more strongly negative than anything she had ever felt for anyone else; and might have grown, if she had let it, into full-blown hate and fear.

She heard a car drive up down below and was glad of the excuse to go to the window and see. It was a sleek, long, black sedan; and the man who got out—she saw him foreshortened from above, could look down on his modeled gray hair—was also sleek and city-bred, in a pale and perfect suit. Kent had come up behind her, and at the sight of the stranger, he turned from the window without a word and went out of the room. Natasha could hear him say from midway down the stairs: "What are you doing here? Who asked you to come?" And the man said: "I had to." The unlived-in, impersonal house had become charged, electric.

They went into the room on the left (the dining room), and Kent shut the door. Natasha followed them downstairs. She could hear their voices—principally the other man's—but they were low and intense, and she would not have been able to make out the words even if she had wanted to, which she did not. By the time she had reached the bottom of the stairs, the man's voice had risen. She still could not distinguish the words, but now there was something in the tone that she recognized only too well. For it was the same she had heard, or rather overheard, in some of Mark's telephone conversations: high-pitched, even shrill, and one would have said feminine if at the same time it hadn't been fraught with more force, more physical strength than could have come out of a woman's body. She sat down on the lowest step, stubbornly; and stubbornly, she did not cover her ears but made herself be present to hear and know. More than anything, she was indignant. She felt that Mark's house was being desecrated by these strangers before he had even had a chance to live in it.

But as she sat there and listened, her feelings began to change. She still didn't know what was going on—in the same way as she had not known the details when she had overheard Mark on the telephone: but as on those occasions, here too a point was reached when she felt she had to intervene. Mark had always been furious when she came in and stood by him while he shrieked down the phone. But it had made him put down the receiver, and after a while he did not seem to mind her presence while he sat holding his head in his hands, trying to hide his tears. He never said so, but maybe he even felt good to have another person there, though a silent one.

Moved by the same instinct as had moved her then, the same inability to stand another person's pain, she got up from the step and went toward the front room. She didn't have to overcome her acute shyness, it just disappeared. Kent stood towering, fierce and gigantic, by the fireplace; the other man was kneeling on the floor, with his arms clasped around Kent's knees and his face laid against them.

When Kent saw Natasha, he gave the other's shoulder a slight push. The man raised his face and looked toward her and then quickly looked away again. He got up; he kept his face averted from her and wiped at it with his handkerchief. Kent remained standing by the fireplace, angry and awkward and not knowing what to do; Natasha was also helpless, and there was a profound and terrible silence in the newly painted, newly furnished, carefully restored dining room while they waited for the other to collect himself. Maybe *he* would know what to do.

And strangely he did—at any rate, he knew to put on a better face than either of them. When he felt sufficiently recovered to turn around toward them, he managed to take charge. This may have been because he was so much older and more experienced than they were. He even managed to smile as he advanced toward Natasha, holding out his hand and introducing himself by name. She saw that his eyes were washed and dimmed not only by these recent tears but by days and nights and years of them.

By the time Marietta came to collect her to take her to the Academy, Louise had so many packages that they had to call the doorman up to help carry them to the car. Before starting off, Marietta phoned Eric to tell him to have Regi ready, so that when they got to her apartment house, Eric had her down there sitting in the marble lobby, and he and Regi's doorman helped her get in the back of the car with Louise. Louise hugged and kissed her for her birthday and pointed out all the parcels and the enormous box holding the birthday cake; and Regi seemed well-pleased—at any rate, she had no complaint. Her only anxiety was for the safety of the birthday cake, until Eric, up front with Marietta, took it on his lap and kept it sitting there the entire way.

The beginning of their journey was dull—getting out of the city, out of traffic snarls, and through decaying areas full of empty, littered lots and broken buildings with ornate fire escapes. All the windows were boarded up except here and there where a furniture maker or other trader going out of business had put his stock on sale. It hadn't started snowing yet in the city, but the sky looked grim. People huddled in their coats and walked with their heads down against the wind, which churned up litter from the sidewalks. The river was choppy and ugly brown, and the pleasure cruiser, which still stood on it, looked incongruous with its smart white paint and little colored flags. But Louise, snug in the back of the heated car with Regi, looked out at everything with excitement and pleasure; and so did Eric who loved a ride.

Then they left the last thinning part of the city and began to strike out into suburbs and scenery. The highway turned into a parkway, and Marietta drove more and more smoothly over better roads: till at last for miles on end there were only trees and little woods to see, and sometimes a field rising to a hill with one house on top. Once, they passed over a bridge and water stretching clear and far on either side; and shortly after that Louise leaned forward in her seat and then she cried: "Look, Regilein, *snow!*" But Regi was asleep and only grunted; what a pity—except that rest was always good—for Regi too had loved snow and winter sports.

As they drove farther north, they came into a landscape that was already white, with snow hardening and still falling. Wherever there was water, it had turned to ice; and once Eric looked around at the two of them in the back to point out a little stream that, in falling down a precipice, had frozen midway into icicles. "Oh, they're both asleep," he then said to Marietta. Louise heard him, and she wanted to cry out, "No, I'm not!" But she didn't—was she really asleep? But how could that be, when she was so excited with the snow, and their outing to the Academy, and Regi's birthday. Too excited perhaps: she couldn't take that much anymore, and it was exhaustion, not sleep, that had overcome her. She opened her eyes for a moment, but they fell shut again almost at once; and really, perhaps she didn't need to keep them open— she could see within herself all the snow and all the ice she had ever experienced, and all the fun they had had in it. Louise had been a very good ice skater: not fast and dazzling and swooping like some of the others, but slow and stately as a swan.

Bruno had proposed to her one day after he had watched her skate on the frozen pond of the Gruenewald. She hadn't known he was there watching—she always went into a sort of trance when she was skating, she got so much enjoyment out of it. She was warm in her cloth coat with fur collar and hem, her head encased in a fur cap matching the muff that dangled from a string around her neck. She didn't keep her hands in it for she had her arms folded; she glided around on the ice with the same ease as she danced, not thinking of her feet at all. Her eyes were half shut so that the bright crystal sunlight came to her dimly, and so did the voices of the other skaters. She didn't notice Bruno till it was time to leave when, with her easy rhythmic glide, she went to the edge of the pond; and there he was, holding out a gloved hand to help her. He sat beside her while she took off her skates; she was aware that he was looking and looking at her, and it made her face glow more. Bruno was also wearing a fur-collared coat, and there were drops of snow melting in it and in his moustache, which was the same color as the fur.

He didn't propose to her there and then, but later in Schwamm's where he took her to warm her up with hot chocolate. Actually, she didn't need warming up—she was glowing, as always after skating—but she noticed his hands were icy-cold when he drew off his gloves. They sat at a round table in a corner by a magnificent gold-framed mirror in which she could see that he was still looking and looking at her. She was glad she was wearing a dress he hadn't seen before—a green and rust plaid wool with a bolero and a big black bow; it had been finished a few days earlier by the old lady who came to sew for Louise's mother every Wednesday. When the chocolate arrived, it was very hot, but Louise had a trick of sucking it out from under the cool cream on top. The only thing was, one had to watch out for a chocolate-and-froth moustache; so she was surreptitiously doing that in the mirror and wiping off a faint trace from her upper lip with her tongue when Bruno began to propose to her. She wanted to get back to her drink—she loved it so—but desisted, for she realized this was a very solemn moment; so she made a solemn face and he talked—oh, so poetically! She was deeply stirred and thrilled and thought to herself it is forever, for life, for the whole of life. And that seemed to her the most beautiful phrase she had ever thought: the whole of life.

Before going on to the Academy for Regi's birthday party, Mark drove to his house. He was surprised to see a sleek black sedan standing in his driveway. "Whose is that?" he asked Natasha, who appeared on the front porch the moment she heard him drive up.

"Did Mother bring Grandma?" she asked.

"Yes, they must have arrived at Leo's. . . . Why aren't you there? Why are you here?"

With these questions they got inside the hall. Now Mark heard voices muffled from behind the dining-room door; but before he could go in, she drew him away into the opposite room.

"What's going on?" Mark said. "Who's in there with him?"

"It's someone called Anthony," Natasha had to say at last.

"Oh, I see." And Mark, looking grim, strode at once to the door.

Before he could open it, she had run in front of him and held on to the knob.

"Don't be ridiculous, Natasha."

Still holding on to the door, she began to plead: "Let's go—I was waiting for you to drive me there—Grandma must be waiting. They're all waiting, Mark. They must have brought the cake. Regi's cake. Let's go. They'll want to cut it." As she spoke, her eyes searched desperately over his face—as if she didn't know it already, better than any other in the world.

Instead of replying, he tried to pry her hand from the door. She knew she couldn't hold on much longer—he wasn't very strong, but at any rate he was stronger than she—and she tightened her grasp on it and became more pleading: "Drive me there, Mark. I want to go. Please drive me." And then she let go of the handle and did something she had not done since their childhood: she flung her arms around his neck and clung to him, her face touching his. This contact, slight as it was—no more than a brushing of her cheek against his—filled her with a deep and poignant sensation; so that to feel him recoil at the same instant with what was at least distaste was correspondingly painful. But she willed herself to keep her hold on him; she even tightened her arms and said, "You're not to go in there."

Then he fought back. He loosened her arms from his neck and flung her aside. There was a look of wild fury on his face; and when he spoke, his voice was shrill: "I think you've gone crazy! You really are crazy! A crazy hysterical woman!" But it was he who sounded liked one.

"No, don't!" she cried and again she tried to hold him, interposing herself between him and the door. And, "Don't," she said again in a quieter voice as she looked into his pale and twitching face; and what she meant now was not only "Don't go in there" but also "Don't look like that. Don't be like that." She wanted him calm, manly, himself.

But at that moment, to be himself was to get rid of her and go into the other room and deal with whatever was going on there. "Get out of the way," he said, and he didn't scruple now to push her roughly. At that, all the fight went out of her. She knew she didn't have a chance. She moved aside, and he opened the door. She followed him into the hallway, and as he went toward the dining room, she went to the front door to let herself out. She didn't want to hear anything of what was going to happen.

However, just before opening the door to the dining room, he stopped short and looked after her and had second thoughts. He called to her, and when she didn't turn around, he went to her.

"I won't be long," he said. "I'll take you in a moment. If you'll just be patient and wait."

She had turned her face aside so he plucked at her hair as if he were ringing a bell; it was what he sometimes did when he wanted to attract her attention. But now she put up her hand and brushed his aside. "Hey!" he said. "What's with you?" And he looked into her face, which she tried to avert from him so that he wouldn't see how sad she was.

But he knew that very well; he knew it exactly. He stood there, torn between her and what was going on behind the dining-room door: but then a raised voice came from out of there, and at that he could not be held a moment longer. He murmured, "We'll talk later"—shamefacedly perhaps, but it was with determination that he left her and went straight into the dining room and let her go out of the house.

The dining room: the way Mark had furnished it was

almost an exact replica of what his paternal grandmother's had been. Yet only the candelabra, some of the Georgian silver, and the carving set on the sideboard had come to him from her, while the rest he had bought at auctions and from antiques dealers. On the other hand, the portraits on the walls really were his ancestors—the senator, the abolitionist, the sweet-faced general's wife who had died in childbirth— but they had been so carefully cleaned, so tastefully restored that they looked as impersonal as the rest of the furniture and might equally well have been bought in antiques shops.

Seated at the table where Mark planned to give his dinner parties—he was getting an appropriate set of dishes together—were Kent and Anthony. They were side by side, and Anthony had laid his hand on Kent's. He left it there when Mark came in—perhaps in challenge: at any rate, the way he looked up at Mark was defiant.

Kent said in his growling, deep voice, "I didn't ask him to come here."

"But he *is* here," Mark said.

"I didn't ask him," Kent said again. He looked down at Anthony's hand on his and seemed surprised to see it there; and only then did he withdraw his from underneath.

"I've come to take him away with me," Anthony said.

"Oh, yes? And what does he say about that?"

Kent didn't have anything to say. He stared ahead of him into horizons of his own, frowning, absenting himself from the scene.

Mark saw that he and Anthony were expected to fight it out between them. He was prepared to do that. He stood by the sideboard (inlaid with matching veneers) and Anthony came to join him there. They faced each other. Trim and fair, with careful haircuts and elegant casual suits, they looked so much alike that they might have been brothers. But there was this difference—that under his boyish haircut and over his young man's suit, Anthony's face was strained and old. Looking at him, Mark might have been looking at his own face twenty years later; but not yet, not now.

Anthony said, "He wants to come and live with me. We've been talking about it. You can ask him."

Kent had his back to them and gave no one any help. He sat there stolidly and now he even supported his elbows on the table and held his hands over his ears.

"I don't think he wants to at all," Mark said. "If he did, I wouldn't try to stop him."

"You can't stop him."

They kept on glaring at each other. Mark felt at an advantage—in years, strength, everything. He wasn't even sure that he urgently wanted or needed Kent, but he was certainly determined that no one was going to take him away.

"Do you want to go, Kent?" he asked.

They both knew there wasn't going to be any answer, so instead Anthony spoke. He said, "Leave him out of this. I'm telling you: he wants to go with me." His voice rose to a falsetto: "Do you think you own him? Do you think you bought him, with this house, as part of the furniture?" Anthony's mouth twitched, so did his hands; Mark could have felt sorry for him—perhaps he even did, especially as he knew so exactly how he was feeling.

"Listen," Mark said. "You'd better drive yourself home now. They said on the radio there's going to be a very bad snowstorm. I wouldn't like anything bad to happen to you driving back by yourself."

Anthony replied with bravado: "I'm not driving back by myself."

This was followed by too long a silence. When Anthony spoke next, the bravado had gone out of him. "Kent?" he said in a trembly voice, turning in that direction.

Kent let Mark speak for him—and Mark was glad to do

so. He felt triumphant and superior, and couldn't help showing it on his face; and he said, calmly: "You must realize
yourself that it was not a good idea to come here."

Anthony did something entirely unexpected: he
snatched one of the silver-handled carving knives out of the
stand—the same Mark's aunt Mary had used on the Thanksgiving turkey—and he directed it toward Mark's heart. Now,
Anthony knew how to wield a carving knife—he could cut up
roast chickens expertly—but not how to plunge it into other
people's hearts. Or perhaps at the last moment caution over-
came his rage. He got as far as Mark's pale blue cashmere
sweater and slit into that, crying, "I'll kill you!" And with
that cry the knife clattered to the floor, and both Mark and
Anthony stared down at it.

Mark stooped to retrieve it and, in his tidy way, to replace it on the stand. He touched the tear in his sweater, and
Anthony, watching him do that, said, "Good God."

"Yes," Mark agreed.

Anthony straightened the necktie under his fiercely
working Adam's apple. He said, "I guess I'm sorry," in a
strangled voice.

"So you ought to be," Mark said. "It was quite a favorite
sweater."

He managed to smile, and so, with more effort, did Anthony. But Kent was devastated—he had buried his head in
his arms laid on the table. The other two had to comfort him,
each placing a hand on one of his huge shoulders, now shaking with sobs. He was still very young, only at the beginning
of his career, and knew nothing of what could sometimes happen among people with very strong feelings.

About these feelings: Leo had once likened them to the
voices of the great castrati, in which a man's vigor was made
to give body to a woman's nervous delicacy. Unhuman voices,
Leo called them; unnatural hybrids. "All the same," Mark
had replied, "no one ever said they weren't beautiful."

* * *

When they arrived at the Academy, Louise was so excited that she embraced everyone, even people she didn't
know. "Where's Natasha?" she asked. Leo looked around:
"Yes, where is she?" No one knew. Louise wouldn't allow Eric
to take off Regi's hat and coat because she wanted to take her
out again at once to show her the Academy grounds. "You
don't come," she told Leo. "I don't want you with a cold." He
didn't hear her. He said: "Where's Stephanie?"

Louise had taken Regi's arm and she carefully descended
the steps out into the garden with her. When Eric tried to
help, she wouldn't let him; she said they could manage perfectly well, this wasn't the first time she and Regi had been
out in the snow together. "Is it, darling?" she said, squeezing
Regi's fur sleeve. But Regi said, "When are we going to open
my presents?"

Louise took her to the sunken garden. Marietta and Eric
and a few students came up behind them, in case they needed
help. But the two old ladies seemed to be managing quite well
on their own, clinging to each other as they tripped over the
hardened snow. Both of them tall and completely encased in
fur coats and fur hats, they looked like two prehistoric animals—cumbersome yet graceful because so perfectly adapted
to their environment. Their high-heeled suede boots made the
first tracks in the virginal snow of the sunken garden. Louise
led Regi to the edge of the fountain basin. She showed her
the stone nymph, whose curves were now packed with snow;
icicles had formed at the stone nipple from which in the summer she pressed a fountain. "Brrrr," Louise playfully shud-
dered at Regi. "Aren't you glad you've got your mink?"

"When are we going to cut the cake?"

The water in the basin had frozen solid—"Just nice for
skating," Louise said; and still in her playful mood, she stuck
out one toe toward the ice and the tip of her tongue emerged
between her lips in pleasant anticipation.

But Regi didn't want to go skating, she wanted to go in where her cake and presents were. She said crossly, in German, "Let me go, you stupid goose": and she jerked her arm free—so that Louise, one foot extended toward the ice, the other on the slippery surface of the snow, lost her balance and fell, striking the rim of the basin.

The others rushed forward to help her up. She was hurt but no one suspected how badly—except Eric who had seen old ladies slip and fall more than once before, on the ballroom floors round which he had led them in the fox-trot, the peabody, and the old-fashioned waltz. They usually broke a hip and had to be taken away in an ambulance; once, one of them had died before they could even call the ambulance. Some of them died in the hospital, but others came out again and hobbled around a while longer. However, none of them ever came back to dance again.

After Mark had gone to join the others in the dining room, Natasha didn't want to stay in the house with them. She walked down the hill to wait for him in Jeff's cottage. She hoped he wouldn't be long because, with the wood stove gone out, it was cold in there. She huddled in the garbage-dump armchair, with her hands in the pockets of her coat; her breath came in vapors. The cold outside seemed to be taking over the deserted cottage as if it were a dead tree with a hollow trunk.

She was relieved when she heard a car and got up to lift the latch from the door. But it was Leo who rushed in—like a wild man, wearing nothing over his monk's robe, his silver ornament swinging. He didn't say anything but his eyes rolled around the room, and when all he saw was Natasha, he said, "Where have they gone?"

She couldn't tell him; she really didn't know. She said, "Has Grandma come?"

He seized her arm as if she were unwilling to go with

him; though at the same moment she was saying, "Take me back to the Academy." He hustled her into his car. She was surprised to see that it was his own car—a very small red sports model that he had had for thirty years. His followers wouldn't let him drive it anymore because it was so old and also because he was such a mad, erratic driver. And he drove madly now, with Natasha beside him: the tiny car lurched and groaned as he wildly, doggedly drove it over the slippery road; it heaved and thumped and boiled. Natasha, who had never learned to drive, didn't realize how dangerous it all was. Instead, she was glad to be speeding back to the Academy where Louise and Marietta were waiting with Regi and the birthday cake.

But after a time she realized that he was driving in the wrong direction, not toward but away from the Academy. It took some time longer before she plucked up courage to point this out to him. It was doubtful whether he heard her: he was hunched over the wheel, wheezing as loudly as the old car, his heavy, sack-like body lurching every time the car lurched from one side of the road to the other. Natasha said it again: "Leo, we're going the wrong way."

He was muttering; he was saying, "I'm going to find her. We'll find her." It was crazy. He looked and sounded crazy. His face was inflamed, his nose swollen, tears were coming out of his eyes and falling down his cheeks onto the steering wheel. He was making sobbing sounds like a baby or a very old man. Natasha was awestruck: "He really loves her," she thought. At the same time, this thought depressed her, for it seemed to her that there just wasn't enough love to go round and never would be—not here, not now—with everyone needing such an awful lot of it.

Although it was still afternoon, dusk was falling—imperceptibly, for all day the clouds had not cleared and there was no sun to set, only sky and white earth to fade together into a colorless twilight. This was relieved by one single star that had appeared and glowed dimly in midair. It didn't occur to Leo to turn on the lights—he was too sunk in other thoughts that made him mutter as he lurched and drove and wept. It seemed to Natasha that the pale twilight, the fading earth were swallowing them up, sucking them in, as into water or clouds. Nevertheless, she was glad to be there with him: not that she could do anything as, blinded with tears, he drove them farther into snow and mist, but at least so he wasn't alone.

They carried Louise into the den and laid her on the leather couch. She sighed when they did that—probably with pain, but perhaps also because she felt satisfied to be there in that hot, close room full of Leo's cigar smell. Regi's cake had been taken out of the box and placed on the round table in the center where it shone pink and festive.

Regi wanted the candles lit. There were four of those—for herself, Louise always had the full amount (on her last birthday, her cake had blazed resplendently with eighty-four candles); but for Regi she left out the first digit. When every-one ignored her, Regi became more plaintive and loud—until she penetrated whatever it was that made Louise keep her eyes shut. Anyway, Louise opened them and said, "Let her"; so then Eric lit the four candles. They made a very pretty sight, and Regi laughed and clapped her hands, and Louise too seemed to smile as she shut her eyes again.

But the very next second something happened within her—it was as if a stone broke through a vein and lodged itself inside her lungs: filling her with a sensation surpassing all others, a pain so sharp that it became transporting. She cried out, though just once and not very loudly, and only Marietta heard her. "I'm coming!" was what Marietta heard—as she had heard her mother exclaim once before, years and years ago when she had watched her and Leo from behind the screen. And Marietta wondered now as she had wondered then—*What's she mean? Where's she coming? Where's she going?*

Regi gathered herself together to blow her four candles out, but although she tried very hard, she only managed three and one remained. Nevertheless, Eric praised her for her effort, and then he said, "Now let's try again—one more time, okay?" So Regi took another deep breath and blew the last one out, terribly pleased with herself.

Printed in the United States
by Baker & Taylor Publisher Services